ALREADY THERE

Diane Dierks

Aha! Publishing

www.aha-pubishing.com

To Merrilee —
A Sweet friend.
Thanks for buying one of first copies!

Diane
Dierks

First printing 2013. Printed in the U.S.A.

10 9 8 7 6 5 4 3 2 1

For information about reproduction rights, address
Aha! Publishing, P.O. Box 1016, Lawrenceville, GA 30046
ISBN -13: 978-0-9745254-1-9
ISBN -10: 0974525413

Join the *Already There* conversation on Facebook & Twitter!
Facebook.com/AlreadyThereNovel
Twitter @AlreadyThereBuz
Pin it at:
Pinterest.com/ahapublishing
Read the author's blog at: **www.AlreadyThereNovel.blogspot.com**

For Eric, my "Nathan"

TELL *me not, in mournful numbers,*
  Life is but an empty dream! —
  For the soul is dead that slumbers,
  And things are not what they seem.

> — Henry Wadsworth Longfellow
> *A Psalm of Life* (1838)

Prologue

As Julia approached her son's grave, her heart sank. As always, it was impossible not to remember the day two years ago when she stared through tear-drenched eyes at Joey's casket as it was lowered slowly into the dark damp hole. Today, it was warmer and cloudier than that chilly spring afternoon. In fact, the sun had shone so brightly on the day of his funeral that it hadn't seemed fair to feel so sullen. Even the birds that had been joyfully singing in the surrounding trees, while the priest was performing the internment service, had felt out of sync with what had just happened in her life. Now, when Julia felt lighter and more in control, how ironic it was that the clouds loomed, casting a humid shadow over the trees that gently rustled and announced a storm. And the birds that usually inhabited them were silent and noticeably absent – as if hiding from Julia's presence. She felt an eerie shiver.

In one ordinary day, Julia Olwen's life had been divided into two parts: the before and the after. In the before, there was predictability, safety, and rules that were meant to protect. In the after, there was only a surreal sense of motionless existence in which nothing could be measured and rules didn't matter anymore. Apparently, rules were absent from Lance Irving Eddy's conscience when he murdered her son and got away with it. So she had rationalized that the rules no longer applied to her either, at which point the plot took root in her mind to make Eddy pay for his heinous deed. The plan was about to come full-circle and Julia had put away any and all reservations about her involvement. She would find pleasure in the aftermath and hoped she would not be eternally punished for the payback, even though she was risking being caught and penalized in the present world. She worried, though, when she occasionally became physically and emotionally charged at the thought of Eddy's suffering. She wondered why she got such tangible pleasure from thinking of his demise. It felt dirty and justified all at once. Godly and devilish. Did that make her similar to him? Was she capable of such derangement? It was a whole new way of seeing herself – a woman whose means could justify the vengeful end. All she had to do was think of Joey when she was confronted with this dilemma. His sweet innocence. A twelve-year-old who in one moment could take on the maturity of a grown man in his intense protection of her. But in the next minute, she would find him huddled in his closet, secretly playing with action figures she had bought him when he was a toddler. He was too smart for his own good sometimes, but too young to have endured the unexplainable tortured sickness of Lance Eddy. She often wondered how she would have helped him cope had he lived through it. Maybe it was God's mercy that he did not survive since who could explain such a horrific ordeal? Especially a parent who is supposed to protect her child from the monsters under the bed. Yet, she knew she would endure anything to be able to touch her son again. To hear his voice. To wipe his tears. She had not protected him in life, but she was determined to avenge him in death.

Cemeteries were never Julia's favorite places to hang out, but now she found herself tied to this one in particular – Precious Gardens. The entry was flanked with gates that were akin to those of a royal palace, gilded with gold, announcing inhabitants of high regard. It was meant to elicit feelings of security and invulnerability, the way a child is supposed to feel in the safety of his own home. The irony pained her. Every time she drove through the entrance and down the curved, tree-lined thoroughfare toward Joey's site, she felt jealousy and rage instead of peace and tranquility as the name would suggest. Just saying her son was at rest in "Precious Gardens" embarrassed and angered her. In all her years of planning for motherhood and completing only twelve years of it, anticipating where her child would be laid to rest was never on the radar. Of course, where Joey went to daycare, elementary school, and catechism training were of the utmost importance. On the day she had to choose his final resting place, though, it seemed like a senseless detail. How can a parent accept such defeat and finality? There was nothing precious about the cold, hard truth of her son's body decomposing in a box underground, alone. It was all incomprehensible to Julia. Not Precious Gardens. Maybe for someone's elderly grandmother, that would do, but not for Joey. He was out of place here.

As she stared at the newly-installed grave marker, she thought she should feel some sense of closure, as everyone was prone to saying she needed. What is closure anyway? And why did she need it? So she could forget Joey? No way. She had waited almost two years to order the marker because it felt like the final gesture of acknowledging his senseless death, and then what? Go on as if nothing ever happened? She didn't know how to do that. Maybe after she executed her plan, she would feel the satisfaction of revenge, but it would never feel fair. Her one qualm about the course of action she'd decided to take was that it would mean never visiting Joey here again. But in some ways, that didn't really bother her. Instead of feeling resolved upon actually seeing the marker for the first time, she felt sadness that it literally marked the end. The familiar disdain for the man who robbed Joey's childhood and her motherhood was ever present. It would never come to a close. The best she could hope for was that it would be neutralized by her impending actions. She felt her heart tearing into shreds as she read the bold brass letters:

Joseph "Joey" Landry Olwen
We are already with you, sweet angel,
for in heaven there is no time.
January 9, 1998 – March 17, 2010

The marker was embossed with his photo – the one they all loved, with him holding his baseball bat, and his cap turned backwards on his dark blond head. The inscription came from an idea Julia got from a pastor in her community who had visited her after Joey's murder. Pastor Tucker had convinced her that because the Bible suggests there is no time in heaven, she didn't have to worry about Joey being lonely there – that all who went before and after him were already there to celebrate his arrival with him. Including her. That was the only thing anyone said in the two years since his death that made sense and that had offered her any sort of comfort. In the aftermath of grief and a long court case, she hung onto those words daily, sometimes hourly, feeling imprisoned by time and space on earth. In these moments when she had to be confronted with the coldness of Precious Gardens, she tried to refocus on the pastor's words. *He is not really in that grave...he is in an awesome place...and we're already there...together.*

Julia reached down and felt the raised letters, outlining each with her finger, one by one. Dual pangs of sadness and anger overwhelmed her once more. So much time had passed, yet it felt like everything was still so fresh. The flame of a mother's love is never extinguished, she thought. It is more like a pilot light that silently remains constant, but whose power can never be underestimated. This moment felt final, but it did not eclipse her love. She would carry that around with her forever, no matter what became of her. She unwrapped the bouquet of roses that she had brought from her cutting garden and placed them in the vase attached to the marker. White roses. White for hope.

Just then, Julia felt a droplet on her forearm, and then several. Within seconds, it was pouring and she knew she had to go. "I love you, sweetheart," she said rather loudly over the background of thunder and splatters of raindrops. She stood up, pulled her light jacket over her head and ran across the lawn to her car. Her tears and sobs were indistinguishable from the thunder or the rain – both were equally profuse and loud. She felt a fleeting moment of guilt, leaving Joey behind like this, but quickly reminded herself that only his memory was there. *Don't forget.* She opened and shut the driver's side door quickly to take cover from the downpour. Julia sighed heavily while wiping the smears of water from her hands and arms. Julia Olwen turned the key and drove away. She had one last task to complete and it was finally time to even the score.

It was June 16, 2012. Within twenty-four hours, she would be gone.

1.

June 17, 2012

In all his years in law enforcement, Nathan hadn't seen so much blood in one place. He wasn't usually prone to nausea at the scene of a crime, but this one caused him to wince and turn away at first sight. The metallic scent of blood was overwhelming.

"Holy….." Nathan muttered aloud. *What the hell happened here?* He had a difficult time getting reoriented to his purpose. He thought he would just find her sleeping late because she drank too much last night, or maybe her employer forgot she was on vacation and she was sunning herself on a Florida beach with no cell phone service. He never expected to find this when he got the call from the hospital that an employee had failed to come to work. She was an RN, and apparently one who never showed up late. But when she had missed almost an entire three-to-eleven shift and no one could reach her, they asked the department to send someone to her home. She reportedly lived alone and had little in the way of close family and friends who would know of her whereabouts. Nathan was available and he agreed to check it out as his last duty before heading out for the night. China Grove Road wasn't too far off the path he usually took to go home in the evening. He expected it to be routine.

"Yeah, we need the homicide team here ASAP," he reported to dispatch. "It's a mess."

Nathan Lee Davis was in his third year as sheriff of Calhoun County, a rural, but wealthy area fifty miles southeast of Atlanta. He was popular for his no-nonsense style of solving and preventing crimes, which appealed to the mostly conservative Republican people of the county. They had an image to protect, and although Nathan came from what would seem like a middle class upbringing, he understood his constituents. They were business owners, seasoned farmers, contractors, and Christians who still believed in corporal punishment in the schools, even though it was no longer practiced. They had a low tolerance for crime and even lower tolerance for politically correct rhetoric. Nathan Davis had the knack for knowing how to speak the mind of the people without being offensive. Most people agreed it was his large stature and teddy bear demeanor that allowed him to use salty language that most other public servants could never get away with. This made him liked by most, but feared by those who would dare consider violating his principles.

He walked slowly and carefully back out of the home the way he came in, making mental notes of the entry and hallway leading to the kitchen where most of the blood was visible. It was everywhere…puddles on the floor, and splatter on the countertops, walls and ceiling. It was a bloodbath. An angry one. There had been a struggle, as Nathan noticed items knocked over on the kitchen counter and a chair from the dinette set on its side. Blood was smeared on the kitchen wall leading to the entry hall, which led Nathan to believe the victim may have been trying to get away, but had been unable to maintain the strength to do so. Then it appeared the smears ran along the floor toward the back door leading from the kitchen to the back porch, where the killer may have exited with the body through that door, but Nathan could not be sure. He was not even sure this was a murder, but the amount of blood pointed in that direction.

Until the team arrived, he didn't want to compromise evidence, so he made his way outside to the street in front of the house and lit a cigarette. As he stared at the scene that looked somewhat peaceful and quiet, he thought that whoever lived there took great care to create a *Southern Living* style, especially at the entrance, where the long wrap-around porch was adorned with a distressed sign hanging over the door that read, "Rest for the Weary." *Ironic.*

It was times like these, demanding his calmness and logic, when nicotine was Nathan's go-to drug. He knew all too well that he had begun smoking years ago precisely because of these kinds of events, when primal fear and instinct were stimulated. He wasn't particularly proud of that, as it went against Nathan's usual sense of self-control. But he was able to forgive himself for the vice as long as it allowed him to have a clear head when it was needed most, like after having walked into a gruesome murder scene that would require him to find the answers. His heart and thoughts were racing as he considered the sheer trauma that must have taken place inside this home, and he was keenly aware of how powerless he was at the moment to make any sense of it.

On the porch near the front door, there were lush green ferns and semi-worn wicker rockers, dressed in colorful fabrics with seams frayed just enough to be inviting. Unfortunately, the woman who'd created the invitation of rest for the weary had an unwelcomed guest...or maybe it began friendly, but turned evil. Nathan was intrigued by the possibilities. This was not a common occurrence in Calhoun County. This was something he might have seen in his younger years, working the beat in south Atlanta. He was already anticipating the media coverage and the many questions he would be expected to answer, but couldn't. Nathan sighed at the thought. He had a disdain for reporters, but knew they were a necessary evil.

Nathan took the last drag of his cigarette and carefully placed the spent butt in a gum wrapper in his coat pocket so he wouldn't contaminate any area around the crime scene. While waiting on the CSI team, he took a casual walk around the perimeter of the property to look for anything that might seem out of place. At first glance, he hadn't noticed evidence that indicated forced entry, although he would need to check out all entry points to be sure. With no break in and with this much blood, it would only stand to reason that it was someone she knew who not only wanted her dead, but wanted to exhaust an enormous amount of rage. In the distance, there were flashing blue lights approaching, followed by the unmarked cars of the homicide investigators. John Weiss got out of his car and walk toward Nathan.

"Hey, man. Sounds like a bad one," said Weiss, one of the department's best CSI officers. His clothes reeked of cigar smoke.

"Yep." Nathan answered, shaking his head in bewilderment. "Do you know who lives here? All I got is someone named Julia."

"*Oh, yeah,*" Weiss said emphatically. "Remember that Olwen kid that got murdered a couple of years ago in Atlanta? This is the mother's house. She apparently moved from the city down here after it happened to get away from the publicity. Bizarre. What did you see inside?"

"Unbelievable. Pretty gruesome, actually." Nathan was still reeling from it. "I haven't seen one this bad in a long time…maybe never. I did a preliminary walk-through of the house, and there's no body, but lots of blood from one, or enough for two or three. It's hard to tell. I hear she lived alone."

Nathan vaguely remembered the little boy's murder, but at the time, he was the newly-elected sheriff of Calhoun County and going through a divorce, limiting his available attention to news going on anywhere else but in his own jurisdiction. Nathan was going on about what he had seen to Weiss while several officers blocked the area with yellow police tape. Others were talking to neighbors who had begun to gather in front of the house. This was a property facing south, set off from the main road, and the closest neighbor was a couple of hundred feet to the east. The west side of the property was lined with a wooded area, and a small farm was on the other side of that. The driveway leading up to the house was open, and the house was visible from the road, but not in detail. The neighbors may have seen some activity there, but it was doubtful they would have heard anything significant. Weiss noted all that Nathan had said and proceeded into the house donned in shoe covers and latex gloves.

The crime scene crew soon found Julia Olwen's purse hanging on a door knob near the kitchen. It contained her cell phone, car keys and wallet, which indicated she had not gone anywhere willingly. Nathan's brain began calculating the possible scenarios. He couldn't help wonder how someone could be so unlucky to have a highly publicized murder in the family recently, only to have something this gruesome happen now in the very home meant to be her retreat. He felt heavy, weighed down by the reality of it. And from the looks of her home, she was no lowlife, nor did she live in the lap of luxury.

This was the kind of home a kid would visit to see his grandmother. Inviting, safe. It just didn't add up for Nathan.

The old sleuthing bug quickly emerged in him as he began to go over the details in his head, causing him to wonder who would do this. Why this way? Why now? Why her? Or was it even her? Could *she* have been the perpetrator? He was reenergized at the end of a day that had begun with an ordinary tenor, as he walked over to his car, got in behind the wheel, and pulled out a notebook from the glove box. This was the part he liked the most about police work – making notes of everything he saw, smelled and heard – and then letting the evidence create the story that everyone hoped would lead to the bad guy. Nathan loved catching the bad guys. And he loved, even more, putting them away. No one would get away with something this heinous in his county. Not if he had anything to do with it.

2.

June 18, 2012

A parking space designated for Nathan Lee Davis was in front of the county building that contained the sheriff's department. But as self-assured as he was, he rarely parked there because it felt too arrogant to do that. It was a matter of privilege, not convenience, as there were only twenty spots in the whole lot. But acting privileged was not who Nathan was. The shady magnolia tree above the space was one benefit, which was a bonus in the hot Georgia summers. But other than that, it didn't make practical sense to Nathan to have it labeled "Reserved for the Sheriff," as if he needed public recognition. That kind of decorum caused Nathan some discomfort, not because he felt unworthy, but because he knew from coming up in the ranks that without good deputies, the sheriff was useless. To communicate that, he had created an incentive, sometimes serious but more often humorous, for his employees to earn the privileged use of the spot. If one of his deputies did something exceptionally well or solved a case or helped an old lady across the street, he might just declare him or her employee of the month, simply to show appreciation for members of his team. He was that kind of leader – the kind who got respect because he gave it. And being able to reign in favors, like asking someone to pull an all-nighter, was worth more than a parking spot. Those on the outside were often amazed at his ability to get things done and tended to attribute that to his charm. Nathan knew better. Police officers went into their jobs because they were attracted to rules, power, and respect for authority. A simple parking spot that indicated those qualities would be a good trade when he needed absolute compliance.

Tommy Braselton, affectionately known to Nathan and the other officers as "Pork Chop," was the current occupant of the coveted parking space. Nathan had forgotten why the nickname had stuck, since Tommy wasn't overweight, but he did have somewhat of a square nose and his body was rock solid. One rumor was that he snorted when he drank too much beer, but Nathan had never witnessed that. After his election, Nathan had hired Tommy to be his chief deputy because of his smarts and his rapport with his fellow officers, so he didn't much care about his snorting, as long as it was legal. Tommy's recent claim to fame that earned him the sheriff's parking spot was arresting a guy who had a meth lab in his mobile home. Nathan had no respect for meth addicts or their manufacturing methods, especially since a lab had blown up last year in the county, killing two toddlers. He had been on a mission ever since to find and shut them all down, so when Tommy busted this one, Nathan thought him deserving of the reward.

"Hey Pork, how's the coffee this morning?" Nathan asked as he walked into the break room, looking fatigued from the events of the night before.

"Not bad," said Tommy. "You okay?" Tommy had turned and noticed dark circles under Nathan's eyes, coupled with a raspy voice.

"Yeah…it was a tough night last night. What's the news from the lab?" Nathan asked as Tommy poured him a fresh cup.

"Blood came from one person, so we assume it's Julia Olwen's, but until we can get a match with her DNA, we can't be sure. They are working on that now."

Nathan nodded. "That's what I figured. The amount of blood was crazy."

"Dang, it's wild, isn't it?" asked Tommy. "Who would want to get rid of that kid's mother?"

"Well, we're not sure anyone is dead, but I'm tellin' ya man, I can't imagine the alternative." Nathan had a brief flashback of the scene and remembered the acrid smell of fresh blood. He rubbed the goose bumps on his forearm. "I've got Tolbert and Busby on the case, tracing the bank and credit card activity, so hopefully something will turn up. If it's quiet, we can probably assume she's gone."

"Okay, boss. Let me know if there's anything I can do." Tommy put a lid on his coffee and turned to walk away. "I'm headed out for a meeting." He would have normally made a sarcastic comment to Nathan or told a dirty joke first thing in the morning, but the sheriff seemed unusually disturbed by the previous night's events and Tommy felt he should be more respectful this time.

"Good deal," Nathan replied as he walked toward his office, without asking about Tommy's meeting, indicating an unusual level of distraction that Tommy rarely saw in his boss.

Nathan knew this was not going to be an ordinary day as he sat down to his computer. His phone buzzed. It was Dorothy, his secretary.

"Sally Tate from WLTA is on line one. She wants to talk to you about last night."

"Thanks, Dot. Here we go…" He let out a sigh as he clicked over to the line that was flashing red.

"*Sall-ee Tater-tot,*" Nathan announced melodically with his southern drawl. Of all the local reporters, he liked red-headed Sally Tate the best. She could take a joke that didn't have to be politically correct, unlike other female reporters he had to treat with more caution.

"Good morning, Sheriff Davis," she replied with a cheery half chuckle. "I'm surprised to find you at the department and not at the murder scene."

"Headin' out there soon, and no one has reported it as a murder yet," Nathan corrected, knowing she would twist anything he didn't refute into fact. "What can I do for ya?"

"Will you be making a statement or having a press conference or anything today? This is big news here, especially since it's tied to the Joey Olwen case."

"Yeah, I know." He was Googling Joey Olwen's name as she spoke. "Uh, give me an hour or so and my secretary will get back to you and the others about a time for the press conference. We'll probably do it in front of the building here…I'm guessing early afternoon."

"Okay, sounds good. Is there anything you might like to tell me before then?" Her voice became more high-pitched, as she tried to woo preliminary information out of the sheriff.

"Not yet. I'll have a prepared statement this afternoon." He was engrossed in his computer search and to Sally's surprise, he didn't playfully scold her like he normally would.

"Well, I appreciate you taking my call," Sally said in a more professional tone.

"You kidding me? *I love* reporters, you know that." He enjoyed teasing her and sometimes called her by her full name, Sally Lynn Tate, which irritated her because it had a Southern cadence, even though she originally hailed from Iowa. In turn, it shocked him that anyone would be ashamed to claim Southern roots.

"Uh huh," she muttered sarcastically. "We'll see you soon, Sheriff."

Nathan hung up the phone as he clicked on the link to an article from an Atlanta paper. Joey Olwen stared out from the computer screen. *Cute kid.* Probably eleven or twelve years old, he guessed. He gripped a baseball bat, wore a baseball cap turned backwards, and had a focused expression on his face, like he was all set to hit a home run. Above the picture, the black headline told the stark truth: "Atlanta Boy Victim of Pedophile." *Shit.* It didn't get any worse than that. Except that yeah, it did. Nathan shook his head. The poor kid's mom never even had the scant satisfaction of seeing her son's killer sent to jail. And now it looked like she might be dead herself.

Nathan clicked through to later articles. Lance Irving Eddy had been tried and acquitted of the murder, some said because of a botched police investigation and a corrupt judge. Apparently, Lance Eddy's father, real estate developer Clyde Eddy, was tight with Judge Seeger. But Nathan had some previous dealings himself with the judge and couldn't imagine him throwing a murder case because of a relationship – unless of course there had been some dirty dealings that Seeger didn't want Clyde Eddy to reveal. *How could a judge influence a jury anyway?* Then he read on to discover that the judge had not allowed a critical piece of evidence to be revealed to the jury, which skeptics now speculated was a dirty move. Rumor had it that the prosecution was set to appeal based on that fact, but appeals after an acquittal were lengthy in coming and rarely successful. Some even said that the D.A. was dirty as well – in cahoots with the judge and Eddy – which meant an appeal was probably going to be purposely delayed.

Nathan decided it would be a good idea to set up a meeting with Leroy Luckinbill, the Marlowe County district attorney who had prosecuted and lost the case against Joey's suspected murderer. He was sure he could get Luckinbill to squirm with the right questions. Nathan resolved to put the interview on the back burner for the moment because he had to gather evidence, and time was of the essence. He kept the idea tucked away, though, because if there was something dirty going on back then, this new development may be tied to it. Nathan felt a natural excitement well up in him. It had been a long time since he had a case that might actually be challenging.

He gulped the remainder of his coffee, put on his sport coat, and headed out of the office, passing Dorothy along the way. "Don't forget these," she said with a smile, while holding up a pair of reading glasses. She knew he was always losing or sitting on his, so she kept several pair in her desk drawer just in case. He grabbed them from her hand as he hurried by.

"You are one sweet girl – and hot, too!" he shouted as he walked out the door. He knew that would get a rise out of her, especially since she was just shy of her sixtieth birthday.

Dorothy shook her head and rolled her eyes in feigned disgust, while smiling and patting her bleached blonde hair. She sat back down at her computer to write the press conference announcement, still thinking about Nathan's comment. *Mm…mm…mm, if I were only twenty years younger.*

3.

Julia - September, 2011

"Has the jury reached a verdict?" asked Judge Seeger in a formal monotone.

"Yes, we have, your honor," replied the jury foreman.

"What say you?"

"As to count one of murder in the first degree, we the jury in the above entitled action find the defendant, Lance Irving Eddy…*not guilty.*" There were gasps, followed by groans, and then sobs coming from the left side of the courtroom.

"As to count two of aggravated kidnapping, we the jury in the above entitled action find the defendant, Lance Irving Eddy, *not guilty.*" Again, the gasps, the groans and the sobs.

Julia didn't hear anything after that. It was as if her body was under water and all the voices were muffled. Her head was swimming in disbelief. Then she noticed that her friend Claire was struggling to hold her upright. *Am I fainting? I want to faint…just fall apart…go away.*

She didn't remember much after that, but later saw the television coverage of the verdict and could tell by the reaction in the courtroom that no one else believed what they were hearing either. A close-up of Eddy's attorney, Wayne Beaudreau, who was one of the best criminal defense guys in the Southeast, revealed an O.J.-like moment – reminiscent of Robert Kardashian's famous look of utter surprise and disgust at hearing that Simpson was *not guilty*, effectively caught on camera. Beaudreau, too, was visibly startled by the verdict, even though he tried to immediately hide it. Then his face turned to something like despair. Julia watched the video clip over and over, taking some odd comfort in knowing she was right every time she saw Beaudreau's faint grimace at the words *not guilty*. And District Attorney Luckinbill fell back into his hard wooden seat at the prosecution table, feigning disappointment, but subtly relieved. She was certain they were all in on the deal to ensure Lance Eddy's acquittal. She just didn't know why or how exactly. To make matters worse, all the television reporters were using words like *shocking, unbelievable, devastating* and *surprise*.

Julia had been in the courtroom every single minute the trial was in session. She knew all the evidence and how it had been presented. There were no obvious holes in the case. It was open and shut, as they say, except for Eddy's weak plea of innocence. So, how could he go free? Important evidence had been disallowed for no apparent reason, but couldn't the jury see what she and everyone else saw? Even more telling to Julia was the video shot of Lance Eddy's face at the reading of the verdict – he showed no expression.

No expression. How does it feel for a grown man to sit in jail for months while a trial is being prepared, especially if he were truly innocent, and then finally hear the words *not guilty*? She was convinced that if it had been her, she would have jumped for joy or fainted from relief. Not Eddy. He was as stone-faced as he could be and that did not sit right with Julia Olwen. For her, that was just one more confirmation that he had done it, yet expected to go free. She smelled a rat, and her mind began to race about the next steps. But nothing materialized for her. There was always a next step, wasn't there? Some recourse to ensure justice? The D.A. had told her they could appeal based on the judge's poor discretion in not allowing important evidence into the trial. However, if she and others were right about their suspicions that Luckinbill was dirty, then his words, "Winning an appeal for a new trial won't happen overnight," were nauseatingly true for Julia. She felt sure he would drag his feet on this until after the next election. So how many children would Eddy hurt in the mean time? The thought was unimaginable to her. For the first time ever, she hated the justice system that protected the acquitted from double jeopardy. All she could do was pray that Eddy's crime would torture his mind forever, but she also knew that as all true psychopaths go, he probably wasn't capable of introspection. The pain was deep and angry and heavy for her. How could she go to sleep with this knowledge, and worse yet, wake up the next morning with no hope for resolution? She couldn't wait for Luckinbill's appeal. She would do *something*.

***

"We'll ask for ten million," said Stu Wheeler, the attorney who had agreed to help Julia with a civil suit against Eddy. "Depending on what the jurors know, you might get more than that. Eddy's family has more dealings than a Vegas casino."

Julia sat staring, not even sure why she had driven to Stu's office this morning. She was still shattered by the disappointing trial and was having trouble putting herself back together. A few weeks had passed since the verdict and everyone seemed to think the next logical step was to begin preparing motions for a wrongful death suit against Eddy – something she was told she had to do to make him pay somehow. In her heart, though, she knew the only benefit to her would be a share of the Eddy family empire, but it would do nothing to assuage her anger and guilt about Joey's death. Why hadn't she installed that security system like she had promised herself she would do? She knew Joey was spending more time alone during her crazy hospital shifts and she had even called a few companies to get estimates, but never made an appointment. Had she done that, maybe Eddy would have been too scared to pursue Joey in the midst of a blaring alarm horn. She felt guilty about not getting that puppy Joey had been begging for, but Julia could only anticipate the extra work and effort it would demand, so she had nixed the idea out of practicality. Now, she wished she would have gotten a pit bull or Doberman that might have scared Eddy to death in his moment of thrill-seeking. These were the thoughts that haunted Julia's sober and drug-free moments, giving her reason to down a rum and Coke with a Xanax, just before bed each night. It was her guilty escape from the unrelenting truth.

"You okay?" asked Wheeler, who realized she had not heard most of what he had just said, as she blankly stared past him toward the window behind. It pained him to see her like this – a mere shell of a broken woman who was once vibrant and positive. He was angry at Eddy, too, for putting Julia through this torture. He had known Julia for years, since she and his daughter Claire met in the fourth grade and became best friends. Wheeler thought Julia had always been too caring and a little too accommodating with men, which is why he figured she ended up with a deadbeat like Joey's dad. But he knew that none of those shortcomings deserved the kind of pain Julia was experiencing now.

"Huh? Oh…yeah." Julia finally looked him in the eyes. "I don't care about the money. I just want someone to say he's guilty, that's all. I need someone to tell me that son of a bitch is guilty. Then maybe I can sleep." It was good for her to feel occasional intense moments of anger that didn't induce tears.

Within seconds, she lapsed back into thought again, contemplating the first days after the verdict which were so difficult. But then she had been in shock. Now, it seemed there was no buffer. The enormity of what had happened was finally settling in and anger was surfacing without a moment's notice. There were no more daily news reports about the case. There were no more regular phone calls from her well-meaning church family, inquiring about her state of mind while her son's name was constantly in the spot light. It was as if everyone around her had accepted the verdict as the end of her ordeal, but to Julia it was only the beginning. As much as it was heart-wrenching in the last eighteen months to have the constant reminders of Joey's murder, it seemed ten times worse to have everything suddenly go silent. She almost welcomed the civil trial in order to not have to be forced to go on with her life. For the first time ever, she had contemplated suicide and often thought that if it was not for Pastor Tucker's words that she was already with Joey, she might have decided to take her life in order to hasten the reunion. But how could she know he was right about that? How could she know there even was a heaven or a God or anything higher overseeing this crazy, deranged world? Julia felt alone. Alone and hostile. Hopeless.

Wheeler sat patiently with her for a few more seconds and then spoke up rather softly, trying to ease her out of the trance she had slipped into again. "Julia…just to be clear. If you win, it only means we have presented a better case than the defense, and the jury will see fit to award damages…they will not be declaring him guilty, per se."

It annoyed Julia to hear the way he emphasized the words *per se*, as if it was his duty to inform her that she would not get the satisfaction from it that she was seeking. "Stu, I don't care about the fucking money, did you hear what I said?" Julia yelled while pounding the heel of her hand on Stu's massive cherry desk. She was surprised by her loud outburst toward Stu, a man she grew up respecting and had addressed as "Sir" for nearly half her childhood. She sat back in her chair and dropped her head. "I'm sorry, Stu. I don't know…"

Julia was confused about what had just happened. She noticed Wheeler had that look on his face that she had seen in many men when she was exasperated. The one that says *I have no idea what to say now.*

To her surprise, he spoke before she did. "You know, it might be a good thing for you to go see someone," Wheeler said.

Not the words she was looking for. "See someone?" Julia looked puzzled. "You mean like counseling or something?"

"Well, yeah…you know…someone who could help you figure this out."

The lump in Julia's throat burst at the words. "Figure this out?" Her voice cracked. All of a sudden it was as if the floodgates had opened and years of hot, molten lava came flowing out of her. This, she thought, was the best therapy ever. "Figure this out?" She said louder, feeling her chest tighten and the anger well up again, the tears coming through the words whether she liked it or not. "There is no *figuring* this out, Stu. I've *got* it figured out!" She was unaware her voice had grown loud enough to penetrate Wheeler's office walls. "Eddy massacred my son and he gets to go to dinner tonight at Longhorn, and ride his motorcycle to the mountains this weekend, and maybe find another little boy to molest and kill, and I'm supposed to figure this out?" she sat up again and dropped her head on her hands on Wheeler's desk, sobbing with audible moans. Wheeler got up from his chair and went around his desk to comfort Julia. He placed his large hand on her bony shoulders and said, "I know sweetie. We'll figure…I'll make the bastard's family pay if it's the last thing I do."

Wheeler reached over his desk and buzzed his secretary to bring water. He nervously walked over to the door to see if she had heard him and then returned to his big chair while Julia sat limply, broken. Moments later, Julia composed herself and smiled apologetically as the middle-aged woman handed her a bottle of Dasani. In silence, Julia drank, while Wheeler fiddled with a stack of papers on his desk, clearly sending the message that there was not much more to say. But Julia wanted to linger a little while longer so she didn't have to face the end of this meeting. Everything seemed to be disappearing. Ending without her permission. She could see that Stu felt helpless and knew it was time to go.

"I guess I'll head out, Stu. Sorry for the…the outburst," she said with a dejected tone, as she rose and gathered her purse and bulging file folder from the floor next to her chair.

"Not a problem, kiddo." Wheeler got up to walk her out. "I wish I could make this all better for you. I really do."

Julia believed him. His eyes were soft and caring, not like the ones she remembered as a child when she and Claire got into trouble. She walked out of his office and to the parking garage across the street, in a distracted state of reflection – so much so that she nearly got hit by a speeding car, laying on the horn as she crossed. She wondered if she could physically and emotionally do this again. *Another trial.* For a moment she had no memory of the spot where she had parked her car, let alone which floor it was on. She stopped and was nearly brought to tears by this inadequacy. Then she remembered that when she first parked the car, she had travelled one or two floors down to get to the street level that led into the high rise office building. She decided to go up the garage elevator to both floors and hit her car alarm, hoping it would guide her to where it was parked.

Safely on the elevator, her brain resumed its obsessive pattern. Wheeler had promised he would do all the work and all she would have to do is testify. He said the case would probably not be heard until January, since the holidays usually slowed down the civil court system considerably. Maybe by then she would be in a better place. The holidays. She dreaded the thought. The last holiday season was awful, but so many people were willing to share themselves and their homes with her. She wondered if anyone would be so gracious this year. Would they just expect her to be over it? The elevator stopped on the first floor. She exited and hit the alarm button on her key fob and heard the welcoming blare of her car horn. She proceeded toward it like a zombie.

On the way home, she thought about what Wheeler had said. She was certain she needed to lean on his strength and attention to detail because she could already feel her brain compartmentalizing the last two years – putting them neatly into a cavernous file cabinet somewhere in her brain's amygdala, where traumatic memories lie. She wanted to pack it away, safe and sound, never to be retrieved again. Yet she knew from her years as a trauma nurse that people often temporarily lose their memory around traumatic events, but if not dealt with properly, the memories would return at the wrong times and trigger a lot of erratic emotion. As much as she didn't want to admit it, Wheeler was probably right, at least about one thing. Yes, perhaps she did need to find someone to help her get this under control. But, while Wheeler was referring to her grief and anger, Julia had a far more troubling problem to deal with: her obsession with a plan that haunted her exhausted soul. A plan to avenge her son's murder.

4.

June 19, 2012

It had been two days since Nathan had discovered the crime scene at Julia Olwen's home — nearly the proverbial forty-eight hours in which law enforcement should crack a case like this, but it remained as much of a mystery now as it did when he had first discovered it. He spent hours looking at the crime scene photos, making notes about every detail, reading the police reports of the neighbors' statements, and trying to think like a criminal to reenact what might have happened at 1126 China Grove Road. Nothing materialized that Nathan could sink his teeth into except for a sighting of a red pickup truck in Julia's driveway the night before, reported by her elderly neighbor. From all accounts, Julia Olwen was a hardworking nurse and a wonderful daughter to her two ailing parents who she had lost a few years before her son's murder. Seemingly, she was a great friend and good neighbor to those she had befriended since her recent move to Calhoun County. People like Julia don't usually find themselves at the end of a gun or knife — not unless it's a random act. He needed to talk to her attorney and see if there were plans for a civil suit, which might shed some light on her state of mind about Lance Eddy. Nathan could only imagine the anger she must have toward Eddy and those responsible for setting him free.

He had also learned that Julia had a burglar alarm system installed in her present home, unlike in the home where Joey was murdered. In fact, according to the alarm company, it was installed about six months ago, causing Nathan to wonder if she was afraid of Eddy or his family, since he had been acquitted and would be roaming free. Had she made contact with him and then worried about the repercussions? Yet, Nathan's suspicions had been confirmed by investigators that there had been no forced entry into Julia's home. He remembered being able to walk through the front door without any trouble the night he was there. He deduced, then, that she was a woman afraid enough to have an alarm system installed, but not afraid enough on the evening of her disappearance to lock her front door, let alone activate the alarm system.

He made a note that she may have been expecting her kidnapper or murderer to arrive. Did she have family members or friends who were angry with her? All reports showed that she had very little family. She was an only child of Donald and Lucy Olwen, who had adopted her as an infant when they were in their late forties. Neither Donald nor Lucy had siblings who were currently alive or living anywhere near Calhoun County. He checked out first and second cousins, but came up with nothing, except for a distant cousin in California she had communicated with occasionally. The current friends she had were mostly connected to her church at St. Oliver's, and all of them said nothing but positive and adoring things about Julia. A common theme among all who knew her seemed to be the disgust they felt about why tragic things happen to perfectly good people.

Nathan then finally turned to romance – the potentially deadliest of all relationships. What about Joey's father? Did she continue to have any contact with him? He had learned that Joey's dad, Trent Karracher, was a ne're-do-well who Julia met when she was in her late twenties and working in the ER at Grady Hospital. Trent had gotten injured on the job at a construction site and she was on duty when he was brought in with a fractured leg and punctured lung. He had fallen from a three-story scaffolding and was rushed to the hospital for treatment. When Nathan looked closer at his background, it seemed he had roamed from job to job and had done a couple of stints in the county jail for public drunkenness. Not a bad guy, but not a particularly good one either. *What was a girl like her doing with a guy like him?* Others described Trent as a charmer with a big white smile as large as his ego. He was known around town as a party animal and a friend of the ladies. Julia was apparently vulnerable to someone like Karracher at the time because she was rebounding from a bad breakup, according to Julia's closest friend, Claire Brownlee. She had reported that Julia always had been extremely responsible and level-headed, but when she was grieving the break-up from her first love, Karracher triggered that throw-caution-to-the-wind spirit in her that felt daring and angry. The relationship apparently lasted only six months, until Julia's good senses returned, but all that throwing caution to the wind produced an unwanted pregnancy. From all reports, though, Julia never questioned whether or not she would have the baby. Her Catholic faith and responsible nature would have never allowed it to be any other way. Karracher took off after discovering Julia's pregnancy, which was not a problem for her since she had learned enough about him to know he would not be the greatest influence on her son. According to her friends, one of the reasons she had named her son *Joseph* was because she had a great deal of respect for Jesus' surrogate father who was betrothed to the Mother Mary. Joseph had stuck by her even when the facts and rumors pointed toward deception. Apparently, Julia wanted her son to be different from his biological father. She wanted him to be a man who would face life's challenges head-on. *Much like his mother*, thought Nathan.

As he pondered that, a memory was uncomfortably triggered in him – one of his own that illuminated his sense of faith and justice as a child. He remembered the day as if it were yesterday, when at age fifteen, he walked into his father's hardware store and saw it in shambles after a break-in. The plate glass window had been smashed and the money in the cash register had been emptied and stolen, along with some expensive tools and woodworking equipment. His father had a look that was burned into Nathan's mind. It was a look of complete violation, but also of anger and determination to bring the thieves to justice. As he had watched the police officers that day assure his father that they would make the criminals pay, Nathan had felt a sense of envy for their power and ability to right some of the wrongs in the world. That experience led him to his profession in law enforcement and whenever he needed to remind himself of why he chose such a financially unrewarding career, he remembered his dad's eyes, which put it all into perspective. As he was deep in thought, a voice startled him.

"The forensics came back on the blood," Tommy Braselton bellowed as he smacked a sheet of paper onto Nathan's cluttered desk.

"Yeah?"

"It's hers. The blood is all hers according to the lab. Coincidentally, she had just had blood drawn at the hospital a few days before for her annual physical, so it was an easy match."

"Amazing," Nathan said softly, as the meaning of what Tommy had said sunk in. "What else?"

"Lab says there were probably five to seven pints lost according to the CSI reports and the photos that were taken. Five to seven pints! That's a half-gallon of blood. C'mon, nobody loses that much and lives to tell about it, do they?"

Nathan remained silent for a few seconds while he stared at the lab report. Tommy followed his lead and stopped talking. He had learned that the sheriff didn't really like him droning on when he was deep in thought.

Finally, Nathan spoke. "Nah, there's no doubt she's gone. Now we have to figure out what happened to the body." Nathan leaned back in his leather office chair, still looking pensive. "Well, Pork, I'm going out for a smoke," said Nathan as he got up from his desk. Whenever he needed to solve a problem, nicotine seemed to relax him enough to help him access a higher form of mental processing. Without it, his thoughts were easily distracted.

"Alright," said Tommy with slight frustration. He wanted Nathan to let him in on what he was hypothesizing, but he knew better than to interfere with Nathan's so-called *process*. A few weeks before, Tommy had overstepped his bounds and pushed the sheriff for his thoughts when he was in one of these moods. "Damn it, Pork, you're worse than a nagging woman," he had admonished Tommy. "When I get it going in the right direction in my head, I'll let you in on it. Got it?" Tommy and the other officers knew it was Nathan's perfectionism that kept him from talking too much before he was ready to reveal his conjecture to others. Nathan Lee Davis did not like to eat his words, so he chose them carefully and accurately, keeping his cards close to his chest. Nathan would say that was the key to his success – letting the apparent truth simmer a while until it was a sure thing. The unspoken truth was his fear of being accused of ever getting it wrong.

5.

Julia - October, 2011

"You let yourself go…you let the anger go, that is," the therapist said softly and knowingly. "Yeah, it was like all the toxins were leaving my body. I hated dumping on Stu like that, but once I did, it felt really, really….good," continued Julia.

This was her first therapy session with Dr. Sonya Pierce, a middle-aged throwback from the seventies, whose facial lines reflected a life of learning the hard way. She was slightly overweight, dressed in a flowing flowery skirt, with a crocheted belt and beaded jewelry. Julia trusted the cliché nature of Sonya's appearance, making it easier for her to reveal her own stereotypical emotions as a grieving mother. Although it felt scripted at first, there was a sense of safety and predictability in it. Dr. Pierce exuded authenticity and Julia was glad to have found someone who might not make her feel judged or pitied. Surprisingly, it was a good fit and Julia reminded herself to thank Stu for the push in the right direction.

"Cleansing?" Sonya guessed.

"I guess you could say that. Although I don't think anything will ever really clean up all the junk that's inside here." Julia nervously chuckled and made a circular hand motion near her midsection.

"Say more about that…the junk."

There was a long pause that seemed like eternity. She could hear Dr. Pierce's clock softly ticking in the background. She noticed her therapist's perfume. *White Linen.* It was difficult for Julia to answer questions that made her have to dig so deep.

"I don't know…I guess…I don't know…the guilt, the anger, the devastation of losing a child. No one ever cleanses that, do they?"

Julia felt unnerved by Dr. Pierce's silence.

"Do they?" Julia asked more emphatically.

"I can't say. I've never lost a child," Sonya explained. "I just know that grief can be a really hard thing to endure."

"Yeah, you can say that again."

"Is there anything about your grief that you find helpful?" Sonya asked.

"Helpful? What could possibly be helpful?"

"Well, some people report feeling a sense of relief from responsibility, for example, when they've lost a loved one they have had to take care of for a long time."

"Yes, I remember that after I lost my dad. It had been a really long haul and even though I hated to lose him, I didn't have to worry about him so much anymore. I knew he was in a better place." She paused, thinking about how she just answered that.

Julia continued, "But I don't feel that way at all about Joey. I loved being responsible for him." She could feel the tears coming. "I loved every single minute of being his mom, even when he drove me crazy with his backtalk or wore me down, arguing like a good attorney." Julia laughed through the tears.

"It's much different…with Joey," Sonya affirmed. "You weren't supposed to lose him right in the middle of loving the responsibility for him."

"No." Julia reached for a tissue out of a leopard-print tissue box on the glass-top table in front of her. "I'm sorry," she said. "It's still so fresh…it's so damn fresh."

"I understand," Sonya acknowledged. "There are no rules about what you should feel or for how long. You get to make the rules about that."

After a few more interchanges, Sonya reached for her calendar, which Julia took as a sign that the session was over. Julia was surprised by how quickly the time had gone, although much of it was taken up by basic getting-to-know-you questions. She hoped the next session would be a little easier and less intrusive. After making the next appointment and handling payment, Julia got up and awkwardly shook Sonya's hand and left her office, wondering what Dr. Pierce would do next once she was gone. Will she write notes about what she said? Will she yawn because she's heard this stuff a thousand times? Did she care what she was going through or was she just really good at pretending? She couldn't know for sure, but one thing that stuck with her was one of Dr. Pierce's last comments. "You get to make the rules." For some reason, that bolstered Julia. She deserved that much at least, didn't she? *I get to make the rules. And the rules, I will make.* For the first time in a long time, Julia smiled with a sense of determination. She wasn't sure about what, but that would come in due time.

6.

June 20, 2012

The clock-radio was blaring *Margaritaville* as Nathan groped for the snooze button. It was seven o'clock in the morning, and he had slept like a rock for the first time in a few days. The music made him long for a vacation instead of the long hours he would likely be putting in on the investigation of the first murder in Calhoun County in twenty years. He groaned and felt his middle age as he stood up and his left knee buckled slightly underneath him. It was an old football injury from high school coming back to haunt him. He limped to the dresser and looked at his flashing BlackBerry, indicating a new message. It was from the clerk in the magistrate's office saying the search warrant for Julia Olwen's house had been issued. He wasn't sure how he had missed that message since it apparently came in at four o'clock the day before. The search would be a big part of the day ahead – trying to learn about Julia's life in that cozy little bungalow with the wrap-around porch on China Grove Road.

He grabbed his toothbrush and mindlessly cleaned his teeth while thinking about what he hoped to find. Maybe there would be something on her phone or computer's hard drive to indicate what her steps had been in the last few days before the murder. His phone was lighting up and vibrating, and nearly fell off of the bathroom vanity before he caught it. He must have been so dead tired the night before, he had forgotten to turn the ringer back on after his late afternoon staff meeting. He made a mental note to be more careful about that, as he wanted to be certain to get every possible call when it came in while there were so many plates spinning in the air around this case.

"Yeah, Davis here," he answered in his scratchy morning voice.

"You awake?" he heard Tommy ask way too cheerfully.

"Yep, just barely. Whatdya got?"

"Just wondering when you are planning to head over to the Olwen house," Tommy said.

"In a few minutes," said Nathan, with a clearer voice and a little more energy. "I'm gonna stop by the QT for some coffee and then I'll be right there. Want some?"

"Nope, got mine already. See ya over there." Tommy hung up before Nathan had a chance to say anything else. He made another mental note to remind Tommy which one of them was the sheriff.

The QuikTrip was just around the corner from Nathan's house, an eighteen-hundreds, Antebellum-style bungalow that had been in his family for generations. Every morning when he pulled out of the driveway he was reminded of how much work needed to be done on the place, but since the divorce a couple of years ago, he hadn't had the money or the energy to put into it. *As soon as I get through this case, I've got to get to work*, he thought as he pulled away once again looking at a yard full of weeds and a roof that needed replaced. As soon as the house was out of sight, Nathan's thoughts turned quickly back to Julia's murder.

The photo of Julia that he kept in his file was the one of her and her son that appeared on little Joey's memorial Facebook page. She was an attractive brunette in her mid-thirties at the time of the photo, with what appeared to be an athletic, but feminine physique. She was about five foot six inches tall, with brown eyes and a kind smile. Nathan remembered seeing her occasionally on the news reports at the time of her son's murder, but he hadn't noticed how pretty she was until now. Maybe because he was going through a bad divorce at the time and he wasn't in the habit of caring what any woman looked like, even if they were drop-dead gorgeous. At the time, women were a symbol for Nathan of what could go terribly wrong in your life, not anything particularly inviting. But he had noticed recently that he had softened his position on women and was beginning to feel like he could at least consider dating again. He glanced at the photo one more time in the folder sitting on the passenger seat before pulling out of the QuikTrip where he usually picked up his morning coffee. Julia Olwen had round, appealing features – silky hair, with doe eyes and a cute pug-like nose. At first glance, she had a Valerie Bertinelli kind of look, but less voluptuous and more down-to-earth. Although, he imagined she had the same kind of spunk. He had noticed in the photo the first time he saw it the gold crucifix around her neck. But this time his eyes glanced below it at a bit of tantalizing cleavage that made him think she might have been a good dating prospect had he not met her in this more tragic way. He did not care for bony women, but liked those who had enough flesh, but not too much. He knew most men felt that way, even though women thought they had to be emaciated to be pleasing. He grinned and silently scolded himself for not being more respectful of the dead.

Nathan pulled into the driveway off of China Grove Road and remembered that the investigation team had taken photos and plaster casts of some tire tracks on the dirt part of the drive that was not paved. It appeared to have been used as a turn-around spot since Julia's drive led out onto a busy county road and was not conducive to a car safely backing out. The tracks had been compared to Julia's vehicle, but didn't match those on her 2010 Nissan Murano, which was still parked in the garage. He made a note in his file to look at those track photos more closely and get one of the guys to work on identifying the make.

He parked his unmarked black Crown Victoria in the turnaround spot, got out of the car and put on his sport coat that had been lying on the passenger seat with the case file. He grabbed his super-sized coffee and walked toward the house when he heard Tommy's cruiser pull into the driveway. Nathan stopped to wait for him and noticed the sides of the car were splashed with mud.

"Looks like you need a wash there, buddy," Nathan said as he pointed to the mud.

"Yeah, I had one on the run yesterday. I pulled over this guy in a Jeep because he was all over the road, and when I got to him, he sped off and took me on a wild chase down Two Bridges Road, which is mostly dirt. After that big storm, there were puddles all over the place."

"Did ya get him?" asked Nathan as he grinned and turned the knob on the front door of Julia's home.

"Did I *get* him?" Tommy guffawed sarcastically at Nathan's question. "Like a scene from Dirty Harry. By the time I caught up with him, backup had blocked the road ahead and his Jeep ran off into a wooded area when he couldn't get by the block. The idiot tried to run, but he was so stoned, he only thought he was running!" Tommy rambled on excitedly as Nathan quietly walked into the front entry.

The smell of cleaning solution used by the CSI unit to clean up the scene overwhelmed him, causing Nathan to remember the shock of what he had seen a few nights before. He walked over to the kitchen counter, laying the warrant down as a procedural gesture. He couldn't help notice how different the kitchen area looked without all the smears and splatters of blood everywhere. He felt a little nauseated.

"Where do you want to start, Sheriff?" Tommy had calmed down and was back in his police business voice.

"Why don't you take the back bedroom and the master, you know, check out her personal items and clothing. I'm going to see what I can find in her office here," Nathan said, pointing to a computer desk in a small room off of the kitchen. He hoped to get some preliminary information from her computer before he had it sent to forensics. Julia Olwen's house was a nineteen-fifties cottage with a wrap-around porch that made the place look much larger than it really was. In the back of the house, there was an eat-in kitchen with an adjoining dining room that she had set up as an office. The living room and master bedroom were in the front of the house, with a smaller bedroom and bath across the hall from the master that shared a wall with the sun porch off of the kitchen.

Nathan had to check his enthusiasm as he sat down at the desk and began rummaging through it. He reminded himself that this was an investigation into a tragic death, not simply a puzzle to be solved. That quickly became a reality the minute he opened a red leather journal with gold-edged pages that was in the top desk drawer. Nathan opened it and found a photo of Joey taped to the inside cover, with a message written below it, presumably in Julia's handwriting:

Your life gave me life; Your death was not in vain; Somewhere, someway, someday, there will be justice for you, my sweet boy.

He hurriedly flipped through the less than ten pages of hand-written entries that appeared to be dated from October through April, 2012. Key words stuck out for him at first glance, such as the mention of Lance Eddy's name and words like *hate* and *depressed* jumped off of the delicate pages, but that wasn't surprising given what she had been through. He also took note of the mention of a Dr. Pierce on the first page who she had written was the one who encouraged her to start the journal. He assumed that would be her physician or possibly a counselor of some sort, and he made a mental note to schedule an interview. He was tempted to begin reading more intently, but with limited time, he didn't want to ignore other possible clues in the house, so he placed it in the evidence box to take back to the office. Most of the journal was blank, so he doubted in contained anything of significance.

Nathan and Tommy finished rummaging through Julia's belongings, securing a few interesting items for testing like a hand towel that was found on the bathroom floor and Julia's computer equipment that Nathan would deliver to the forensic tech guys. He glanced at his watch and shouted to Tommy that they needed to wrap up. He didn't want to miss the meeting he had set up with Luckinbill. He walked out of Julia's house, pulling the door shut behind him, still amazed that from the outside, everything looked as cozy and inviting as the first night he saw it. Certainly not like the home of a violent murder victim.

7.

Julia - November, 2011

"For God's sake, Julia," Claire admonished. "You lost your son and the guy got away with it. You are still allowed to feel pissed off." She was Julia's closest friend, but occasionally felt frustrated with Julia's emotional perfectionism. Claire stared at Julia with her piercing blue eyes for a few seconds before turning to pour herself another glass of Pinot Grigio, which was sitting on the wicker coffee table in front of her.

It was a cool evening, but unseasonably warm for November, even for Georgia. The two women were cloaked in sweatshirts and jeans – Claire covered with her husband's oversized Georgia Bulldogs hoody, and Julia in her navy pullover with a pink breast cancer awareness motif. In a moment of alcohol-induced nostalgia, Claire nearly laughed out loud at their fashion choices that seemed to scream party girl versus humanitarian. Yet, although they couldn't be more different, Claire loved and cherished their closeness.

Julia's front porch was one of their favorite talking spots, especially when they could drink wine without Claire's children around. Julia had moved to Calhoun County after Joey's murder at the cajoling of Claire, who knew Julia had little in the way of family and would need a support system, which she quickly found in Claire and in the church they now both attended at St. Oliver's. As Julia went on about her worries, Claire felt an intense admiration for her lifelong friend and knew that if the same thing had happened to her, Claire would be doing more than whining. Chances are, she would have ended up killing herself or someone else. Julia was the strongest person she knew. She just wished she could convince Julia how special she was.

"I know… I guess I meant, well, it just feels like this tape is always running in my head…you know, in the background, but I'm pretty sure no one else wants me to talk about it anymore." Julia was struggling to explain her reason for apologizing to Claire for the hundredth time for droning on about Joey's murder. "I'm sure your dad has had enough of my whining." Julia had propped her feet up on the worn cushion on the front-porch ottoman and looked down at her wine while twirling it around in her glass.

"Forget about pops. He loves you like you're his own kid." Claire smiled affectionately at Julia and then grew quiet, while looking out over the front yard where a doe had just galloped past with fear in her eyes. "I don't know how you do it, actually," Claire finally said more forcefully. "If anything close to what happened to you had happened in my family, I'm sure they would have admitted me to a mental ward by now or I'd be in jail for killing the bastard."

Julia loved Claire because no matter what happened in either of their lives, there would never be any judgment from the other. Julia reminded herself, though, that when Claire gets more than two glasses of wine in her, she tended to be overly boisterous.

"Yeah, I know. Well, nobody knows what they would really do until it happens. And even then, it is surprising how calm you can be…or maybe how much denial just feels like a good drug." That was the first time Julia had admitted she coveted the feeling of normalcy, in spite of nothing being normal. It was a two-edged sword. If she confronted her true feelings head on, it felt crushing, like colliding with a semi-truck. If she chose to relieve herself and ignore any of it occasionally, the guilt of not remembering Joey for even one day filled every pore of her body until she was weighed down with the sludge of it. It often seemed to Julia as if there was no way to process it all without feeling the weight of it.

"You are not in denial, sweetie," said Claire, with more empathy. She reached over and put her hand on Julia's. "You've done everything you were supposed to do...and more...as a grieving mother." Claire paused for a moment to wait for Julia's next thought. The air remained silent, as Julia sat pensively.

"Daddy tells me he's encouraged you to see someone for the depression," said Claire delicately. Claire never talked to her father about his cases, but he had been so worried about Julia after their last meeting, that he had called Claire to find out what he should be doing better to soothe her through another court case.

"Oh, yeah." Julia looked away, half embarrassed at the thought of Stu and Claire discussing that day in his office. "I started a couple of weeks ago. Her name is Sonya Pierce. Do you know her?" Julia was aware that Claire and Steve had gone to some marital therapy a while ago.

"No. Do you like her?"

"I guess...I don't know. I've never done that kind of thing before. I don't know what I'm supposed to say or talk about exactly."

Claire chuckled. "There is nothing you are supposed to do. Just tell her how you are feeling."

"And what good is that?" Julia was staring through her half-full glass of wine, while thinking about her session with

Dr. Pierce. She noticed how the liquid refracted the moonlight into different shades of gold.

"To relieve *me*, for one reason!" Claire exclaimed, slightly slurring her words.

Julia smiled, still pensive. "See? I meant it when I said I was sorry for being such a load."

Claire got up from the table, grabbed Julia's glass from her and put it aside. "C'mon," she said, while pulling Julia by the arm. "Let's go watch a movie or something. You are not going to ruin our girls' night by being little Miss Sourpants."

Julia reluctantly got up, but she was smiling because Claire always knew how to get her out of the dumps. She was right. It was a rare occasion that Steve was willing to stay home with Zoe and Chase so they could have an evening together. Gone were the days of clubbing, but drinking wine, eating chocolate and watching Kate Hudson in *How to Lose a Guy in Ten Days* one more time was all Julia and Claire needed to feel young and giddy again.

Julia pretended to watch the movie and occasionally laughed at the familiar parts, but for two hours, her mind stayed on what Dr. Pierce had said. *I get to make the rules now.* When Julia snapped out of her distraction, she could hear a hearty, but sinister, laugh coming from Claire, who was relishing in the mishaps of Ben and Andie on the screen. Claire had no idea that Julia was thinking she didn't need a therapist to help her understand her feelings. She needed payback.

8.

June 20, 2012

Leroy Luckinbill's office was covered in awards, trophies, and commendations. Nathan noticed one plaque that said "Rotarian of the Year," and he chuckled to himself. *Even if I got that award, I would be embarrassed to display it,* Nathan thought as he sat in front of Luckinbill's desk, waiting for him to return with coffee. Luckinbill was a former marine, turned attorney, who did have some accomplishments that Nathan could acknowledge, but he had found the guy to be more interested in his own image than anything else. He was courteous enough, but Nathan never had a good feeling about him. He was the kind of district attorney who cared more about reelection than he did about the right thing, which sounded cliché to Nathan even as he thought it. As he reviewed Luckinbill's wall of degrees, he noticed a Yale law school degree and a University of Florida bachelor's degree in communications. Being a Georgia Bulldog fan, Nathan grimaced. *Yeah that's about the best you'll do at Florida.* He'd had his share of *communications* at Georgia-Florida football games in the past.

"Here ya go, Sheriff," chanted Luckinbill as he handed Nathan a mug and moved into his big leather chair behind his palatial desk.

As far as Nathan knew, Marlowe County was hurting for money, but you wouldn't know it by the accoutrements in Luckinbill's office. He was noticing a fancy crystal carafe and water glasses on his credenza when Luckinbill interrupted his train of thought.

"So, you wanna know about the Olwen murder?" Luckinbill inquired.

"Well, Leroy…I've got his mother's murder to solve now, or at least we have a pretty good idea that she's been murdered. I figured that you might be able to shed some light on why someone might want to silence her." Nathan maintained a poker face, but Luckinbill showed an air of defensiveness.

"I don't know why you think I would know anything about that, Nathan. We weren't investigating her, ya know."

Nathan cringed at the sound of Luckinbill's fake southern drawl. He was from Indiana, and granted, he had been in Georgia for twenty years or so, but that accent was developed to win elections.

"Yes, I understand that," said Nathan, "but as you know yourself, my man, when you've got two tragedies in the same family this close toegether, there might be a connection…even if it's just a slight one."

"Sure, I didn't mean to imply…" Luckinbill's voice trailed off.

"Yeah, well, can I ask you a few questions just in case?"

"Shoot…" said Luckinbill confidently, as he leaned back in his cushioned chair. Nathan pulled out his case notebook and flipped a few pages.

"From all accounts, Ms. Olwen…Julia Olwen…had no enemies, was a hardworking nurse, a grieving mother, and moved down my way to get away from the memories in your county." Nathan looked up from his notes. "Do you remember anything about her? Was she making any threats after the acquittal? Did she know anything that someone might not have wanted her to talk about?"

Nathan stared intently at Luckinbill expecting him to squirm a little. Luckinbill sat up in his chair. He folded his hands on the desk.

"No, I can't think of anything like that," said Luckinbill, shaking his head slightly while rubbing his chin, as if to help him remember. Nathan hadn't noticed before, but Luckinbill reminded him strangely of Buzz Lightyear, with bulging eyes and a large chiseled chin.

"There were reports of a botched investigation," Nathan continued, "and speculation that Judge Seeger and Clyde Eddy had a business connection. Is there anything there that I should be looking into?" Nathan already knew the answer, but he wanted Buzz to know he was not going to overlook any possible avenue to solving this case.

"Of course not. The key words are *reports* and *speculation*. Nathan, you know how these reporters are. If you're talking about Sally Tate, she is the worst one of them all. I heard that she got dumped by Seeger's nephew, so who wouldn't expect her to try to trash the family?" Luckinbill maintained his composure, but Nathan was enjoying reading his eyes, that were darting back and forth. The eyes never lie.

"So just rumors and innuendo, you think?"

"Absolutely. We tried the case fair and square and unfortunately, the jury found that there was reasonable doubt that Eddy murdered that boy. "

"C'mon, Leroy. You know as well as I do that the guy did it. I could tell that just from reviewing the case file. He got off because Seeger wouldn't allow critical evidence to be admitted, among other things. Remember? That pair of little boy's underpants found in his apartment that the mother identified as her son's? Add that to the fact that Eddy had the best legal team in the country that could have convinced the Nazis to doubt Hitler." Nathan felt his blood pressure rise as he thought about how exasperating it must have been for Julia Olwen. He waited for Luckinbill to respond, but he just stared at Nathan unaffected. "That must kill you to think about it," he continued. "I mean, the highest profile case to ever be tried in Marlowe County and you aren't going to investigate Seeger for misconduct?"

Nathan knew Luckinbill was covering for someone — either Clyde Eddy or Judge Seeger — but it was clear he wasn't going to get him to fess up about it.

"Sorry, Nathan," he said stoically. "I'm afraid I can't be of much help to you." Luckinbill got up from his chair to indicate the meeting was over. "You've got the case file and there's really nothing more I can add to it."

"Okay, then. I appreciate your time, Leroy." Nathan got up as well and put his hand out to shake Luckinbill's.

They parted and Nathan felt comfortable he had ruffled Luckinbill's feathers a bit. Now he was anxious to talk to Sally Tate to find out what personal connection she had to the case. As he walked out of the Marlowe County administrative building, he pulled out his BlackBerry and found Sally's contact number. He was surprised that she answered.

"Afternoon, Tater," Nathan exclaimed, while making his way across the street to the parking deck.

"Sheriff Davis," she replied cheerfully.

"I'd like to buy you lunch. You got time today or tomorrow? Maybe come visit me down in my neck of the woods?" He could feel her smile on the other end.

"Sure," said Sally. "Perfect timing. I'm actually in Regal today covering the murder investigation. How about in an hour or so? That little diner on Maple?"

"You mean Lana's?

"Yeah, that's it."

"Okay, see you then." Nathan hung up and made his way to his car, thinking he wished he would have gotten his hair cut like he had intended to before this crazy week began.

9.

Julia - December, 2011

Julia was startled out of her sleep by the reoccurring nightmare that haunted her every couple of weeks. "No!" She had cried out, sitting straight up in her bed, her body covered in sweat and her heart pounding furiously. It took her a few seconds to gain her composure. Then the tears came, usually in quiet sobs, as she lay back down and curled up in the fetal position to wait for the memory to fade. The nightmare was always the same. She saw Lance Eddy enter her house on Del Mar Street through the back door. She was behind him, trying to yell for Joey to get out of the house, but she couldn't seem to make a sound. She ran into the house and went from room to room, but Joey was nowhere to be found. Just as she got back to the kitchen where Eddy had entered, she saw Joey in Eddy's arms, limp and lifeless. Eddy and Joey went out the door, and as he turned around to shut the door behind him, he cracked a sinister smile and entered the moonlit night with her son. Then she would cry out for him, but was unable to move or scream or anything. She was just simply helpless and crushed at knowing he was gone.

"Isn't there some kind of medication I can take to stop this crazy nightmare?" Julia had pled with Dr. Pierce after one of her episodes.

"I wish there was," explained Sonya. "Unfortunately, you just have to go through it. You will get to the other side eventually." Her voice was soft and reassuring.

Although Julia knew she was right, the pain was often unbearable, as it was on this night. She was afraid to tell Dr.

Pierce that there were times when she couldn't feel the ground underneath her. It was as if everything was rocky and there was nothing holding her up except her own will. In those times she wanted to just disappear into thin air – evaporate as if she never existed. She wondered if anyone would notice. *Joey is gone. Mama and daddy are gone. What is there to live for?* Then she would grab onto a piece of her anger, like sliding down a slippery mountainside, suddenly halted by a tree branch that supported her weight. For a time, the anger kept her from sliding further and even allowed her to stop and see hope in the distance.

Lately, when the nightmare had come back to haunt her, she had found herself lying awake, plotting against Eddy. She desperately wanted him to feel the kind of agony that she felt every day for the rest of his life. But getting a psychopath to feel bad about his crimes was like asking a three-year-old to solve an algebra problem. It was simply beyond his capacity. In fact, Eddy would be delighted to know she was suffering because that's what feeds someone who is truly evil. Julia had never believed in satanic spirits prior to Joey's murder. Even though Catholicism teaches that evil spirits exist and may need exorcised in the worst cases, she always passed that off as sensationalism – akin to people seeing the shape of the face of the Virgin Mary in their oatmeal. Julia became a believer in demons, though, when Eddy raped, tortured, mutilated and murdered her precious child. There was no good in a man like that. And by definition, a man who possesses no good, is pure evil. The thought of him being free and some other little boy, or some other mother, going through this was incomprehensible to Julia. Her obsession with Lance Eddy was beginning to frighten her. For the first time ever, she was thinking murderous thoughts. No one would believe it. She was a nurse. A healer. Not someone who would ever desire to destroy a life. But this was different.

Tossing and turning, sleep eluding her, Julia became convinced it was time for a visit to Father Sheehan at St. Oliver's. It had been years since her last confession and she needed to disclose and receive a word of redemption. Her biggest fear was that he would bring up the word *forgiveness*, which is why she had avoided confession until now. But maybe he could shed some light on how God might make Eddy pay in some supernatural way that only God could accomplish so that she could get some relief from the obsession. *Vengeance is mine, sayeth the Lord.* She needed to know that Eddy would pay, even if it wasn't at her own hand. And he needed to be isolated from every other little boy in Calhoun County...in Georgia...in America...in the world. With that train of thought, Julia drifted off to sleep again, the clock reading 3:12 a.m.

In what seemed like only minutes, the alarm woke her at six o'clock. She had a seven-to-three day today, her favorite shift, especially in the winter months when the days were so short. She had been working as a nurse in the cardiac ICU unit now for the last year and it could be intense at times, with the threat of death always looming. At least there were a couple of hours after work before dark that she could walk and feel somewhat alive.

Julia drug herself to work and throughout the day, faint memories of the nightmare visited her but she managed to quickly put them aside to focus on her work. During her lunch hour, she sat in the break room like usual and watched television to pass the time. She typically didn't like to watch crime investigation shows as there was always the chance she would see something that would remind her of Joey's murder. For some reason today, she felt numb to it, which she took as a sign of improvement. As she listened to investigators talk about the mounting evidence against a particular serial killer and the evidence that finally ended his killing spree, Julia reflected on Eddy's trial and the judge who obviously ignored the so-called smoking gun. She thought to herself how she wished she could go back in time, with what she knew now, to warn that it wouldn't be so cut and dry as the D.A. seemed to think it would be. Luckinbill was smart, but sleezy. He kept saying the case against Eddy was airtight, but Julia never trusted him. He frequently blew her off when she thought of one more detail he should know about her son or what she had discovered in her own personal investigation of Eddy. His overconfidence comforted her at times, but in her gut she always felt he was too cavalier and smiled way too much for the cameras. She had been right, but that didn't make her feel any better. She wanted so much to go back and fix it. Make Eddy pay. Send him to prison where he would get raped and beat up by the inmates who hated child rapists. Maybe he could feel what Joey felt. She shuttered and shook her head to bring herself back into the present moment where she became aware that her co-workers were engrossed in a conversation at a table behind her.

"In the end, the serial killer got what he wanted, which was notoriety," the investigative reporter explained. "But the families of the victims made sure he paid a high price for his infamous crimes." Before signing off, he explained that since New York did not have the death penalty, the killer would have to spend the rest of his life in prison. One family member they interviewed had the last word. "I'm glad capital punishment was not an option. Death would be too easy. We wanted him to live in fear the rest of his life and the best way to do that was to send him to prison forever."

Julia understood exactly what that meant. Without realizing it, she had stood up suddenly and the molded plastic chair underneath her had screeched back on the linoleum floor, drawing attention from the two people who had been talking quietly at the table behind hers. She looked over at them and apologized, and they promptly looked back at each other as if nothing had happened. Julia pulled the chair back and sat down again, gathering the remnants of her half-eaten lunch. It was the word imprisonment that had startled her. She was in her own private prison and Eddy was keeping her there. Full of fear and guilt. The wrong person was living in fear, she thought. *The wrong person.*

10.

June 20, 2012

Nathan walked into Lana's Diner and looked around, but didn't see Sally anywhere. He looked down at his watch. It was five after twelve. The place was beginning to fill up with customers, so he spotted an open booth and nodded to a waitress that he wanted it. She nodded back with a smile. He sat on the side facing the door to watch for Sally. He always chose a seat facing the door no matter where he was – it was his cop instinct to never have his back to the action.

"Hey, Darlin'," Nathan said to Tish, the waitress who approached the table with a water pitcher. "You doin' okay today?"

"Well, hey there, Sheriff. I'm alright," she responded, her eyes lighting up at the sight of Nathan. He was tall, good-looking, and that dimpled-chin was irresistible. Kind of a cross between Dennis Quaid and Richard Gere. Then when you added that Southern drawl of his, it was almost more than a girl could take. She knew she was blushing at the thought, so she composed herself and tried to make small talk.

"Haven't seen you in a while," she said in a melodic, southern tone, as she poured iced water into his glass. Why his wife had done him wrong, she would never know. She had heard he was a good guy, not a cad, like most cops.

"Yeah," he said with a laugh. "Not since last week."

Tish felt embarrassed.

"Oh, I guess I was off that day, huh? You gonna be alone today?" She took her order pad from her apron pocket.

"No, I'm meeting Sally Tate here – you know that pretty newscaster from WLTA." Nathan's eyes sparkled when he grinned. He enjoyed inducing a little female competition.

"Well, well," Tish responded. "Sounds like there must be a story brewing in Calhoun County. Hey, I heard about that murder on China Grove Road." Her voice had lowered to a gossipy whisper.

"Yeah, it's a shame," he said. She seemed hungry for information, but he just wanted to eat his lunch. "I'll have a cup of coffee while I'm waiting." Nathan put down the menu and looked up at her matter-of-factly with his soft grey-green eyes that she noticed took on the muted color of the sage-colored tie he was wearing.

Tish felt slightly rebuffed. "Comin' right up," she replied and walked away.

Nathan heard the restaurant door's bell clang as Sally strode into the diner, with a briefcase in one hand and her cell phone in the other. He smiled at the sight of her, a thirty-something redhead with long hair and legs, and a navy-blue business suit that complimented her fair skin. When she spoke, he swore he saw a glimmer from her white smile like in the cartoons.

"Hi, Sheriff, sorry I'm a little late. Traffic getting here is a bear," she said while putting her cell phone in her briefcase. She took a deep breath and let it out before going on.

"So…this is a first – you requesting an interview with me!" She smiled charmingly. "Do you mind?" she asked Nathan as she placed a mini-recorder on the table.

"I don't think you are going to want that there," Nathan said apologetically.

"Really? I'm intrigued. I was sure this was about the Olwen investigation."

"It is, but I need some information from you. I had a little get together with Luckinbill this morning and he's not that enamored with you." Nathan smiled while sipping his coffee.

"That's an understatement. We got crossways when I started digging around and finding that Clyde Eddy and Judge Seeger had something going on under the table. What did Luckinbill say about me?" Sally's curiosity looked defensive.

"Nothing specifically, other than you were the worst of the reporters who blew things out of proportion. He was trying to derail my suspicions that Julia Olwen's murder may have had anything to do with her son's murder investigation or Eddy's acquittal. That's kind of why I wanted to chat with you. Do you think there is anyone who might have wanted to silence Julia Olwen?"

"I'm not sure how I would know that," replied Sally. "I mean, I was just reporting what I was digging up, but I had very little contact with Ms. Olwen."

"I guess I'm wondering if she may have dug further into your story after the case was over…that it might be possible she found out something and confronted someone with information that might have gotten someone in big trouble." Nathan was being vague on purpose.

"Wow, I don't know," Sally lifted her voice a little. "Are you saying that someone like Clyde Eddy or even Judge Seeger would have wanted her dead?"

"I'm not saying anything at this point, other than I want to know what facts you found out so I can eliminate any possible suspects, if you get my drift." Nathan was doing his best to be cryptic because as much as he liked Sally, he could not afford to give a reporter anything directly that might hinder the investigation.

"Got ya," said Sally, as she looked across the diner in thought. She focused back on Nathan and was about to answer when his phone rang. She grinned, as it wasn't surprising that his ringtone was the theme from the old television show Bonanza. She had only seen it on TV Land when her father would watch reruns. *He is such a throwback*, thought Sally with affection.

"Yeah, Davis here," Nathan answered. "What? Sh...." He stopped himself as he looked up at Sally. "Crap," he said disgustingly while flipping his phone off.

"Something wrong?" inquired Sally.

"I am so sorry, but I'm going to have to go. I gotta snitch in trouble and I need to find out what that's all about. Raincheck?"

"Sure, name the day and time."

"How about dinner sometime?" Nathan smiled, showing his dimples.

Sally was taken aback by his forwardness, and how handsome he was when he was in pursuit.

"Call me later," she said.

Nathan got up and slapped a five-dollar bill on the table. Tish saw him leaving and cried out. "Hey, you didn't even order yet!" She watched Nathan go, and then looked over at Sally, who was leaving the table as well.

"Duty calls, I guess," Sally said to Tish, taking a sip from Nathan's water glass before retrieving her brief case from the booth. She was smiling all the way to the door, not knowing that Tish was extremely annoyed by her beauty.

11.

Julia - December, 2011

The site of Saint Oliver's cathedral on a crisp December day was comforting to Julia. It was decorated to the extreme with garland, holly and all the Christmas trimmings that were supposed to signify hope and peace. Although these things had a much different meaning for her now. Or maybe they had no meaning at all anymore. She wasn't sure. Julia was a regular attendee, but she had not gotten too involved since moving to Regal, Georgia, last year. Whether it was depression or guilt, she had simply lacked the energy to face some of her fellow parishioners, who she was sure had been exposed to her dramatized life through the media. She generally slipped in and out of mass, often without being noticed by anyone. She liked it that way, although many of the older women would manage to catch her before she left to invite her to an activity or social. She didn't suspect they were gossip mongers. She hoped they were genuinely able to ignore what they had heard about her and love her anyway. That alone had increased Julia's faith and her strong connection to St. Oliver's. It seemed to be a true place of grace for her, which was also a source of inner conflict. Would God punish her for not feeling like extending grace to the one who had ruined her life? Was she placing too much importance on this carnal existence and not thinking about eternity – the afterlife? Her racing thoughts were halted as she approached the building and needed to find her way to the confessional.

There were large stained-glass windows towering above the numerous concrete steps leading to the double wood and metal doors. The tall white bell tower and spire soaring toward the clouds, all reminded Julia that there was a higher power that bound those in her little town of Regal together with more than their families and vocations. They all relied on the faith of a God unseen to get through the unexplainable, and sometimes senseless, problems facing any of them. Julia pulled the scarf around her neck closer to her face, feeling a cold breeze that had kicked up as she turned the corner to go around the front of the building. She had a sense of peace and resolve as she confidently walked the sidewalk along the north side of the church, approaching the side door leading into the vestry where she thought the confessional booth was located. She had not been to confession in this place before. A pang of guilt returned as she opened the door, which she secretly wished would be locked. Upon entering, the smell of burning candles struck her. There were signs leading her to the location. She entered and sat down, waiting for what seemed like a long time before a shadow appeared on the other side of the screen that separated her from the blurred figure of a man.

"Forgive me father, for I have sinned," Julia said quietly in the dark confessional booth. "It has been….years since my last confession."

"Yes, my child. Name your sins." It didn't sound like Father Sheehan, but she couldn't be sure.

"I have been thinking…cruel thoughts." Julia struggled to find the words. "Thoughts about the man who murdered my son." She thought she heard the priest let out a long sigh, as if he knew who she was. She wanted to run, but knew that would only make it more embarrassing to see him again.

After some silence, the priest said, "Go on."

"I'm having murderous thoughts. I want him dead. I want him to suffer like my son suffered. I want him to live in fear and pain and anguish." She could feel her heart pounding a she rubbed together her clammy hands.

She continued. "I know it is wrong to harbor these thoughts, so I need to find some peace. I need to know that God will deal with this man so I don't have to think about it anymore. Is that possible? I'm sorry...." She knew she was going off topic. *Focus, Julia, focus on your sins, not the solution.* "And for all other sins for which I may be unaware." She wanted Father to know that she was finished with her confession.

"Your feelings are understandable," the priest said in a calm, steady tone. "God understands our humanness. That's why he sent his Son to live among us...to be one of us for a time. He knows your pain and your anguish. You must have faith and let God be the judge of such things. We can only see life through a small keyhole in our time and space. Your Father in heaven sees the whole world at once, and all of time all at once, so He is the only One who knows why things happen as they do. You must trust him as the Creator and Perfector of His will for the world. You are absolved of this sin. Say your prayer of contrition."

"Thank you, Father," Julia obediently replied. She was silent for a moment, trying to remember how to pray this way.

""Dear God," Julia started with nervousness. "I am heartily sorry for having offended Thee. I fear the fires of Hell but most of all because it offends Thee my God who art all good and deserving of all my love. And I firmly resolve to go forth and sin no more."

"Recite ten Hail Marys and five Our Fathers and you will be on your way," the priest aptly instructed.

After doing as he asked, Julia stepped out of the confessional booth and walked down the long, dark corridor of St. Oliver's, being blinded by the daylight when she opened the heavy wooden door to the outside. The priest's words went around and around in her head, as she opened her car door, sat down, put her seat belt on, and turned the key.

Have faith, have faith. Starting today, I will turn over a new leaf. She spoke to herself as an alcoholic leaving an AA meeting, knowing that by the time she got home, the urge to imbibe the sinful elixir of cruel thoughts would once again overwhelm her. And it did.

12.

June 20, 2012

"Centipede…you crossin' me? You crossin' me?" screamed Nathan, while holding Nashaun Jones by the neck, slamming him up against a dumpster off of Barrel Street. Jones had the fear of God in his eyes as he tried to defend himself against Nathan's grip. "You know better, don't ya, man?"

"I do!" Jones strained to yell back, as he attempted to pull Nathan's hands away from his neck, but his slight build couldn't match the strength of the sheriff's dominance. Jones had tears in his eyes, but the enraged sheriff failed to notice.

Nathan and Tommy had affectionately nicknamed Jones "Centipede" because he had a lengthy rap sheet so diverse that he was said to have his hands in every crime imaginable. Nathan found him to be a good snitch for a number of purposes, so Jones was treated well by the sheriff's department.

Finally, Nathan let go and Jones fell to the ground, gasping for air.

"Damn, Sheriff! You was gonna kill me." Jones eeked out the words while still breathing heavily.

"Yeah…" Nathan was out of breath as well, standing over Jones with his hands on his hips, feeling the adrenaline rushing through his veins. "It's because of me that you're not rotting in prison right now, Cent. So, you best be careful or you'll be there before noon tomorrow."

"I understand, sir. I really do." Jones sat up and leaned against the dumpster, exhausted.

Tommy Braselton pulled up in time to see the two breathless, but alive. "Wha'd I miss?" Tommy said as he got out of his squad car.

"Nothin," said Nathan. "Our friend here thought he would get the bright idea to start blabbin' his mouth about our little arrangement." Jones would exchange information about drug dealers with Nathan for meals and cigarettes, and the promise of not going to jail if he wanted to partake in the lifetstyle now and then. Their deal required him to not reveal his role to anyone, even if it was a homeless drunk on the street. Nathan had been told that Jones was talking a little too much for his own good, which required a less-than-friendly visit from Nathan and a reality check for Jones.

"Uh-oh. That ain't good, you little insect," said Tommy as he started toward Jones. Just then, Nathan stepped forward to keep him at bay.

"It's all good now," Nathan said calmly. "I think we're back on the right track, ain't that right, Centipede?" Nathan stared at Jones with conviction.

"Yes sir, you got that right sir. I ain't gonna tell nobody about nothin'." Jones got up and was rubbing his neck where the sheriff had gripped it.

"All right, then," said Nathan as he handed Jones two packs of cigarettes. "Now, get on outta here."

"Thanks. You men have a blessed day now." Jones wanted to tell the sheriff that he had given him the wrong brand of nicotine, but he thought better of it as he felt the pain in his throat. He shoved the packs in his shirt pocket and walked briskly toward the package store across the street.

"I'm getting too old for this, Tommy," Nathan said as they walked back to their cars together.

"I know, but here's something that will lift your spirits." Tommy was looking at Nathan like a Golden Retriever eyes his owner.

"What's that?"

"You know that neighbor of Julia Olwen's who said she saw a big red truck leaving Olwen's driveway the night before you went to the house? She called and said she remembered one more thing about it."

"Okay," Nathan was distracted and frowning, still not recovered from his encounter with Centipede.

"Well," Tommy continued, "she said she remembered it had a large green alligator decal pasted in the rear window...and we have tire track impressions from the driveway, remember?"

"Okay, so I'm not impressed until you find out who Julia Olwen knew with that truck description."

"You'll be impressed when I tell you that Clyde Eddy owns a 2012 Ford F150." He waited for Nathan's approval. "You think he's a Gator fan? I can't imagine that." Tommy squinted, with the glare of the June sun in his face.

"Jeez, Tommy. How the hell did you find that out?" Nathan wiped the sweat from his forehead.

"Well, when you told me that you were worried Julia Olwen could have information that certain people might not want her to leak, I just thought I'd check into Seeger's and Clyde Eddy's recent business dealings, like real estate deeds, vehicle titles, and such. And there it was, plain as day. Eddy has a new Ford F150 registered in his name."

"Interesting," said Nathan. "But those trucks are a dime a dozen. We can't be sure there is a connection between the sighting at Julia's house and Clyde Eddy. At least it confirms we're probably looking for a red truck, no matter whose it is."

"Agreed…but…anyway, I thought it sure was a piece of interesting information." Tommy felt a little deflated that Nathan was not more interested.

"Hmm…" Nathan went into his quiet mode, thinking, while Tommy stood and impatiently waited for the boss to speak again.

"I think it might be time to pay Clyde Eddy a visit," announced Nathan. "See what kind of vehicles he has parked in his big ole garage."

While driving away, Nathan's thoughts went back to the photo of Julia and her pleasant smile. *Such a waste*, he thought. He had patience for a lot of weaknesses prone to men, but the need and greed for money and power were vices he had little sympathy for. In fact, he actually respected Centipede's struggle with addiction and crime, and at least understood how he came by his deviant behaviors. But murder to protect power and millions of dollars in assets? He had no understanding of that. He reached down and turned on the radio to redirect his frustration. The Beach Boys were belting out *Kokomo* in perfect harmony, reminding Nathan he needed a vacation.

13.

Julia - January, 2012

The first time Julia's plan crystallized in her head, she was sitting on a swing at Peacock Park, a little county-run oasis that she and Joey used to go to when he was only five or six years old. It was a drive for her to come back here, but she occasionally did because she felt more of his presence here than in the cold and overly groomed cemetery where she knew she was supposed to go. Joey loved to be pushed on the swing and she delighted in his playful "Weeeeeeeeeee...." She was going back and forth, back and forth, back and forth, letting the wind blow her shoulder-length hair to and fro. She was pumping her hips with purpose, to go higher and higher. There was something about swinging that relaxed her mind and allowed her to think more linear and focused. It was freeing and a little risky. Eventually, she would get so high that she would be jolted by gravity, free falling until the swing pulled her back again. She hadn't noticed that a group of children were watching her with concern, wondering what this middle-aged woman was doing swinging like a fearless monkey. She returned to the moment and slowly swung back to a normal pace, eventually dragging her feet in the dirt below to come to a full stop. When she got up to walk away, she felt light-headed, almost drunk, and stopped for a moment to regain her balance. It was good to feel a natural high for a change. She smiled at a little girl who looked back at her sheepishly and sweetly, causing Julia to wonder how anyone could ever begin to hurt a child in the way Eddy did her son. Joey would have been fourteen this year, maybe a foot taller and with a deeper voice. Had he lived a little longer, maybe he would have been strong enough to fight Eddy off. Maybe he would have been hanging out with friends after school instead of going dutifully home like she had always instructed him to. Maybe....*Stop it!* She knew she had to arrest these kinds of destructive internal monologues. At least that's what she and Dr. Pierce had been working on. Julia felt her nose running from the cool air. She found a tissue in her coat pocket and began a brisk walk toward her car, trying to put Joey out of her head and her plan back into focus.

Walking into her quiet foyer, she realized she had turned her obsessive thoughts about Joey into ones about the execution of her plan against Eddy, and she wasn't sure if that was what Dr. Pierce meant by *redirecting*. Regardless, she was feeling better and more energized. She got a notebook out of her desk drawer and thought she should start making some notes while her thoughts were clear and methodical. It felt good to have something other than her anger to dwell on. She was surprised at how well she was able to compartmentalize the plan and separate it from her emotions. It didn't feel like she was doing anything wrong or inappropriate or even crazy. Instead, she felt in control for the first time in almost two years. She felt justified, unbridled, as if she were a novelist, plotting out a story with an ending she had the power to create, or not. She saw no sin in the planning, as that was only in her head. And if it made her feel better and more in control, then what was the harm? The execution would be yet another story, but Julia resolved to not think about that just yet. For all she knew, there was no way to execute such a plan without discovery, so she would just work on the idea of it and then she could decide at any time whether or not the rewards would be worth the risks. The adrenaline rush she got in just putting pen to paper was surprising to Julia. She could imagine how exciting it would be to start doing some actual research on the internet about some of the elements that were not so familiar to her. She reminded herself that she had to be careful, though. The same rules of cunning would have to be applied to her covering her tracks as well as to those she wanted discovered. It would be an interesting balance. For now, she felt like a modern-day Angela Landsbury in reverse.

Julia's thoughts were interrupted by her doorbell ringing. She shoved the notebook back into the desk drawer and ran her fingers through her hair to be sure she was presentable. She opened the door to a brown package, lying on her porch in front of the door. The UPS driver waved as he drove off. It was a box of supplies she had ordered for Mrs. Timko, her elderly neighbor who was a diabetic, and for whom Julia had offered to help acquire the appropriate syringes per her doctor's orders. Mrs. Timko said she was frequently confused by the long list of insulin supplies and didn't want to order the wrong ones. Julia took the package into the house and pulled off the tape.

"Darn…this isn't what I asked for," she said aloud. She had ordered insulin syringes, not these. She was frustrated and couldn't understand how the lady on the phone could make such a mistake. *Can't anyone do their job right?* She set the mistaken order aside, vowing to call first thing in the morning to set them straight. She was disappointed she was going to have to tell Mrs. Timko that she wasn't any better than her at getting the orders right.

It wasn't until much later, when she was lying in bed before drifting off to sleep, that an idea took root that made her believe in divine intervention. She got up and retrieved the notebook from her desk, deciding that from now on, it needed to be kept in her bedside table for moments like these. Once it was written down, she could sleep soundly until morning, when she would have to divert her thoughts back to Calhoun County Medical Center. Sleep was coming much easier these days and she would be glad to share the news with Dr. Pierce at their next session. She rolled over and put her therapy session out of her mind so that she wouldn't get fixated on that instead of simply relaxing to fall asleep. Julia drifted off with a greater sense of control.

14.

June 20, 2012

Lance Irving Eddy sat in his boxer shorts, mindlessly picking at a scab on his chin. His boredom with Facebook was increasing as the never-ending status posts of his so-called friends reminded him of their shallow idiocy. He felt proud of himself to have garnered so many supporters who had never met him face to face. *Who were these people?* He smiled as he clicked on the "Like" button under a photo of a prepubescent boy with an innocent grin, posted by one of his NAMBLA friends. Chad Davidson, whoever that was, obviously had a penchant for bleachy tow-heads. Eddy preferred the darker blonds.

Given Eddy's fairly recent acquittal in which he was accused of more than just molesting a child, he was careful not to blatantly violate the law, but he knew that showing favoritism to a fully-dressed child was not illegal. He also knew that the cops were probably looking in on him, since none of them believed in his innocence. But Eddy liked playing the cat and mouse game, giving them just enough tantalizing information, such as "liking" a little boy's photo, without really crossing the line. He relished the thought of someone in law enforcement watching his internet movements – most likely one of his fake Facebook friends. He imagined them getting frustrated by Eddy's obvious proclivities, but not being able to do anything about it.

His association with the North American Man Boy Love Association was transparent enough, but his support of his friends' family photos that included cute, smiling little boys, and his pool of friends who were noticeably odd, would all point to a suspected child molester. Yet, Eddy had never been charged or convicted of such a crime, so he was not required to register as a sex offender. The best they could do was count on his stupidity, but Eddy had no such plans. He impressed himself with his own ability to avoid discovery. It was the only accomplishment that made him feel successful and he wished it was the kind of thing he could brag to his father about, but he knew Clyde Eddy would always take credit for any legitimate success of his son's. Frequently, Lance Eddy watched the video of the acquittal verdict to remind himself of two things – that he couldn't be too careful and that he was smarter than the blockheads who tried to convict him. Just hearing the words "not guilty" one more time never failed to cause a rise in his confidence.

To satisfy his cravings, he liked hooking up with eighteen and nineteen-year-old so-called men who wore a youthful glow. He had begun to talk with them frequently through his favorite internet gaming sites, and required them to send him a copy of their driver's license before meeting to prove that they were of age. He had to avoid accusation of anything other than adult consensual sex. They were easy targets. Eddy preyed on young adults who came from abusive homes, who were high school dropouts or drug addicts, and had any number of dysfunctions in their lives that he could capitalize on to draw them into his sickness. Eddy had a knack with these types since he could relate so well to a young man's tattered history and warped sense of reality. After all, his own family had conditioned him to think he deserved every beating he had received from his filthy rich father. His mother found her escape at the bottom of a vodka bottle, and Eddy himself had eventually learned that strategy as well. Yet, there was nothing more satisfying to Eddy than enticing a pre-adolescent boy into a sexual encounter, which was usually followed by his own self-loathing, causing him to become enraged at the child. The tender pleasure followed by the satisfaction of mutilation was ultimately realized with Joey Olwen, but Eddy was well aware that he nearly paid a high price for his unique appetite. For now, he would use the older boys as throwaways, saving his ultimate pleasure for a more calculated endeavor that would take some patience to plan. The next time, he would ensure he could not be caught. The next supreme encounter would require a great deal of delayed gratification. He became aroused each time he contemplated the possibilities.

Lance Eddy logged out of his Facebook account and switched over to his favorite online game – *Slash and Burn* – that combined the thrill of the kill using knives and primitive weapons along with some pyromaniac fantasies. Eddy noticed that Skateman3 was playing again, the online identity he chatted with last night. He wasn't quite sure if this avatar was an adult or not, but he liked his enthusiasm for the game. He cautiously toyed with him over instant messaging using his usual screen name, Buddy666.

Buddy666:	*You again!*
Skateman3:	*Yep…ready to burn?*
Buddy666:	*Bring it*
Skateman3:	*No doubt*
Buddy666:	*What kind of stuff do u do when yer not here?*
Skateman3:	*Duh….Skateman????*
Buddy666:	*Got it*
Buddy666:	*So when yer not skating*

Skateman3:	*Nuthin. Hang out.*
Buddy666:	*Where?*
Skateman3:	*What are u...some sort of pervert?*
Buddy666:	*Whoa...man. Take it easy. Yer probably just a little kid anyway*
Skateman3:	*U wish.*
Buddy666:	*Nah...just looking to hang out with my SandB buds*
Skateman3:	*Sorry. No offense.*
Buddy666:	*None taken*
Skateman3:	*BTW, I'm turnin 21 this weekend*
Buddy666:	*Congrats...time for alcohol initiation. Let me know if u wanna crash course*
Skateman3:	*Ha! Already know that game. Maybe I'll meet ya somewhere*
Buddy666:	*Need to know u are of age first*
Skateman3:	*Right.*
Buddy666:	*Well, lets talk later. In the meantime, I'm up for a SandB challenge. You game?*
Skateman3:	*Like u said...bring it!*
Buddy666:	*U will be sorry.*

This is so easy, thought Eddy as he virtually entered into yet another young man's life with a possible meeting in the future. Eddy knew that would only happen if he could get more information from this guy and know that he was into some of the same sadistic activities as himself. That would take some time to discover, but the prospect was always a welcome challenge to Eddy's otherwise boring and mundane existence. One thing he knew was that anyone who enjoyed *Slash and Burn* already had a fair amount of sadistic energy.

After an hour or so of battling online, Eddy went out for a pack of cigarettes and a six-pack of beer. As he pulled out of his driveway, he noticed a couple of little boys playing across the street from his new two-story townhome. He marveled at the fact that he was able to live in a place like this without anyone knowing his secrets.

Lance Eddy's father, Clyde Eddy, had purchased the townhome in Riverbridge Commons, a multi-use community connected to the Riverbridge Hills Country Club where his parents lived in the summer months. This was the most affluent part of Marlowe County. Clyde Eddy needed to protect his own image after the trial, so he set up Lance in the Riverbridge community, bought him a brand new truck, and hoped he would stay out of trouble for a while. Lance readily accepted the gifts, as he felt his father could never do enough to make up for the past. It was the last time he had talked with his father – when he called to let him know the truck was ready to be picked up in Albright, a little town north of Regal in Calhoun County. As far as Lance was concerned, and Clyde for that matter, there was no need for the two of them to talk or have a relationship. They did best when they simply stayed out of each other's way. "Keep your name out of the papers, son—do you think you can do that for a change?" Clyde had said with disgust when he handed his son the townhome keys. Every time Lance Eddy recalled those kinds of interchanges with his father, he felt more justified in his deviant pleasure.

"Pack of Marlboros," Eddy barked at the store clerk without making eye contact. He was staring at a piece of paper with a phone number on it that he had stuck in his billfold.

"Regular or menthol?" asked the clerk.

"Regular," Eddy said sharply, as if the clerk should know him by now. He looked up and noticed that he was a young blond kid who must be new to the store.

Eddy smiled as he walked out with his goods. How could he help himself? These things just seemed to fall in his lap.

15.

June 21, 2012

"Yes, Patty," acknowledged Nathan. "This is Sheriff Davis in Calhoun County. Is Mr. Eddy in?"

"I'm sorry, he's unavailable. May I take a message?" Clyde Eddy's personal assistant asked in a tone that caused Nathan to suspect she was only covering for her boss. He hated how protected the wealthy were from the real world.

"When will he be available?"

"I'm afraid not for a while, Sheriff Davis. He and Mrs. Eddy are out of the country until the middle of next month."

"I see. Well, I really need to meet with him as soon as possible…" His voice trailed off and Patty remained silent. Nathan wanted to meet him face to face. He couldn't get a good read on Eddy over the phone, and he hoped to check out his vehicles, wherever they were parked. That gave him an idea. "Hmm…I thought for sure I saw his red pickup in the parking lot over there this morning."

"Oh you must be thinking of someone else. Mr. Eddy usually drives his Cadillac into the office," Patty drawled politely. She obviously wasn't going to say whether or not Eddy had a red pickup – just that he doesn't drive it to the office. Nathan left it at that.

"Oh, well, I stand corrected. Could you get a message to him that I would like a call back when he gets a free minute?"

"I'll relay the message to him the next time he calls in, but he usually does not like to be disturbed when he is on vacation with his wife. I'm sure you understand. Can you tell me what this is about? Maybe that will make a difference."

Nathan was annoyed but not shocked. A regular Joe who had gotten a call from the sheriff would not be so casual about returning a call, but guys like Eddy, with more money than God, never thought the rules applied to themselves. "It's not a social call, Miss Patty. I can assure you it's official business and I think it would be in Mr. Eddy's best interest to return my call at his earliest opportunity."

She sounded annoyed. "Like I said, I will relay the message."

Nathan hung up and doubted he would be hearing from Eddy before he returned from his trip. He was determined that was not going to stop him from checking out the whereabouts of that truck Tommy reported Eddy had recently purchased. Nathan knew a few old boys in the car business who could snoop around for him and find out if Clyde Eddy had been wheeling and dealing on a truck in the area. He made a few phone calls and hit pay dirt when he found out that a salesman in Albright had been bragging about selling Clyde Eddy more than one vehicle. Nathan grabbed his sport coat and ran out of the office, plucking his reading glasses from Dot's hand like clockwork. He was on a mission and loved the adrenaline he was feeling. It gave him more focus and he tended to be a little less absent-minded and negative under the influence of his own natural drug.

Albright was due north of Regal and just southeast of Atlanta, near the airport. Traffic going north was a little heavy, which annoyed Nathan who had a disdain for people who didn't know how to drive courteously. Twice en route, he had been cut off by hurried drivers, causing him to pound his steering wheel and shout an expletive. It was one of his ex-wife's pet peeves about him – impatience – the kind that caused him to be prone to tailgating and yelling at perfect strangers. She could never understand why he couldn't accept that he was not the only one on the road. He could never comprehend how she didn't see his point of view, until he realized that she was the kind of driver he was likely to despise. That was a microcosm of what was wrong with the marriage at the core – they misfired on just about every cylinder. Nathan had a fleeting memory of her nagging him from the passenger seat and he relaxed for a moment, realizing that he had taken for granted how much easier life was in the last couple of years without her stressful influence.

Clementine Ford in Albright was in an industrial part of town, on a street that seemed reserved for car dealerships. Nathan pulled into a customer parking space and upon getting out of his car, was immediately assaulted by at least two salesmen who wanted to welcome him to a friendly car shopping experience.

"Mornin'," Nathan said with a charming smile while flashing his sheriff's badge. One of the men, who was about to bust a button on his too-tight dress shirt, stepped back and let the thinner one shake Nathan's hand.

"I'm here to see someone named Smiley?" Nathan inquired of the two salesmen.

"Oh, yeah, sure," the thinner man said nervously. "I think he's inside with a customer."

Nathan walked into the showroom and the smell of fresh leather and floor wax enticed him to look at the inventory. While waiting, he began ogling the shiny new Fords and was startled at the list prices. *Jeez…how do people afford these things?* Just then, a short, bald man approached Nathan and quickly belied his nickname.

"Can I help you?" the man tentatively asked with a frown. His co-workers had told him a man with a sheriff's badge was looking for him. "Are you Smiley?" Nathan tried to maintain a jolly disposition in order to not put him on the defensive. "Yes, sir. I heard you asked for me by name. I'm not in trouble am I, Sheriff?" Smiley laughed nervously.

"Yep, a buddy of mine in Regal said you were lettin' them steal cars up here, the deals were so good." Nathan joked and Smiley relaxed. "Thought I'd come by and check out your F150s." Nathan stared into the window of a black model with a GPS screen in the dash and a luxury leather interior. *Trucks sure have changed since the one my daddy and I fixed up when I was a teen.*

Smiley slinked into his salesman demeanor, glad that the sheriff was there on personal business. "You came to the right place, then Sheriff. Who was it? The guy who referred you to me? A customer of mine?"

"Ya know, I can't really say. It was a buddy of my buddy's, if you know what I mean. All I know is that I was supposed to ask for Smiley." Nathan was walking around the vehicle with his hands in his pants pockets, trying to avoid Smiley's detailed inquiry.

"Well, I'm glad you found me on a work day. I'm usually off on Fridays, but we've got a big sale going on this weekend, so we're full up on inventory and sales staff. And zero down, zero interest, if you're interested."

"Great, so can I drive one of these babies?" Nathan thought it couldn't hurt to have a little fun while at work.

"Let me go get a set of keys." Smiley started to walk away and stopped in his tracks. He turned back and said, "I'm gonna need a copy of your driver's license."

Nathan shot him a raised-eyebrow look that conveyed. *Are you serious?*

"Right," said Smiley quietly, and he proceeded toward the office to retrieve the car keys.

Nathan and Smiley took off in a dark blue F150 and jumped on the freeway entrance toward Atlanta. While Smiley was droning on about the vehicle's high-tech revolutionary engine with the capacity to haul over eleven thousand pounds, amazing torque, and best fuel efficiency in its class, Nathan was embarrassed to think that he didn't know anything about what Smiley was talking about. So, he nodded knowingly, feeling like it was the macho thing to do. What he really wanted to know was how to get his IPod to play his favorite tunes through the elaborate sound system that Smiley was showing him.

"See? Satellite radio and top of the line Pioneer speakers."

Nathan was annoyed by his enthusiasm. As they were rounding the corner to turn back into the dealership, Nathan knew it was time to talk turkey, so they settled into Smiley's cubicle to "run some figures." While Smiley went off to get them both some coffee, Nathan noticed photos of what he assumed were Smiley's family – a pudgy woman in her forties and two teenage boys standing next to the Grand Canyon. He also noticed a photo of Smiley in front of his own Ford truck, with a large Confederate flag decal that covered the entire rear window.

"You from around here, Smiley?" asked Nathan.

"Born and raised…well, technically I was born in Alabama, but came here with my folks before I was two, so I consider myself a native."

"Yeah, that's what I thought." Nathan shot him an approving smile and Smiley affirmed while pulling up a program on his desktop computer.

"Ya know, I like this truck a lot, but I heard it's gettin' real popular with the country-club folks, who like to pretend their southern, if you know what I mean." Nathan was hoping to massage Smiley's bragging sensibilities.

"Don't I know it. In fact, there's been a rash of folks comin' down here from Marlowe County who don't look a bit like they should be buying a truck – you know more like a BMW or somethin' – but I don't much care. I'll sell it to ya if you got the cash." Smiley sat back in his chair and made eye contact with Nathan again.

"Well, you and I know we can tell the difference between authentic and wannabes, can't we?"

"Yep, but like I said, if your money's green, I'll take it...that is, if it's legal and all," Smiley corrected himself remembering he was in the presence of the law.

Nathan laughed to put Smiley at ease.

"Yeah, I even hear that some pro golfer from that Riverbridge Hills club is drivin' around in one of these things. Did you make that sale?"

"Nope...the closest thing to celebrity I came to was that Eddy character from Riverbridge...you know the one whose kid almost got fried for murdering that young boy." Smiley was sitting up in his chair, proud to report his gossip. "Eddy..." Nathan looked pensive, as if trying to recall the name. "You mean that guy who they were sayin' was in cahoots with the judge?"

"Yep, that's the one. Well, a couple of months ago, he came up here and bought three Fords all at once." Smiley's pride was showing.

"My goodness," Nathan shook his head in feigned disbelief. "I'm sure he was after the luxury cars, huh?"

"Sort of. He bought himself an Expedition, his wife a Mustang, and then his kid picked up the F150 a couple of days later. Do ya believe that? When I was thirty years old, my daddy never bought me squat."

A Ford guy. Figures.

"Oh I know what ya mean there, brother. So, I suppose he got a white one – for innocence," Nathan joked and leaned back in his chair, watching Smiley's agreeable eyes. He was getting everything he wanted without much effort. "No, actually it was red." Smiley shot Nathan an inside-joke kind of glance, and he wanted to say "for blood," but wasn't sure that was in good taste with the sheriff. "Ha…well, that's surprising for sure, especially after the trouble he caused that family," Nathan continued hoping to get a little more.

"Uh-huh," Smiley backed down a little as if he knew he was probably running his mouth too much about a wealthy and possible repeat customer. "Well, here's what we're looking at." Smiley had scratched some figures on a slip of paper and then drew a line with an "X" in front of it, presumably for Nathan to accept the deal and sign.

Nathan cleared his throat loudly when he saw the offer. He tried not to look shocked.

"Yeah, well, that's pretty good. But I'm not one to make a deal on the same day I drive a truck. I like to think about it, if you know what I mean."

"Sure, but let me go talk to my manager and we'll see if there's anything else we can do for you today."

"Naw, really, I'm on a limited time schedule. I've got to go meet someone, but I appreciate your time." Nathan got up to leave and Smiley frowned. "Here's my card and don't forget I've got the best deals around," Smiley shook Nathan's hand and Nathan put the card in his pocket. "Have a good one." Nathan bid Smiley a good day and walked to his ten-year-old Crown Victoria.

So, the younger Eddy has the truck. Cha-ching. Nathan lightly hit the steering wheel with a victorious fist, and he backed out of the parking lot. He retrieved his cell phone and called his partner. "Tommy, get me Lance Eddy's address. While I'm down here, I want to see how the pervert lives."

"Did ya get the dirt on his dad?"

"I'll tell ya about it later." Nathan could hear Tommy's sigh of frustration on the other end. He enjoyed keeping the facts to himself for a little while. He was creating a hypothesis in his head, but refused to reveal any of it until he had more answers than questions.

Nathan set his Garmin to take him to 911 Terrace Way in Riverbridge Commons.

16.

Julia - January, 2012

The end of January had to be the most depressing time of the year, thought Julia as she sat with her first cup of coffee, looking out at a bleak landscape from her breakfast room window. It was Tuesday and a day off for her, but she felt a sense of undoing. Her planning had come to a halt since she was forced to work ten days straight due to some layoffs at the hospital, which created a staff shortage. January also seemed to be a month in which elderly people were more prone to acute illness, so the ICU was exceptionally busy.

In quiet moments like these, it was difficult for her to keep her thoughts from straying to Joey and how she missed being a mother to him. But going to that place also had the consequence of rekindling her anger toward Eddy, which she had successfully avoided in her exhaustion over the last week or so. Julia considered retrieving the notebook from her bedside table to make a few more notes, but she wondered if she really had the energy to go through with her scheme, or maybe going through the planning was simply a productive way to process her grief. Another thing she might talk to Dr. Pierce about in her upcoming session.

She got up and took her coffee into the den to watch some mindless television, hoping Kelly Ripa, and whoever her guest of the week was, would give her something to laugh about. She made a place for herself on the couch and pulled her University of Georgia fleece blanket over her legs to take the chill off. She thought of how many times Joey sat in front of the television, watching cartoons or the latest action hero series on Saturday mornings. As he got older, playing video games was his favorite pastime and she got into a fair share of arguments with him about what was appropriate for his age. Many of his friends were allowed to play games that she thought were too violent or vulgar. The latest trend included online interactive games that allowed players to voice communicate without being in the same room. Julia was adamantly opposed to those and would only allow him to talk to players with the keyboard using instant messaging. Even then, she didn't allow the online games while she was at work. Joey, of course, didn't think that was fair, given that his friends' parents were supposedly not so cautious, so he pouted in protest when she would once again refuse him that luxury. Even so, Julia would give anything to have him back, even if it meant they would argue every day.

She looked below the television where there was Joey's Xbox system and a stack of games that she had saved and set up for Claire's kids when they visited. It comforted her somehow to have them there. If she had given them away, it would have felt like she was removing Joey from her life and she wasn't quite ready to do that. At the risk of feeling crazy or morbid, Julia had saved a nearly empty tube of toothpaste from Joey's old bathroom drawer and placed his old toothbrush in the stand on the counter of the extra bathroom just to feel as if he might be returning someday. His lips had touched the brush and he would have announced very soon that he needed another tube of Crest – the special kind because his back molars were sensitive to hot and cold. She was careful not to reveal this to anyone, especially Claire, for fear they would tell her the she needed to put them away in order to truly move on. She had no interest in moving on from the memory of her son, no matter what anyone thought.

In her moment of nostalgia, Julia punched the keys on the remote to change it to game mode just to see if Joey's ID would come up. It occurred to her that the stack of games sitting in the television cabinet with his Xbox 360 were harmless, but she was probably paying something extra on her cable or internet bill to have the online gaming option that was never used. Without thinking about it, she had simply transferred what was on her old account to the new one when she moved. Again, the thought of changing it to something more basic felt like she was getting rid of remnants of Joey, as silly as that seemed. She smiled when she remembered the day the cable company salesman was at her house explaining all the options. Joey had known more about it than she did from spending time at his friends' houses who apparently had more than basic cable. She had fallen victim to the salesman's slick pitch and Joey's big brown eyes as he said, "Pleeeese, Mom."

She never could resist his sweet charm, especially when it came to things like this. "Okay," she remembered saying. "Just so you know that there will be no online game playing when I'm at work – only the Xbox games you have, and if I catch you breaking the rules, the system is gone." It was an expensive package and it felt like she was going to pay for her son to find trouble. The salesman had looked at her with a judgmental gaze, as if he had never encountered a distrustful mother. He was barely an adult himself.

Julia played around with the remote and eventually got a game to load on the television. *JoJo0109* popped up on the screen. Joey's game identity. *Yes! That was it.* Her memory was returning and she was proud of herself to have figured out how to get to the right spot. She also remembered that the password was set by her – one she could remember so she could check up on his playing. *NurseJO1973* had been a password she used for everything online, including her banking, in the last ten years. She knew she should probably change it, but her memory wasn't so keen lately, so she was glad she hadn't so she could still operate the game system. Once she got in and thought she'd try her hand at playing, it occurred to her that if any of Joey's old friends saw his identity pop up, it would freak them out, so she fiddled with it until she figured out how to create her own avatar. *Hmmmmm.* It was fun to try to create a name to go with the picture she had constructed for herself. She had chosen a boy avatar and needed to choose a new screen name. *How about Wonka1126?* She had combined her favorite kid's movie – *Willy Wonka and the Chocolate Factory* and her street address. It was accepted. Then she typed in NurseJO1973 twice for the password and she was ready to play.

She paged through a list of available games, with ratings next to each one. *Oh, this one sounds like a winner. Slash and Burn - rated "M" for mature.* Exactly the type she would have argued with Joey about. It reminded her that in the long investigation of Joey's murder, the detectives had studied Joey's online game-playing patterns and concluded that he had not interacted with Eddy, who was an avid game-player and whose online identity was Buddy-something. Just the thought of it turned her stomach. She had been relieved to find out that her vigilance with Joey had at least paid off in that he was not in the same game sites as Eddy had been. The fact that Eddy stalked her son in person was even more disturbing. Julia shook her head abruptly to rid her mind of the memory and went back to trying her hand at what looked like a very bloody competition. A few names came up and then one asked if she wanted to play. *BadAssTroy* sounded like a worthy competitor. *Sure*, she typed with confidence. *What am I doing? I have no idea how to do this!* She was energized by the thought of this kid having no idea she was an almost-forty nurse and mother from "Podunk" Georgia.

Julia put on the headphones to get the maximum sound experience, and braced herself in front of the television with the game controls firmly in her hands. *Here we go.* At first, she was all thumbs as she tried to figure out how to throw the knives and grenades to set things on fire. She was killed and burned several times before she got the hang of it and actually was able to make a killing herself. She was slightly disturbed at how real the flow of blood looked and how easily a murder could be performed without consequence. She was glad she had held the line with Joey. This was more blood than she saw on the job in a year. The rush was surprising as she jumped up from the couch and said, "Yes!" She felt like a kid again, and for a moment it rekindled a memory of Joey, him shouting the same way upon winning the cash in the middle of the Monopoly board.

She relaxed and took a little break after the last victorious move and saw *Buddy666* pop up on the screen, with a message to her that said, *Yer new.* Her heart went cold and her memory was restored. How could she forget? It was the *666* that gave it away. "You bastard," she spoke out loud to the television. At first she wondered if it was really him. Surely, he wouldn't continue to use the same name after the intensive investigation into every part of his life. Then she remembered how arrogant and taunting he was to the authorities. *Of course he would.* That's how he continues to piss off those of us who are angry about his acquittal. She put the game control down and grabbed the remote to exit out of the game screen. She turned off the television and sat shaking with emotion on the couch. She couldn't distinguish if it was anger, fear, sadness, or a combination of the three. After a few minutes of sitting silent and allowing herself to calm, she got up and went to the bedroom to get her notebook. Her energy for revenge had returned.

17.

June 21, 2012

Lance Eddy's house had clean lines and was surprisingly well-groomed like the other homes in the neighborhood. An orange and blue University of Florida flag hung near his garage and a landscape crew was in the middle of putting the finishing touches on his lawn maintenance. Nathan walked up the sidewalk, giving the workers a nod, and approached the front door. He pressed the doorbell and waited. He noticed the doormat in front him that said "Welcome," with brightly-colored pansies painted around the edges. A flower pot next to the door had brown sticks coming up through the dry dirt, which probably used to be full of live flowers and greenery that had not been watered sufficiently. Nathan imagined Eddy was a mama's boy who allowed her to add her feminine touch to his place, but he had no intention of maintaining it.

The door came open in front of Nathan and an overweight man with dark hair and a two-day old beard looked through the screen door. Nathan detected a combined smell of beer, cigarettes and body odor.

"Yeah?" Eddy looked like he might have just gotten out of bed. He wore a stained t-shirt that bore the 1996 Atlanta Olympics logo.

"Sheriff Nathan Davis from Calhoun County," said Nathan as he held up his badge. "I'd like to ask you a few questions if you have a moment."

Lance Eddy hesitated, as if calculating in his head the number of possible scenarios that could bring a sheriff to his door.

"What's this about?" Eddy said clearly and defensively.

"A murder. Julia Olwen's murder, in fact." Nathan waited for a reaction

"Who?" Eddy's expression was quizzical.

Nathan realized by the look in his eyes that Eddy genuinely did not know the name at first mention. *Amazing*, he thought.

"Surely you remember the Olwen kid, whose murder almost sent you to prison for life," Nathan replied smugly.

"Oh." Eddy was obviously confused. "Listen, man, I have nothing to say about any of that. Remember? They said 'not guilty'. You have no right..." he said sarcastically before being interrupted by an annoyed Nathan Davis.

"No right?. Oh, I have a right, Mr. Eddy. There's been a murder in my county and a truck like yours was seen in the vicinity of the crime scene. You wanna talk to me now?"

"That's bullshit." Eddy looked flustered. "I don't know what you are talking about, but this is harassment."

"I'd like to take a look at your truck, if you don't mind. Is it in the garage?"

"Yeah, but I'm not gonna let you plant evidence just so you can say I had somethin' to do with it," Eddy said, obviously irritated. Nathan was unaffected and moved on to the next question. "So, have you ever been to 1126 China Grove Road?" It took Eddy a second to process the information, his eyes revealing to Nathan that he was familiar with the address.

"No," Eddy said unconvincingly.

"I see." Nathan stared through Eddy, waiting for the next clue to his guilt. He was disgusted by Eddy's demeanor, not to mention his large belly and small feet. He knew the type. He probably had another small feature that made him attracted to little boys, thought Nathan.

"Well, looks like I'll have to call for a search warrant for the truck, then. I'll be sittin' right out front here, so you make yourself comfortable." Nathan was determined he would not let Eddy out of his sight before Tommy arrived, even if he had to wait for hours.

Eddy said, "Knock yourself out." Nathan turned and walked back to his car as Eddy shut the door. He pulled out of the driveway and parked along the curb in front of Eddy's house.

"We need to get a warrant to search the truck and get a plaster cast of those tires," Nathan said to Tommy.

"He's not cooperating, huh?"

"Nah, he thinks he's golden because of the acquittal…cocky S.O.B. I'm gonna hang out here to be sure he doesn't go anywhere. Can you put a rush on it?"

"I'll do my best, boss. Call ya later."

"Thanks, Pork." Nathan hung up and prepared to sit for a while. He picked up his notebook and made some notes about his encounter with Eddy. He was sure Eddy knew the address by the look in his eyes, but the name Julia Olwen didn't seem to register at all, which Nathan found to be odd, but not unbelievable for a narcissist like Eddy. Maybe he misread this guy, but he had to remind himself that Eddy was a psychopath who probably had the ability to commit murder and then actually believe his own lie that he was innocent. Nathan knew he would have to keep going with the evidence and not get hung up on Eddy's lack of conscience. Otherwise, he would start feeling crazy like he had in his marriage. *Stay focused, Nathan. Stay focused.*

Within thirty minutes, Tommy arrived with the search warrant and a few guys from the team to execute the search. Nathan was there when they opened the garage door.

"Bingo!" Tommy shouted when he flipped on the garage's light switch and pointed to the University of Florida Gators emblem in the rear window of the truck. Nathan's blood began to boil. *Gators.* With every development, he was losing more respect for this guy.

"And what's this?" Tommy had opened the passenger side door carefully with a gloved hand and saw a Wal-Mart bag sitting on the floor of the truck. He peered into in and saw a roll of duct tape, box of large garbage bags, and rope. "Well, well, well. I predict it happened in the study, by Colonel Mustard, with the rope," Tommy announced to Nathan, knowing Lance Eddy was watching from the garage door that led into the house. Nathan noticed that Eddy looked blank, as if he had an answer, but it was the wrong one. Eddy remained silent.

After the initial search was completed, one of the officers drove off with the truck to take it to the impound lot for more evidence gathering. Eddy was enraged that they were removing his truck from the premise.

"What? So, you can plant some crap in it? This is wrong!" he shouted while the truck was leaving his garage. Tommy stood by to keep Eddy from doing anything stupid.

I wish I was the kind of guy who could do that – frame you, you bastard. Nathan shook his head in disgust and walked down the driveway back to his car. He drove off thinking he had to keep on Eddy's tail or he would be out of the country in no time. He made a call to the office to request twenty-four-hour surveillance of Eddy's activities. Lance Irving Eddy was going down if Nathan Davis was ever going to sleep at night.

***

"Hey, Miles, Nathan Davis here." This was a call he dreaded making since Calhoun County's District Attorney Miles Thornton and the sheriff were often at odds about how the justice system should work. It reminded Nathan of when his father used to complain about his accountant wanting to tell him how to run his hardware business. "What does a bean counter know about what my customers want?" his father would complain to his mother, who would quietly listen while preparing the evening meal. As much as Nathan didn't want to admit it, his father's voice still rang in his head when it came to being bull-headed.

"Nathan, how are things coming with the Olwen case? Did the search warrant produce anything of value?"

"Matter of fact, there are a couple of things." Nathan tried to sound hopeful.

"That's good. Lay it on me."

"The truck that the neighbor said she saw in Olwen's driveway the night of the supposed murder? It could very well be Eddy's. It fits the description of a large red truck with an alligator decal in the back window. Parked right in his garage. Also a bag of suspicious material he recently bought was in his garage – rope, duct tape – the kind of stuff he used, or allegedly used, in the Olwen boy's murder."

"You know we can't go there, Nathan, and so what? The bag of stuff was in his garage, not at the crime scene, right? There was no body, no rope there, no duct tape that you know of?" Thornton sounded annoyed. "What I don't understand, Nathan, is why this guy would put himself so visibly at the murder scene – I mean, drive his big red truck up there for the neighbors to see? Doesn't that seem a little suspicious to you?"

"Not if you are in a rage." *Here we go.* Nathan felt deflated already.

"I suppose, but what else do you got? Those trucks are everywhere and there are plenty of Gator fans in these parts." Thornton was clearly not buying Nathan's hypothesis.

"A gun was found tucked away in his closet, so we're getting the forensics on that right now."

"And? This guy has a lot of enemies. If I were him, I'd carry a gun, too. If that's all, it's not enough, Nathan." Thornton sighed.

"Well, we're waiting for the forensics to come back on the gun, so in case we find the body, we'll have that information on hand. Also, we'll see if the serial number matches any registration information, so we'll know if he actually owns it or if it was stolen."

"Okay, but I gotta tell ya, it's not gonna be enough if he owns that thing legally. He's allowed to have a red truck and a gun – we live in Georgia, remember?"

"Yep." Nathan was ready to be done with the call. "The guys took a plaster cast of the tires at Eddy's place, so when that info comes back, I'll be in touch." There was silence for a couple of seconds. "I'd like to bring this guy in, Miles. His family has a lot of money, so he could easily run. Now that he knows we're on his trail, I've got my guys hanging in front of his house twenty-four seven. That should keep him from being stupid, I hope."

"That's fine, but I'm sorry. You just don't have enough to make an arrest. You can do it but we can't keep him more than a day or so and then we'll really piss off the family, and the media will be all over the fact that we just want to nail this guy because he got off on the kid's murder. You better dig up something close to a smoking gun. Otherwise, no deal on my end."

"I understand." Nathan sighed this time.

"Okay, thanks for the update." Thornton hung up as soon as Nathan sounded ready to say goodbye, which told him he was too busy to hear anything but hard and direct evidence. He could only hope that the tire cast was clear enough to identify the truck as the one in Julia's driveway the night of the murder.

18.

Julia - February, 2012

Sonya Pierce sat comfortably in her brown tapestry chair, staring at Julia who was looking down at the crumpled Kleenex in her hands. Julia was usually annoyed when Sonya stayed silent after she had broken down in tears. She had come to understand, though, that this was a necessary part of her therapy – to "sit with her pain," as Dr. Pierce would often refer to it. She was allowed to simply cry and sit in silence until the next thought came to mind.

"It was as if everything came back all at once," Julia squeaked through her tears, as she described seeing Eddy's screen name pop up on her television.

"It became real again," Sonya acknowledged.

"Oh, yes. It was like he was in my living room and I felt so much rage. If I could have mustered the courage, I would have played a round of *Slash and Burn* with him just so I could murder him online." She was silent for a moment. "For Joey."

"I understand. That sounds pretty normal to me. Why didn't you? Play a round and murder him, so to speak?"

"Not me. Remember? I'm a healer, not a killer. But, is it normal? That after this much time, I still hate so much?"

"I don't know. What would you expect of someone in your shoes?"

Julia became silent again, and then she continued.

"I guess it just feels like I'll never be able to let it go. Even the thought of actually murdering him online was not enough to make this anger go away. Ya know?"

"What about the journal writing that we discussed? Have you been able to make any entries when you have these kinds of feelings or episodes?"

Episodes. Julia felt sure Dr. Pierce thought she had some sort of disorder, but was not revealing it.

"Yes, I have made a few entries, but it doesn't seem to help. What has helped...." Julia hesitated, not sure if she should continue.

"Go on...." Sonya encouraged.

"Well, I was gonna say that I have been thinking about my future. You know. What I should be doing to get my life together so I can move on from this." This was a lie, but she could not trust Dr. Pierce with the truth at this point – that her real relief came when she would plot out her revenge. This train of thought was safer.

"That sounds like a plan," Sonya agreed. "Can you tell me what some of your thoughts are about that?"

Julia spent the last half hour of their session reciting to Dr. Pierce what sounded like a perfectly normal plan for moving past the grief. Possibly going back to school for a doctorate degree, getting back to her love of photography, trying online dating....the list went on. She left Dr. Pierce's office feeling like a fake and wondering why she was paying for therapy that didn't give her any hope.

In the car on the way home, Julia made a mental note of something she needed to add to the list in her notebook.

Buy a handgun.

19.

June 21, 2012

"What the hell, Lance?" Clyde Eddy barked at his son through the phone from Australia.

"I don't know what they're talking about, I swear," Lance Eddy replied in a high pitched voice like a small child.

"Jesus. If the cops are snooping around, they must have somethin' on ya. They can't just make this stuff up." Clyde Eddy's voice became more intense. "I swear, you little piece of shit. If you've gone and gotten yourself in another mess, you're gonna have to just admit to it and do the time. Your mama can't endure another trial like the last one."

"There's not gonna be a trial. I didn't do anything. I'm telling ya...they're out to get me because they didn't get their pound of flesh and maybe they're gonna frame me for this one. Isn't there something you can do to call off the dogs? One of your connections?"

"I could if I knew what was going on. I don't have any pull down there in Calhoun. And I hear that sheriff is ruthless. Damn...Patty told me he was calling to question me, but I had no idea it would be about you." Clyde Eddy sighed with disgust. "I just thought he was fund raising or something." Eddy could hear his mother in the background, asking if everything was okay. His father's voice became muffled, as if he had put his hand over the receiver. He heard him say, "No worries...I'll be there in a second." Apparently, his mother would not learn that Lance was on the other end of the call. He wished he could talk with her. She would understand and say what he needed to hear, like "Of course, dear. It's a shame that they have this vendetta against you. Can I make you a grilled cheese sandwich?"

"It's about my truck. Someone saw one like it in the area of the crime scene and now they think it was me. They came today and I think they took a cast of the tires to match it to what they found there."

"Well, if you weren't there, then there's nothin' to worry about, is there?" Clyde Eddy was clearly agitated, knowing his son was prone to pathological lying.

Lance was still perplexed about 1126 China Grove Road and his unproductive visit there. He certainly was not going to reveal that to his father, though.

"I guess not, but what's to stop them from making it all up? I mean, they would have to prove that with pictures and stuff, wouldn't they?" Lance struggled to steady his increasingly shaky voice. He felt like crying, but he knew better. The last time he cried in front of his father, he earned a black eye. Even on the phone it would be risky if he ever wanted his father's backing again.

"Listen, your mother is waiting for me to take her to dinner. Just sit tight and don't say anything. I'll call Wayne Beaudreau to let him know you might be calling if they put the heat on you."

"I hate that guy," Lance said emphatically.

"Hey, he got you acquitted, didn't he? You better learn to not look a gift horse in the mouth, son. I swear, your mama spoiled you bad and I'm not gonna stand for your whining anymore. It's my way or no way, ya hear?"

Lance took a deep breath to keep himself from hanging up in anger or saying something he would regret. He always had more courage when talking to his father on a phone call, so he was tempted to give it back to his dad, but knew he had to play the game as always.

"Okay....okay." Lance relented while thrusting his fist into a pillow on the couch.

"Call Beaudreau and I'll talk to you next week."

"Okay. Bye." Lance Eddy hung up and walked in circles around his living room. He hated his father, who controlled him because he owned everything in Lance's life – his house, his truck, his computer…everything. If he could get a job and get out on his own, he would, but it wasn't that simple. He was a pariah in his community. And he never had any luck holding on to a job. It was ironic that he had trouble with authority and didn't like being told what to do, yet his whole life was built on that concept. He couldn't take a shit without his father's approval. He knew he was right in most situations, but in order to remain an heir to his family's wealth, he had to pretend that his father knew best. *What a joke.* Eddy was feeling the burn again. He muttered out loud for a few minutes, holding his ears, as if that would stop the tortuous thoughts of young, innocent flesh breaking open at the touch of his hands. This is when he was most vulnerable to doing something that would prove deadly. He sat back down on the couch, using the pillow to wipe the profuse sweat from his face. Then he reached down and turned on his video game system. When the list of names came up, he felt a sense of calm strangely sweep over him again.

20.

June 22, 2012

The sun was peeking through Nathan's bedroom window at six forty-five in the morning – earlier than usual, but the days were longer this time of year. He rolled over, thinking he would sleep for fifteen minutes more until his alarm went off, but his brain began working on the case within seconds. After a few minutes, he got up, turned the alarm to off, and put on his shorts to go downstairs to make coffee. He got the brew started and he walked outside to retrieve the morning paper. He noticed on his way to the driveway that a few more roof shingles had flown off into the yard during one of the recent afternoon storms. He knew he was running out of time before he would be dealing with an indoor leak. That thought quickly exited his mind the minute he unfolded the paper to see Clyde Eddy's name and photo on the front page:

**ATLANTA REAL ESTATE DEVELOPER
KILLED IN PLANE CRASH**

Nathan stopped suddenly, shocked by what he had just read. *What?* He stood barefooted in the middle of his driveway, reading the article. According to the newspaper story, Clyde Eddy and his wife, Penelope, were scheduled to fly to Melbourne late the evening before on a short business trip after a dinner together in Sydney. Apparently his wife, Penelope, felt ill after dinner and Eddy decided to fly alone, planning to be back in Sydney later today. Aircraft malfunction was reported to be the cause of the crash and there were no survivors after the private Cessna Citation jet went down in the Alpine National Park northeast of Melbourne.

His mind was racing, wondering what impact this would have on his investigation into Eddy's role in the Olwen murder. He hurried through his morning routine and got to the office by eight, making his first phone call to his favorite news reporter.

"Sheriff Davis," Sally seemed to sing his name every time she said it. "I wondered when you were going to finally call me for a rain check after leaving me stranded at Lana's the other day." She knew he would get a kick out of her damsel in distress tone.

"Yeah, sorry about that, Tater," Nathan replied with his usual charm. "Let's make a date...I need to talk to you about Clyde Eddy."

"I know...did you hear about the crash?"

"Just this morning. I read it in the paper. That's crazy. I just called him yesterday and his secretary told me he was out of town until the middle of next month."

"We're still waiting on the details. So what's the latest on the Olwen case? I've got a stand-up this afternoon outside of Eddy's office and thought I might tie it in with the latest evidence. Any solid suspects yet?"

"Let's get together and I'll tell ya what I can," said Nathan.

"Too busy today...can't you tell me something over the phone?" She switched from her business voice to something sounding more like a little girl pleading with a parent.

"There's not much to tell, really. I've got a couple of good leads, but we're not close to an arrest yet. How about dinner tomorrow night?"

The phone went silent on the other end. For a moment, Nathan thought he had lost her.

"You there?" He asked.

"Yeah, sorry...I got distracted. Dinner? Uh, I guess I could do that. What do you have in mind?" Her business voice was back.

Nathan was smiling because he had rattled her a little with what probably sounded like a date request. He meant to confuse her. He knew she was slightly attracted to him and he wanted to capitalize on that knowledge.

"Are you willing to drive down here to Regal? If so, I know a nice little Italian place in town. They have great eggplant parmesan for you vegetarian types."

"Who said I was a vegetarian?"

"I dunno. I thought every media liberal was a lettuce cruncher," he teased.

"Hey, I grew up on an Iowa cattle farm, so I can eat beef with the best of 'em." Sally had switched into her southern drawl for Nathan's benefit.

"Stop it, girl. You are getting' me all revved up. You gonna meet me tomorrow night or not?"

"Sure. What time?"

"Let's say about seven. The place is Mantovani's on Main Street. I'll call and make reservations." Sally went silent again, as it became more apparent that he was arranging a date.

"Sounds good. I look forward to it."

Nathan hung up and was surprised that he felt a bit of excitement at the prospect of wooing Sally Tate with his charm. Until now, it was just flirtation, but it was moving into a direction he hadn't really planned consciously. He reminded himself to be careful that he didn't compromise information by mixing business with pleasure. She was too young for him and he knew it, but it had been a long time and good sense was not what he wanted to rely on to satisfy his curiosity about Sally Tate.

"Dotty!" Nathan yelled from his office. "You know that Italian place on Main? Can you get me their number?"

In less than thirty seconds, Dorothy was standing at his door giving him a look that said she deserved to know why he needed that phone number.

"Really? You're going to Montovani's and I don't know who she is yet? I'm crushed." She was smiling from ear to ear, happy that Nathan was making an attempt at a social life.

"Who said there was a *she*?"

"Are you kiddin' me? I've never known you to go out to anything but McDonald's, let alone a place like that. What time do you want the reservation and I'll get it done."

"You're a doll, Dot. Seven is good, tomorrow night – for two." He smiled, enjoying Dorothy's desperate interest.

"And you're really not gonna tell me who she is?"

"Not yet. You know…I don't wanna jinx it."

"Okay," Dorothy said with disappointment. "But no runnin' off to Vegas without my approval first, ya hear?"

Nathan laughed heartily at the thought. *It would be a cold day in….*

21.

Julia - February, 2012

"I don't know, Claire. Not tonight. I'm tired." Julia was pulling into her driveway after a long dayshift. She was on the phone with Claire, who was trying to cajole her into a night on the town.

"It'll do ya good. C'mon, it's Valentine's Day next weekend and you're gonna need a date. I hear there are some pretty hot single guys at this new place downtown."

Great. Thanks for reminding me. "Single guys? You're married."

"Yeah, but you're not. And you work too much. You need some excitement in your life. I mean, what do you do when you're not working?"

Julia smiled as she got out of her car and walked to the end of the driveway to retrieve her garbage can. If Claire only knew what she had been doing in her spare time, she would be horrified.

"Is Steve okay with this? With you gallivanting around town with me?" Julia was hoping to use guilt to back her off from this idea.

"Oh, yeah. He and the boys are going to his parents' cabin in Blue Ridge tonight for some guy time, and his mother and I are going to meet them there tomorrow afternoon. He just told me I can look, but not touch."

"Okay. But I'm driving myself so if I want to leave, I can just go. Deal?"

"No way. That will be too much of a hassle. If you get tired, I promise we'll go home. So, I'll pick you up around eight?"

"Eight? That sounds awfully late." Julia was hating the idea more and more.

"Are you kidding? Nothing interesting happens until after nine. We're going to get a drink or two in us before then."

Julia wondered if Claire remembered their ages. In less than a year, she would be forty years old and Claire wasn't far behind her. Maybe she was having a mid-life crisis or something since the boys were in their early teens now.

"Whatever," said Julia as she looked at her watch. "It's three forty-five now, so I have a few hours to think of a good excuse not to go."

"Whatever, back at ya," bantered Claire. "See you at eight."

Julia no sooner got into the house when she heard a knock on the front door. It was Mrs. Timko.

"Hey, sweet lady," Mrs. Timko said. "I hate to bother you, but I just saw you got home and I wanted to see if my supplies came for the month."

"Yes, they're right here." Julia had left them near the door so she wouldn't forget to take them to her. "Thank goodness they sent me the right syringes this time."

"I hope you don't mind doing this for me. You know I get so confused every time I get on the phone with those people to make an order."

"No, I understand completely." Julia handed her the box. "In fact, if you are satisfied with the product, I can put you on a monthly standing order, so they can come to your house every month, no questions asked. That way you don't have to reorder every month. I didn't want to say yes until I talked with you first, though."

"That sounds great." Mrs. Timko's face looked relieved, but there was a tremor in her right hand. She seemed to be aging in years every time Julia saw her.

"Good. I'll call them today and let them know. Then if anything seems strange or out of order, you just let me know, okay?"

"Thank you so much, Julia. You are such a dear. I don't know what I'd do without neighbors like you." Mrs. Timko's voice was high pitched and strained.

Julia reached out and affectionately patted her arm. In many ways, they had adopted each other as mother and daughter, especially since Mr. Timko passed away last year. They were never able to have children, so he was all she had. *I'm gonna miss her*, Julia thought, feeling a lump form in her throat. She walked with Mrs. Timko back to her driveway, retrieving the newspaper and the mail on her way back to her house. She opened the paper and saw a handsome man on the front page.

CALHOUN COUNTY SHERIFF
MAKING HEADWAY ON JUVENILE DELINQUENCY

Julia had heard good things about Nathan Davis and he was the kind of guy she would have voted for had she been living in the county at the time of his election, especially because of his focus on juvenile crime and getting young people off the streets and interested in a vocation. She stared more intently at the photo and felt attracted to his genuine face. Julia always had the ability to look at a photo and discern a lot from the quality of a smile. She was surprised to find herself attracted at all, and quickly folded the paper back together, trying to squash any thoughts of getting involved with a man right now. She moaned at the thought of her planned night on the town with Claire later. She knew Claire was right, but also knew her best friend had no idea what she was really doing with her life.

Once inside, Julia went upstairs and changed out of her work clothes and put on a pair of sweat pants and a sweatshirt, trying to forget she had plans for later. She had a few more hours before then, so she pulled her notebook out of the desk drawer and reviewed her next steps, refining the details as she went along. She had a running to-do list that was keeping her on track.

- *Mention the dark thoughts to Dr. Pierce; ask her if it's normal to think about homicide*
- *Finish collecting samples*
- *Find Buddy666 online again*
- *Purchase the gun*
- *Stake out LIE's house*

Julia looked over her notes repeatedly. She had gathered internet research about various subjects that would be helpful, so she was reading over the copies she had printed. She couldn't afford to make any mistakes. In a few short months, she would be ready, so she had to be patient and methodical in the planning. Three hours went by more quickly than she had planned and when she looked up at the clock, she was surprised to see that it was almost eight. She hadn't noticed that the sun had gone down and darkness had overshadowed the whole house, except for the one desk light she had turned on at four o'clock.

She hurried upstairs to put on something that would look presentable for bar-hopping or whatever Claire had in mind, but not too inviting. Before long, she could hear Claire's knock at the door.

"Hey, there." Claire said as she walked through the door. "Really? You're going to wear that?" She was pointing at Julia's faded blue jeans and bulky blue sweater. "You look like a fourth-grade teacher, not a hot nurse." Claire was wearing her tight black leggings, high-heeled boots, and a silk blouse.

"It's freezing out there and I feel perfectly fine in this, thank you very much." The last thing Julia needed was to attract a man who might want to snoop around her cryptic life.

Claire rolled her eyes.

"I tried to call you earlier, but you didn't pick up," said Claire, as they walked to the car.

Julia remembered the phone ringing, but she was too engrossed in her research to be bothered with a call.

"Yeah, my cousin called from California, so I was probably on my cell with her."

"Who? You have a cousin in California?"

"Uh-huh," Julia said confidently.

"Wait a minute…I've known you since we were kids and you never once mentioned a cousin in California."

"Really? Surely I have at some point. Anyway, we're not that close, but lately she has been having some financial trouble…she's got three kids and her husband left her. So, I've been trying to help her out a little. You know…I don't have much family."

Claire seemed skeptical. "What's her name?"

"Celeste...she's a distant cousin...one of those second or third removed types." Julia wasn't sure she should have named her and became distracted at her possible mistake.

"Oh...well, be careful. You know how family can take advantage once you start getting involved in their drama. I know you, Julia. You'll give your last dime to someone if you can."

"I know. It's not like she is a deadbeat or anything. Actually, she is a nurse, too, but it sounds like her husband left her with a lot of credit card debt, so I think she just needs to get out of this hole and then she should be fine."

"Well, we should take a trip out there sometime, shouldn't we?" Claire had accepted her story.

"Yeah, sure. That would be fun." Julia was staring out of the window of Claire's car. She hated to lie to Claire, but it was best this way. She felt a chill and noticed that it had started to snow a little, which was a rarity in Georgia.

"Look, Jules, it's snowing!" Claire exclaimed. "I hope the roads don't get icy later."

"Well, if they do, we just won't go home," Julia laughed.

"Now, that's the spirit."

She was going to miss Claire, too.

22.

June 23, 2012

Montovani's was a small hole-in-the-wall establishment in downtown Regal, run by a local Italian family who was rumored to have Mafia ties, but Nathan just chalked that up to small-town boredom looking for drama. He found them to be honest, hard-working people who could make a lasagna to die for.

He arrived a few minutes before Sally, and secured a table near a street-side window. He considered sitting on the patio, but it was a humid evening, so he decided an indoor table was best. The tables were covered with traditional red and white checkered tablecloths and every chair in the restaurant seemed to be different, which gave the place a flea market look, but its eclectic style created a quaint, comfortable atmosphere. Nathan wasn't much for fancy places and there weren't any of those, as far as he knew, in Regal. A plump young dark-haired woman came by to take his drink order. Nathan ordered the house red. He knew nothing about wine, but he figured it wouldn't look very sophisticated to Sally if he was sitting there with a beer.

Nathan looked up from the menu and saw Sally walk in and say a few words to the hostess, who directed her to Nathan's table. He rose from his chair to greet her.

"Well, hello, Ms. Tate." Nathan's eyes lit up with approval. She was wearing a snug black skirt and satin blouse.

"Hello yourself Sheriff Davis," Sally put out her hand to shake his. He took it into his and patted it with his left hand.

"You look stunning, I must say. And no need for the formal sheriff stuff. Nathan is fine with me." He pulled out a chair for her to be seated next to him and helped her scoot it close to the table.

"Well, thank you…Nathan." Sally hesitated as if the word was foreign to her. "This place is so cute. I wouldn't have pegged you as the romantic type."

"Now, wait a minute…don't go gettin' any wild ideas about me. But I do have some class, especially when it comes to beautiful women." His white smile stretched from ear to ear.

"Well, I'll take that as a compliment," Sally blushed a little as she picked up a menu. "What's your favorite dish here?"

"Definitely the four-cheese lasagna. But I don't think you can get a bad meal here – at least that's what I hear. I always get the lasagna." Nathan hated admitting his propensity for boring routines.

"I could have figured that about you. When ya find a good thing, stick with it. Why venture out, right?"

"I guess…I'm not sure if you think that's a positive or not." Nathan was peering over his reading glasses like an old man assessing his grandchild. With self-awareness, he pulled off his glasses and put the menu down, realizing he really had no need to look at it.

"It wasn't meant to be either one. I just think I know your type." She was smiling playfully while reading the menu.

"And what, pray tell, do you think my type is?"

She laid the menu down to answer his question without distraction.

"I would say Nathan Davis is a rule follower, a facilitator of justice, freedom and the American way. There is a right way and wrong way to do things, and once he knows what is right, there is no need to go looking for trouble. Just do the right thing and everybody will be the better for it."

She stopped to get his assessment and folded her hands in front of her in a confident gesture.

"Damn, girl," Nathan joked. "You hit the nail on the head and aren't you so proud to know it?"

"Yeah, well, you're not that tough to figure out. It's quite attractive, and even refreshing in some ways. You know…the protector and hero every girl wants to rescue her from life's dragons."

"Sounds like there's a history there, but I won't ask you to reveal it just yet. So, wanna know what I think of Miss Tater Tot?"

"Jeez, Nathan, I wish you wouldn't do that…it's so…so countrified."

"Yeah, and I'm a country boy," Nathan began to laugh. "And I do it mostly because it annoys the heck out of you."

"Okay, okay. I'm dying to know what you think you know about me." Sally had picked up the menu again to look it over.

"Let's see. Sally Tate is a country girl at heart, turned Atlanta jet-setter, who doesn't like to be told how things really are. She likes to fantasize about how things could be. So, she gets offended by comments that aren't so politically correct, even if they come from a hero like me." He softened his voice for effect. "But deep down, she likes the safety of someone who tells the truth, even if it's a little scary." His eyes softened and as they did, she melted into them as she looked up from the menu. For a moment, she was silent, as if she had been undressed, hoping not to call attention to herself.

"How'd I do?" Nathan refused to take his eyes off of hers.

"Fair to midlin'…" She was not going to admit he was spot on.

"Fair to what?" Nathan looked confused.

"You know, fair to midling...so, so...almost there, but not quite. It's a Midwest saying."

"We don't talk like that down here, Missy." Nathan was exaggerating his southern accent, while letting her off the hook for not admitting he was right about her.

Sally laughed at his fake drawl, which was interrupted by the waitress who asked for her drink order.

"I'll try the Malbec, thank you."

"Are you ready to order?" The waitress inquired politely.

"Give us a few minutes to chat over our wine first, if you don't mind." Nathan was enjoying Sally's company and didn't want to be bothered with the food details yet.

"Nice," acknowledged Sally. "I had no idea you would know how to conduct yourself in such a chivalrous manner. You just took charge there, didn't you?"

"I invited you, so it's my party tonight."

"Okay, I'll accept that. Soooo, was there another reason we were meeting tonight or did you just want to harass me about my Midwest colloquialisms?"

Nathan knew that was a trick question to get him to commit that this was either a date or a business meeting. He was not going to reveal himself that easily.

"My first goal was to tease and harass you about many things, which I'm not done with, by the way. And my second purpose was to pick your brain about Clyde Eddy."

"Well, there is a lot to tell. Have you got all night?" She didn't seem to want the flirting to end.

Nathan cleared his throat on purpose, to let her know he wasn't sure how to answer that question.

"Is that an invitation?" He felt like he had just achieved a checkmate. She was cornered now.

She began to respond with a look of sarcasm when Nathan's cell phone rang with the ring tone he used for urgent calls. Sally stopped in mid-sentence when he looked down at his phone.

Nathan looked up at her. "I need to get this. Do you mind?"

"Of course not, go ahead." Sally took another sip of her wine.

It was Tommy reporting that the lab was able to match Lance Eddy's truck tires to the tire tracks at the scene and that the gun found in Eddy's home was registered in Julia Olwen's name.

"Ya don't say," Nathan responded with reserve in front of Sally, although he wanted to jump up and say *hot damn!* "Okay. Get the warrant and I'll meet you at his place in about an hour." Tommy then told Nathan that Eddy was at a family gathering at his mother's home. "That complicates things a little," Sally heard Nathan reply, "but we'll figure it out. Thanks, Buddy." Nathan ended the call, looking like the Cheshire cat.

Sally looked confused.

"Don't tell me you are gonna cut out on me again. I'm starting to get a complex, Nathan Davis."

Nathan smiled like a ten-year-old on Christmas morning.

"Do you want an exclusive?"

"What?"

"Do you want first dibs on the story of the week?"

"You have one? Of course!"

"Then call your camera crew and tell them you are going to Marlowe County. We're arresting Lance Eddy tonight for the murder of Julia Olwen." Nathan got up from the table and threw down a twenty dollar bill. He grabbed Sally's hand and said, "Let's go."

Sally's eyes lit up with excitement, not only for the story, but for the man who liked being a hero.

23.

June 23, 2102

Lance Eddy tried to get Penelope Eddy to sit and relax, as he watched her wander around her kitchen, still in a daze from the news about her husband, combined with the Xanax her doctor had prescribed to keep her calm. Eddy soon accepted that she needed to busy herself with cooking for the family in order to not have to face that her life was crumbling around her. He had resolved that it was his job to take care of her and he had to work at not thinking about what losing his father was going to mean to him, as well as her. Being an only child of a wealthy megalomaniac had not been easy. There was a lot of pressure, given the fact that Lance's aunts and uncle, his father's siblings, were a bunch of country-bumpkins who somehow managed to raise college-educated children, some of whom were doctors and lawyers. Eddy wondered if his father had ever understood that all the money in the world could not create the child he really wanted, and he felt the anger in him well up again. Yet, something was different now. The anger still came, but he felt a sense of control now that he knew his father was no longer a factor in his life. Then he thought of the money he stood to inherit and he literally became giddy at the prospect. Yes, he was sorry for his mother's loss, but he felt that even she would have to feel some sense of relief to not have him constantly telling her what she could and could not do. As he watched her flit around the kitchen, he thought that maybe he was wrong – that it would not be a relief for her. She needed someone like his father to control her and Lance thought that would be another perk of his father's death – that he would step into the role of making sure his mother knew what to do at all times. He smiled, feeling a sense of real power over his family for the first time in his life.

"Lance, dear, can you take these trays into the dining room?" Penelope was handing Eddy two silver trays covered with pinwheels, meats and cheeses.

"Mother, I don't know why you just didn't have all this stuff catered. No one expects you to be doing this."

"I know, but I have to stay busy. You know how I love to entertain. Now, move along." Penelope had always been good at dismissing him with a task.

Eddy walked into the dining room where there were a dozen people standing around talking about the crash and what the authorities had said about the wreckage. Would Clyde's remains be found? How long should they wait to plan a memorial service? Would there be an investigation first? The Australian government was being as cooperative as they could be, but the area where the plane crashed was heavily forested and it would be some time before they were able to make an assessment about why the plane went down.

Eddy was aware that he should be having feelings of sadness or wonder about how his father died and whether or not he experienced pain, but he just couldn't get to those emotions. He wasn't sure he really even cared about it. This was just another event that was centered on his father's status and wealth – something he had become bored of many years ago. Yet, there was something different about this gathering than those in the past. Usually, the only pleasure for Eddy in these kinds of family moments was in watching the faces of his aunts, uncle and cousins show pity toward his father for the pathetic son he had raised, causing silent, but evident, humiliation that pleased Lance Eddy. Without his father in this setting, he could not revel in that embarrassment. Instead, it felt empty. He didn't know these people outside of his father's gaze, so he felt awkward, abandoned, and devalued, emotions he didn't tolerate well. He went outside onto the large stone patio off of the kitchen to have a cigarette, hoping to calm the anxiety. The moon was large and low in the sky, looking almost alien. Lance mindlessly stared at it, inhaling the sweet elixir of nicotine that helped him erase any feelings of anger or discomfort.

Just then, Lance's Uncle Charles opened the patio door. "Lance, there's a Sheriff Davis from Calhoun County here to see you. Says he needs to talk to you." Charles Eddy looked worried. "Now," he reprimanded.

Lance stomped his cigarette out on the patio. *Unbelievable.* His anger took hold instantly. His first reaction was to begin running, but then he remembered that he had his father's money and they could arrest him, but there would be no evidence to prove anything. He decided to remain calm, even though his heart was pounding and the blood had rushed to his head. He wasn't sure what lengths the cops were willing to go to in order to get him behind bars. He remembered the last words his father had said to him.

Call Beaudreau and I'll talk to you next week.

24.

June 23, 2012

Nathan felt the adrenaline flowing as he and Sally sped up the freeway toward Marlowe County. He had placed his flashing light on top of the car and got into the express lane to speed by all of the Friday night drivers. He looked over at her and he could see she was excited by the action and the story she stood to gain from it. They exchanged approving glances and Nathan wondered if they could resume their date after the excitement was over. He was amazed by how beautiful she looked in her tight black skirt and high heels. She had a natural beauty that didn't need make up, but she had taken care to look gorgeous for him and he needed to be careful to not move too fast with her. He thought about how sly women were – they knew exactly what men wanted and dressed accordingly, but then would play dumb about their intentions, driving men crazy. It was Nathan's biggest pet peeve about women, even though he loved everything else about them.

"So, we're going to interrupt his family's memorial gathering to arrest Eddy?" Sally asked with concern.

"I know. It's cold, but we can't waste time. I will get him outside and hopefully whisk him away before his family knows what happened. You'll keep the crew down the street, right?"

"I'll do my best." Sally felt unusually nervous and wasn't sure why.

They arrived at the home of Lance Eddy's mother and as much as he hated to do this to Mrs. Eddy, he was concerned that Lance Eddy would be a flight risk, especially since he would likely be distraught about his father's death. Men such as

Eddy were prone to high anxiety and would do whatever necessary to avoid arrest or incarceration. Nathan didn't want to take any chances. With Eddy's father unable to save him this time, Lance would be like a caged animal.

He had asked Tommy to explain to the magistrate judge that the arrest warrant was based on the tire tracks matching Eddy's vehicle and the gun found at Eddy's house. Nathan wondered how Thornton would react at the news of Eddy's arrest, but he decided it was better to act now and ask for Thornton's forgiveness later. He couldn't worry about any of the politics now. He was happy just to be getting Eddy in custody.

Nathan saw Tommy's squad car parked along the street in front of the Eddy estate and the Channel 3 news van parked a little further down. When Nathan and Sally got out of the car, she ran toward the news van and Nathan and Tommy walked up the long walk toward the front door. After ringing the door bell, an older man opened the door and waited for Nathan to speak. Nathan flashed his sheriff's badge.

"Sheriff Nathan Davis, Marlowe County. Is Lance Eddy here?"

The man who Nathan later discovered was Clyde's older brother, Charles Eddy, hesitated and then looked away toward the back of the home.

"Well, yes, may I ask what this is about?"

"I'm sorry sir, I know this is a difficult time for the family, but we are on official police business and need to speak with Mr. Eddy, if you don't mind. "Can you have him come outside here – away from the family?" He gave Charles Eddy an astute look, hoping he would take the hint and let him arrest Lance discretely.

"I understand," said Charles, as he walked through the house to retrieve his nephew. Nathan stepped off of the stately front porch and retreated to the sidewalk on the front lawn to wait.

When Tommy spotted Eddy coming through the door, he said, "Lance Irving Eddy?"

Eddy said, "Yeah...what's this about?" Tommy then revealed the handcuffs and announced he was under arrest for the murder of Julia Olwen.

Eddy resisted at first and then he seemed to go into a trance, as if he knew there was nothing he could do in the moment. Nathan was pleased to see that Sally and her crew were ready, but waiting until after the arrest to film Eddy being led to the squad car.

"You have the right to remain silent," continued Tommy, while Eddy scowled at Nathan.

Once in cuffs, Nathan began walking toward Tommy's car, alongside Tommy and Eddy. That's when Sally put a microphone in Eddy's face and asked, "Did you murder Julia Olwen?"

Eddy remained silent and expressionless, ignoring her and the camera, as Tommy pushed Eddy's head down into the back of the squad car. Sally was introducing the story and Nathan could hear her in the background. Once in the car, Eddy blurted out, "You guys are unbelievable. Can't you see my mother is grieving?" Nathan and Tommy scoffed and shut the door as Eddy was still ranting.

Sally was now in her element, reporting the event. "Breaking news here in Marlowe County tonight. Lance Irving Eddy, as you may remember, was acquitted last year of twelve-year-old Joey Olwen's kidnapping and brutal murder, but he has now been arrested for the murder of young Joey's mother, Julia Olwen."

Nathan stepped aside while Tommy drove off, staying back to watch Sally reporting, smiling at her as she answered questions from the evening news anchor. He had forgotten that they were doing this during a prime time news hour. *Sweet.* Eventually, Sally and the crew walked over to get a statement from Nathan. He winked at her away from the camera, but she didn't acknowledge it, as she held the microphone in front of him.

"Sheriff, can you tell us what happened here tonight?"

"Yes, some new evidence came to light this evening that led us to secure a warrant for the arrest of Lance Irving Eddy for the murder of Julia Olwen."

"Can you tell us what that evidence was?"

"Not while the case is under investigation, however, we are going to do everything we can to thoroughly investigate the murder and make sure that justice is served for the Olwen family."

"I'm sure you are aware that the Eddy family has suffered a terrible loss today. Was there a reason you decided to arrest Lance Eddy here, while the family is gathering to grieve?"

Nathan felt stung by the question, but he knew Sally was simply asking what her viewers would want answered.

"We are sorry for the loss in the Eddy family, but it is simply a coincidence that the evidence came to light today. We felt that Lance Eddy could be a flight risk if we didn't have a warrant before we formally questioned him. That's all I can tell you for now."

"Thank you, Sheriff." Sally turned toward the cameras.

"We will be continuing to follow this story as new details unfold. Sally Tate, reporting from Marlowe County for Channel 3-WLTA News." She signed off and walked over to talk to the crew for a few minutes while Nathan leaned on his car, relishing in what had just transpired. Sally then walked toward Nathan smiling from ear to ear.

"Good work, Tater Tot," Nathan teased. "You were kind of rough on me tonight, though, weren't you?"

"Well, you have to admit, it's pretty cold to arrest this guy in front of his freshly grieving mother."

"Yeah, well you didn't see the Olwen crime scene, did you? Talk about cold. I have no sympathy for this guy…and I'm sorry for his mother."

"So, I rode here with you but my car is still in the parking lot at Montovani's." Sally seemed embarrassed that she was just realizing that fact.

"I know that," Nathan said confidently. "We weren't done with our date, were we?"

"Uh, it's nine o'clock. And isn't there some sort of questioning you have to do with Eddy tonight?"

"You watch too much television," he laughed. "It'll do him good to sit in jail for the night to think about what he's gonna say. I'll get to him first thing in the morning. It's the weekend and I doubt he will be arraigned until Monday anyway."

"Okay, well, I've given the station everything they need and they're tickled pink that I broke the story first, given this was my evening off."

"Sounds like we both have some celebrating to do, then." Nathan opened the passenger door to his car and motioned for Sally to get in.

"Where to?" She asked after Nathan had started the car.

"I know a cool Antebellum-style joint that serves good beer," Nathan suggested.

"Huh? That doesn't sound right..." Sally frowned and smiled at the same time.

"You'll see..." Nathan drove off feeling sure that they were both going to get a little tipsy and maybe more before the evening was over. He glanced at Sally who had that look he had seen before from women who went on a police call with him. For some reason, the ladies loved watching a man with a badge take control of a situation. He smiled and flipped on the radio, and Sally instantly began singing along, looking drunk with accomplishment.

25.

Julia - March, 2012

She stood motionless, with a nine millimeter Glock 19 in her hands, as the salesman explained the features. Julia had never seen a handgun up close, and certainly had not ever held one. Her heart was pumping fast and for the first time in many weeks, she began doubting whether or not she had the guts for this.

"Miss? Do you have any questions?" The sporting goods salesman was repeating his question, pulling Julia out of her trance.

"Uh….no, I guess not. Can you show me what I need…like ammunition?" She said in a weak voice, still staring at the gun in her hand.

The salesman smiled wittingly. "You've never held a gun before, have you?"

Julia looked up for the first time and smiled with relief. "How did you guess?"

"It's okay," he assured her. "Most people feel intimidated at first, as you should, since these are powerful weapons that can hurt the wrong people if you're not careful." He reached under the counter and pulled out a brochure.

"Why don't you register for one of these classes? They are designed specifically for the novice shooter so that you understand how to use your gun if needed, but more importantly, how to keep it from firing in the wrong situations."

Julia took the brochure from him and thanked him for the information.

"That's a great idea. I'm sure I just need some time to get used to it." She turned it over several times to exam it, although she did not know what she was looking for.

"You said you wanted it for personal protection…in your home, right?" The salesman said with interest.

"Why, yes, of course. What other reason would there be?" Julia answered with a hint of defensiveness.

"I meant nothing by it other than to warn you that if you have children in the home, you'll want to pay attention to the safety features and you might not want to keep it loaded. You know, keep the ammunition somewhere else so that it's not quite so easy to discharge, but close enough so that if you do suspect an intruder, you will know the steps to get it loaded. For some people, that takes a lot of practice."

Julia was struck by how easy it was for him to make an assumption that she had children. She always knew that she looked like the motherly type, and just the mention of it reminded her of Joey and instantly empowered her to buy the gun.

"I'll take it," she said emphatically and the salesman looked pleased. Julia felt a strange rush of excitement and guilt at the same time that had little to do with her plans. She was the daughter of two parents who would turn over in their graves if they learned she had bought a firearm. They were not "gun people." After completing all the necessary registration paperwork, she walked out of the store with a gun in her shopping bag, making her feel like a bad girl who had given in to her angry urges. She sat in her car, feeling the warm sun burning through the windshield, and beads of sweat began to form on her forehead. Before turning on the car, she contemplated getting out and returning the gun to the store.

Maybe she could accomplish her plans without it. Maybe there was another way. She momentarily reviewed the plan in her head again, turning over the details that had kept her awake on many nights – the details which she could meticulously recite verbatim to herself in that space of time before sleep and wakefulness. She knew that if she began to soften her resolve or change the details she had worked so hard to puzzle together, it would lessen her chances of success. *No, I've got to be sure. There is no room for error.*

Julia Olwen turned the key and started the car, flipping the air conditioner on to a high blast to cool the sweat that was now running down her chest, between her breasts. As she pulled out of the mall and turned right onto Route 42 toward her home, her car was on autopilot and her brain was thinking about her parents, Joey, her friend Sheila who she lost last year to breast cancer. They were in another world and might possibly be looking down on her wondering why she was doing this. Or were they? She fantasized that they might be talking to each other about her recent behavior and her plans to do something so bizarre and risky and out of character for her. Would they understand or would they expect her to be better, stronger, more resilient than this?

The piercing sound of a blaring car horn jolted Julia out of her daze and caused her to swerve to miss the car she almost sideswiped. She cried out in fear, slamming on her brakes to let the angry driver pass by. Shaking, she slowly moved over into the right lane and then pulled off onto the berm of the road. She gently laid her forehead between her hands that were still gripped to the steering wheel and she began to cry, quietly at first, but then it built to a violent sob as she allowed herself to cry out in pain. Julia hadn't felt this kind of anguish since the day of the acquittal.

After the tears subsided, she sat back, closed her eyes and struggled to breathe through her swollen sinuses. She felt exhausted, but relieved and somewhat at peace. She wanted desperately to pick up the phone and call her mother or go home and make dinner for Joey like she used to when she needed to forget about the cares of the day. She wished she could go back to those times and embrace the mundane things of life again. But for some reason unknown to her, she had been dealt this ridiculous set of circumstances that no one could ever explain, not even Father Sheehan or Dr. Pierce, who should have some answers, shouldn't they? Julia felt her frustration building again, but she talked herself out of resuming the tears and started her car to head home. It was dusk and difficult to tell the difference between the latent sunlight or the moon's reflection of it. It was quiet and calm, the end of winter and beginning of spring. Everything seemed natural and normal, except for the gun lying next to her on the passenger seat. Her new identity, which was totally unnatural and unwanted to Julia, was that of a vigilante.

Just then, she was startled once more, this time by blue lights flashing behind her car.

"Crap," she said out loud. *Can't a girl just pull off the road to cry without drawing attention to herself?* Julia was annoyed until she realized what she had with her. *The gun!* She hoped the officer would not ask to see what was in the shopping bag in the passenger seat.

She rolled down her window as she saw him approach. He was not in uniform, which surprised her and caused her immediate alarm.

"Evenin' ma'am," he said while pointing a small flashlight at her. "I'm Sheriff Davis." He showed her his badge. "Is everything all right?" Julia relaxed, glad that she was not under arrest for concealing a newly purchased weapon.

"Yes of course, Sheriff. Someone came close to sideswiping me a minute ago – I don't know, maybe a drunk driver," she continued with a nervous laugh. "So, it rattled me enough that I thought I should pull over and compose myself. I was just getting ready to leave." She noticed him looking at the shopping bag and into the backseat. She also noticed that he was as good looking in person as he was in the paper. She was consciously aware of how her tear-stained face must look under her pulled back hair that was wrapped in a girlish ponytail.

"All right, then. Just thought I'd see if you needed some help." He hesitated again, taking one last look at the front passenger seat. "You drive safely, now."

"I will," Julia responded shyly, not wanting to look him in the eye. She rolled up the window and watched him walk back to his car, with the light still flashing on the dash. He was tall and had a confident gait. She liked that and wished she could have met him under much different circumstances. *In a different lifetime, maybe.*

She pulled out slowly and the sheriff followed her until she turned left onto China Grove Road toward home. She couldn't wait to get there, where she would feel safe from any judgmental eyes.

26.

June 23, 2012

Sally lit up the instant Nathan pulled into his driveway. The front lawn spotlights were shining on the face of the eighteen hundreds Antebellum, a stately bungalow. The curved and pillared portico that gave it such a pleasing curb appeal was a part of the home Nathan rarely noticed, since he always entered through the back door after parking his car in the detached garage behind. This time, though, he parked the car midway in the drive so he could take Sally through the front door. Nathan was pleased that the property's dilapidation was not evident in the dark. He was not quite sure if his front door key would work since he used it so rarely, but he tried to appear as if this was his usual routine.

"Why, Nathan, I do declare," Sally teased with her Scarlett O'Hara imitation. "This is absolutely gorgeous." They were at the front door about to enter and Nathan was fumbling with his key chain. He found the right one and unlocked the door that creaked a little upon opening.

"After you, my lady," Nathan said with a slight British accent while motioning for her to enter. A Tiffany-style lamp was on in the foyer, illuminating the antique tapestry hanging on the wall.

"Wow." Sally was holding her purse straps in both hands in front of her, while planted firmly on a round Persian rug, taking in the romantic feel of the past. "You continue to surprise me, Nathan Davis."

"It's a place to stay," Nathan said teasingly as he led her through the front hall into the kitchen. Sally followed, still dazed by the details that she wanted to explore. Nathan went right to the fridge and pulled out two beers.

"Miller Light okay with you?"

"What? Oh, yeah, of course." She was still distracted. "I want a tour," she said excitedly in a schoolgirl tone.

"I don't know…I didn't clean up – I had no idea we would end up here tonight…really," Nathan said, trying to convince her that he wasn't a cad, as it might appear. She didn't seem to get the reference, still looking around at the artwork on the wall.

"This isn't meant the way it is going to sound, but did you decorate this place yourself?" Sally looked genuinely perplexed by the Nathan she knew and the Nathan who inhabited this home.

Nathan laughed heartily. "No. In fact, not much has changed since my mama passed away. She was a history teacher and spent a lot of time on the family tree, so a lot of this stuff she picked up at yard sales and flea markets to try to restore this place to its original ambiance. It's been in the family for almost two centuries, so I can't bring myself to sell it, but it's not really me, either." He took a long swig of his beer while leaning against the large butcher block island in the middle of the kitchen. "There's a lot that needs to be repaired, but I'm not exactly the handy type."

Sally looked away from the painting she was studying and shot him a playful glance.

"You know what I mean…." Nathan retorted with a sheepish grin. "C'mon, let's go sit outside and chat."

The kitchen was attached to a large screened-in porch, which led to an old slate patio surrounded by mature greenery. As they made their way outside, Nathan pulled out a chair from the white antique wrought-iron patio set, motioning for Sally to take a seat on one of the orange-flowered seventies-style cushions. Sally smiled as Nathan took the seat next to her and leaned back in it to look at her more intently.

"Nathan, this place is amazing. I can't wrap my head around you living here. I mean...you know...you're the smart-ass sheriff, with a goofy sense of humor that I have grown to like. But this...this is quite another side of you that screams of culture and history and..."

"Sophistication? Thanks, Tater." Nathan was flashing his pearly whites again.

"Well, you know what I mean, don't you?"

"Yeah, I know exactly what to do if I want to impress the women. Just ask them over to my place." He was joking, but halfway meant it. "It's almost as good as owning a puppy."

Sally laughed and sat back, too, to relax and sip her beer. She crossed her legs and Nathan noticed how perfectly smooth they looked – sexy lines leading from her heels to her thighs, hidden beneath her black skirt, teasing his eye, that wanted to explore further. She noticed his interest, and seemed pleased.

"Do you mind?" Nathan held up a cigarette to indicate he wanted to smoke.

"No," Sally replied, shaking her head, in a way that showed he didn't have to ask to smoke on his own patio.

"I'm trying to quit, but I've decided to wait until after this case. My sleuthing skills are better when I'm able to access the nicotine." He lit up and took a slow drag.

"Speaking of that...off the record...what can you tell me?" Sally looked serious for the first time that night.

"Off the record? No tape recorder?"

"Of course not."

"Okay then," Nathan paused and then felt relieved to process his thoughts with someone who was genuinely interested. "I think we finally got the smoking gun, literally. First of all, a neighbor reported seeing a big red truck with a Florida Gator emblem in the back window in Julia Olwen's driveway the night before I discovered the crime scene. Tommy heard that a local salesman had been bragging about selling some vehicles to Clyde Eddy, one of which was a Ford F150. So, I visited the dealership and pretended I was in the market for one, and lo and behold, the same salesman couldn't help himself and spilled the beans and told me Clyde Eddy had purchased a red Ford F150 for his kid. With that information, I paid a visit to Lance Eddy and obtained a search warrant to take a plaster cast of the tires from the red truck that was parked in his garage, which by the way, had a large Florida Gator decal in the back window. We also searched his home and the guys found a nine millimeter Glock 19 hidden in his bedroom closet. By that time, I was talking to Thornton, the D.A. here in Calhoun County. He, of course, didn't want to issue the arrest warrant with only the tire track match and the neighbor's citing. But after some cajoling on my part, he agreed that if I could get one more solid piece of evidence to connect him to the murder, he would agree to the warrant. That's when the information on the gun came back...guess who it was registered to?"

"Who?" Sally was engrossed in the details Nathan was reporting.

"Julia Olwen." Nathan finished up his cigarette and put it out in the ash tray on the table.

"Julia Olwen? So, what do you make of that?"

"Well, I have a theory, but you know me, Sally, I don't like to speculate until I have the puzzle pieces put together more securely."

"Ah, c'mon, Nathan." Her eyes sparkled in the limited glow of the porch light, making it difficult for Nathan to resist her pleading. "I'm intrigued and find this stuff really interesting. Do you think he found the gun at her house and used it on her?"

"Off the record," he emphasized, "I'll tell you this much. I don't think he killed her with the gun. There was too much blood. It looked more like a brutal stabbing – especially with the kind of blood splatter there was. Also, no forced entry, which tells me she may have let him in voluntarily, and she made a few personal journal entries that indicated she was very angry at Eddy after the acquittal and wanted him dead. So, it's a stretch, but I'm wondering if she lured Eddy to her home, intending to talk to him, threaten him or even kill him, but something went wrong. Maybe he wrestled the gun from her and then became enraged and killed her, taking the gun and hiding it – keeping it as one of his trophies."

"Wow. Yeah, he liked his trophies, didn't he? Remember, a huge reason he ended up with an acquittal was because Seeger didn't allow the underwear in his apparent trophy box to be admitted into evidence. Unbelievable."

"Yeah...but they had been laundered," said Nathan, "so no DNA. It's possible Seeger was just being extra cautious, not necessarily dirty." He still had difficulty believing Seeger could stoop so low.

"C'mon Sheriff," Sally countered. "Even if you give Seeger the benefit of the doubt, they weren't your average tighty whities. According to mom, they were his favorite

Atlanta Falcons boxers, and a mom knows her only kid's clothing."

Nathan grimaced at the thought, but then got a whiff of Sally's woodsy perfume, causing him to momentarily lose track of the conversation. "Anyway, it's only a theory – that Julia was intending to kill Eddy," he continued. "I'm still waiting on the techies to tell me what was on her computer hard drive, and I have a few more people to interview, like her therapist and her best friend, who was interviewed briefly at first, but not in depth. I need to know what frame of mind she was in and what she may have been capable of."

"I guess I can relate to why she would want to get rid of him," Sally speculated. "They say she didn't have any family left…that Joey was who she lived for. So, I suppose if you get in that state of mind, you don't care if you end up in jail or dead. But still, it's a pretty bold move to invite your son's killer to your own home. I don't think I'd have the guts, but maybe she was at the end of her rope with all of it."

"Well, I intend to find out," Nathan moved closer to Sally with a different look in his eyes that told her the conversation about Julia Olwen was coming to a close. "So, enough about murder and intrigue. Tell me about yourself."

"What's to tell?" She said while tipping her second bottle of beer to finish it off. "Like you said earlier, I'm a Midwest girl hoping to make it big in the South."

"You know what I mean," Nathan pleaded. "How old are you? Have you ever been married? When's the last time you had a boyfriend? How long did that last? And can I see your latest blood test and credit report?" He laughed, hoping his exaggeration would put her at ease.

"Whoa," exclaimed Sally. "You don't waste any time, do ya? And I'm disappointed you don't already have those answers – I would have guessed you'd do a background check on me, Sheriff, before you ever decided to buy my dinner – which you didn't, by the way," She enjoyed the teasing. "In any event, I will indulge you. I am 32, never married, broke off a three-year relationship last year, and I have no diseases and pretty good credit if you don't count the school loans I'm still paying for."

"Spoken like a truly unbiased reporter," Nathan acknowledged. "And I'm sorry about the dinner, but I got you a story, didn't I?"

"Yes you did, thank you very much. And what about you?"

"Me, let's see, well…I'm forty-four, almost forty-five, divorced from my first and only wife two years ago, and that marriage lasted seven years. No diseases. Impeccable credit."

"The seven-year-itch got ya, huh?" Sally looked tentative, as if she wasn't sure she was allowed to pry.

"Who knows why things don't work out…I love women, but I can't say I understand 'em much," Nathan smiled while twirling the ash tray around on the table. "Billie, my ex-wife, just couldn't find peace in her life and it always ended up being my fault somehow. In the end, she decided her dentist was more her type and that ended that. You know, it just seemed so weird that she had to keep getting all that dental work done, but she never complained about any pain. Of course, I investigated the chump to find out what his story was, and found out his last two wives were former patients. So, he obviously had a thing for wooing pretty women in the dental chair."

"Well, I don't know how she could give up such a fine upstanding husband like you," said Sally.

"Oh, I was no saint." Nathan replied. "I had my own faults and I'm sure I could have improved my husbandry skills." He gave the last words a sarcastic emphasis.

Sally laughed at his misuse of the phrase. "Husbandry? So, you farm much?"

"What? Wha'd I say?" He feigned ignorance while watching her amusement.

"Maybe you meant 'husbanding'?" Sally was laughing hilariously now. "Or 'spousing'?" Nathan could tell she was beginning to feel the two beers she had drunk.

"You journalism types are so smug aren't you?" He began mocking her in a whiny voice. "Oh, Nathan, I think you misused a word."

"Yes, and now I'm cachinnating," She spit out some of her beer as she began to cackle louder.

"You're cacka what?"

"Cachinnating…laughing loudly," she could hardly get out the last two words.

"Come here," Nathan pulled her close to him and kissed her lightly on the lips. Sally instantly stopped laughing and responded. It had been a long time since Nathan had kissed a woman – he and Billie had stopped kissing passionately a long time before the marriage ended – but he hadn't forgotten the intense rhythm and sheer exhilaration of it. After a few moments, Sally reached between his legs to feel for him and pulled away from his lips to say, "Wanna go to the bedroom?" Nathan stopped and looked at her quizzically. He didn't know how to respond at first, but eventually said, "No…that's not what this was about."

Sally pulled her hand back and looked awkwardly at Nathan. "Oh, sorry."

"No, it's okay," Nathan tried to recover without embarrassment. "It's been a long time since I've had a date, but I definitely won't go there with a woman right out of the gate." It was his attempt to let her know again that he was not that kind of guy, but based on her eagerness, she didn't seem to care much about his integrity.

"Hey, that rhymed," teased Sally in an attempt to break the tension. Nathan couldn't tell if she was more disappointed in him or herself.

"Yeah, I guess it did." Nathan sat back in his chair again, trying to discern Sally Tate's motives. They sat for another minute or two, without much conversation.

"Well, I should be going," Sally said abruptly. "Take me back to my car?"

"Oh, that's right…we left it at Montovani's. Will you give me a rain check for dinner?" Nathan asked, knowing he probably wouldn't be taking her out again unless she insisted on collecting on the offer.

"Sure. Thanks for showing me your house. It's wonderful."

"Thanks for a fun evening." They walked out to the driveway and Nathan opened the car door for her, as if nothing strange had happened.

The drive to Montovani's was quiet and formal. When they arrived there, he walked with her to her car, they hugged goodnight, and he waited until she drove out of the parking lot before he left to go home. He flipped on the classic rock station, and Firefall was singing a sappy seventies love song, which reminded Nathan of being in the sixth grade when a girl he liked broke down in tears, as he told her he didn't want to "go out" with her. Back then, going out meant you called each other boyfriend or girlfriend, and you were technically off the market, but you never really went anywhere, which Nathan thought was stupid. Nathan felt restless.

Women haven't changed a bit.

27.

Julia - April, 2012

It was a Saturday and Julia was relieved to have a day to herself, as she was finding it increasingly difficult to live a double life. It was becoming emotionally draining to pretend to her co-workers, friends and even her therapist that she was healing, when in secret, she was working out a diabolical plan to teach Eddy a lesson. She thought about going back to the confessional and telling Father Sheehan what she was doing, but she knew that would require her to ask for forgiveness and agree to turn from her sin. But she was not willing to do that. This had gone too far already and in some strange way, she actually felt the hand of God in her life as she pored over every detail, checking and rechecking her thought process. Trying to figure out what every possibility was that would cause her plan to fail. Eddy was evil. Judge Seeger had turned out to be evil. Eddy's father who apparently bribed the judge was evil. She couldn't see how what she was doing would produce anything but justice. Even though she knew that God had said, "Vengeance is mine," she also felt that she was merely an instrument of His in following through with a plan that would prevent Eddy from hurting another little boy. She felt Joey's strength in her as well. At every turn, another memory of him would propel her into being sure that she was on a right and good path.

After finishing her coffee, she got up from the kitchen table where she had been watching the bluebirds go in and out of the perfectly placed birdhouse at the edge of the backyard. They were preparing the nest for the little spotted eggs that would fulfill their purpose in life. Julia felt satisfied that she was doing the same, only on a much higher order. She decided today would be the day to begin communicating with Eddy, giving him just enough to peak his interest, even though she still had a couple of months before she would actually entice him fully. She picked up the remote and turned on the system, choosing the gaming component and signed in with Wonka1126, typed in her password and paged down to *Slash and Burn*. There were a number of gamers on the system, but she didn't see Buddy666. She would have to figure out when his prime play time was. It was ten in the morning, so maybe he slept late and would not get on until much later. She hoped he was not a night owl, which would force her to be up past her bedtime, but she would just have to deal with that. She thought about entering his identity name to request a game, but that felt too obvious. It had to be his idea, so she would wait. After about an hour of sitting and waiting – flipping through her latest issue of *Southern Living* magazine, the system beeped. She looked up and Buddy666 had messaged her. Julia's heart began pounding hard, as she picked up the keyboard to write back. She looked at the screen.

Buddy666:   *Haven't seen you here in awhile.*

He had remembered her screen name. *What a creep*, she thought.

Wonka1126:   *Yeah, my mom's not too cool with this game. she's at work today*
Buddy666:   *Bad boy*
Wonka1126:   *I guess. Wanna play?*

147

Buddy666:	*sure. you any good?*
Wonka1126:	*nope. Remember? I'm not usually allowed to be here*
Buddy666:	*gotcha. I'll be easy on ya*
Wonka1126:	*no need…i will figure it out*
Buddy666:	*LOL we'll see*

They played a game and Buddy666 annihilated Wonka1126. She decided to give Eddy a stroke of approval.

Wonka1126:	*awesome playing…sucks for me tho*
Buddy666:	*yull get better*
Wonka1126:	*oh I think I hear my mom comin home for lunch. Thx for gamin*
Buddy666:	*ok…be good*

Julia quickly signed off, and feeling suddenly sick to her stomach, she ran to the bathroom and vomited up her morning coffee. Communicating with Eddy was going to be the toughest part of the plan.

After taking something to calm her stomach, Julia sat down at her computer and worked on the computer searches on her to do list. She typed "life in a women's prison" in the Google search line and clicked on the various links, reading with interest. It was good that she did this just after communicating with him. The anger was genuine and real. After twenty minutes or so, she searched for "using a Glock 19 to kill." She reminded herself to go to the driving range to practice and she wrote that down in her notebook. An hour later, Julia felt exhausted and hungry. She wrote a few words in her journal to please Dr. Pierce, but they were meaningless.

The last time she was there, she felt she had successfully convinced Dr. Pierce that she was dealing with her anger appropriately through journaling, but managed to drop a couple of hints to her that she was still having very dark thoughts about Eddy. As usual, Dr. Pierce agreed with her feeling, but challenged her logic.

"I can understand how you would feel that way," she would say, "however, dwelling on the thoughts about hurting Eddy only feeds your anger, don't you think?"

Those kinds of words always struck Julia as true, but so very clueless of Dr. Pierce. She obviously had never lost a child and didn't understand how important it was to hang on to the anger. Otherwise, you had to come to some acceptance of what happened and that seemed too disrespectful to the child who seemed to die in vain. Ending her grief felt like forgetting Joey and the injustice attached to his murder. This was the only way, she resolved to herself again. This was her only chance to get justice for Joey and allow herself to move on from this emotional prison she was doomed to be in otherwise. No matter what happened this summer, she would be able to finally let go and move on. That thought alone gave Julia a great sense of peace. She stopped for a moment, closed her eyes, and said her usual prayer. *Forgive me Father for what I am about to do in the coming months. You know my heart and my motives. If you cannot bless my plans, please bless my son's memory no matter what happens to me. Amen.*

Julia felt an unusual sense of accomplishment and lightheartedness, and decided to treat herself to some retail therapy.

"Hey, you have time for lunch and the mall?" She had called Claire on a whim, hoping she could pull herself from her family duties.

"Uh, sure…" She sounded surprised at Julia's enthusiasm. "Give me about an hour."

"Okay, I'll come get you." She hung up and noticed the sun had come out and revealed a bright blue sky. *Everything's gonna be okay.*

28.

June 24, 2012

Being in a cell again brought back bad memories for Eddy, although this one was a little different from the one in Marlowe County. It was smaller with a little better clientele. He was sure this stay would be shorter than the last, though. He spent more than a year in the one in Marlowe County and did not intend to stay in this one long. He was getting restless and wondered what was taking Wayne Beaudreau so long to get to the jail. He had been told that the sheriff was ready to question him, which was not going to happen without his attorney present. His cell mate was a forty-something loser who had gotten into a Saturday night fight at a local bar and apparently broke a man's nose for eyeing his girl. Eddy had no sympathy for the types who couldn't hold their liquor and did stupid, violent things as a result. It reminded him too much of his father's weaknesses. Eddy sat for a moment and wondered what was happening with his mother, who had been crying as he had been led into the police car the night before. He hoped there was enough going on with his father's crash investigation that she would not get the idea to come and visit him. He was in no mood to have to deal with her whining.

"Your attorney's here," said the deputy who opened the cell door.

Relieved to hear it, Eddy quickly got up, succumbed to the hand cuffs, and walked out with the deputy. He hoped he would not have to return to the cell after the sheriff realized he had no case. Eddy felt nervous knowing he did not yet have access to his father's money if he needed to make bail, and that his mother would not know what to do if asked. And he certainly couldn't count on his Uncle Charles to help, since he was the one who consistently told his father to stop rescuing Lance from his troubles. But Eddy always knew how to work his father's need for a stellar image. He would make promises that he never intended to keep, like finishing college or learning the commercial real estate business. That nearly caused his father to have orgasmic reactions, but then Lance would never follow through, garnering his mother's support for how horribly he had been treated by his father as a child. The game was so simple and easy that Lance Eddy had stopped needing to think about it in recent years. He could just set it in motion and let the chess pieces play themselves. It assisted him in getting what he wanted without much effort and he could feel particularly cunning in the process. But now that the game had changed, he was pretty sure so had the rules.

Eddy spotted Wayne Beaudreau outside of the interview room and shook his hand. They talked for a few minutes, with Wayne reminding him to hesitate before answering any questions, so that he could interrupt if needed. Eddy nodded in agreement and they walked into the room, greeting the sheriff, who was sitting at the oblong table.

"Nathan Davis," the sheriff said while extending a hand to Beaudreau.

"My pleasure." Beaudreau returned Nathan's firm grip.

"Mr. Beaudreau, I have reason to believe that your client has been involved in the disappearance of one of our citizens."

"Okay, what do you have on him?"

"I'd like to ask a few questions of your client." The sheriff put his elbows on the table and rubbed his hands together.

"Well, my client has convinced me of his innocence, so ask away," Beaudreau said with confidence.

Nathan turned to Eddy. "Do you know who Julia Olwen is?"

"Yeah, that's the bitch who falsely accused me of killing her kid," Eddie bit back.

Beaudreau interrupted to remind Eddy to be respectful in his responses.

"How well do you know her?"

"I don't know her at all."

"Have you ever been to her home?"

"No." Eddy was staring ahead blankly.

"Have you ever been to 1126 China Grove Road?"

Eddy looked at his attorney quizzically, which caused Beaudreau some alarm.

"Don't answer that question," said Beaudreau after a short pause. "Where's this going, Sheriff?"

"Maybe your client needs to explain why his truck was at that address on the sixteenth of June," said the sheriff.

"What evidence do you have of that?" asked Beaudreau.

"A witness saw a red F150 in the driveway that evening. A truck sporting a large Florida Gator emblem in the back window – like your client's."

"Gators? Are you crazy?" Beaudreau looked more annoyed by Eddy's disloyalty to his father's Bulldogs than the fact that he might be lying about his involvement in the murder.

"Those trucks are a dime a dozen. It could have been anybody," said Eddy. He got a bit of satisfaction at this interchange. Eddy had no real connection to the University of Florida other than they were major rivals of the Georgia

Bulldogs, his father's alma mater and pride and joy. Eddy found it pleasurable to display his loyalty to the rival team just to get under his father's skin. As far as Eddy was concerned, the Georgia Bulldog team was like a favored sibling – and he had to rebel.

"Except that the tire tracks at the house matched those on your truck, Mr. Eddy, and on top of that, a search of your house revealed that you were in possession of a gun registered to Julia Olwen. Would you like to explain that?"

"This is bullshit!" exclaimed Eddy, after pushing himself away from the table and standing up. "They didn't get their conviction before, so now they're gonna frame me for this one. I don't know who is killing these Olwen people, but it's not me!"

"Shut up and sit down, Lance," chided Beaudreau. "I think we're done here, Sheriff."

"Whadya mean we're done here? I didn't do anything wrong!" Lance was beside himself.

The sheriff got up and left the room, and Beaudreau and Eddy followed, while Beaudreau insisted that Eddy keep quiet while under surveillance. Once they were in a private room, Beaudreau lit into Eddy.

"What the hell?" Beaudreau's ears were red. "It's not bad enough that I've just gotten the news about your daddy, but then this? How do you get yourself into these messes boy?"

Eddy hated being called that. He felt his blood pressure rise. "Screw all of you!" Eddy got up and banged on the door for the deputy to let him out. Beaudreau sat with his head in his hands. Eddy was cuffed and escorted back to his cell as he heard Beaudrea yell out, "I'll see if I can speed up the arraignment to this afternoon."

Eddy didn't care. It was obvious he was in for another jail stint and he felt like spitting on the guy in his cell who was still recovering from his booze binge the night before. *Screw the whole world.* He sat on his cot with his back up against the wall and his wrists resting on his bent knees. Too bad he hadn't gone on a killing spree like they thought he was capable of. He could think of a few other people who needed to be gone besides his pathetic father.

29.

June 24, 2012

When Nathan had returned to the department office, he was stepping lightly and Tommy noticed it.

"So, how'd the interview go?" Tommy inquired with anticipation.

"That dude is guiltier than sin," said Nathan. "He got all indignant when I announced we had the gun and he said we were framing him, but even his attorney wasn't buying it. It was rich. We'll get some more on him and I predict we'll get a confession eventually."

"Sweet." Tommy was beaming with pride. "So, isn't it bizarre about the old man and the plane crash?"

"Yeah, weird timing. If I didn't know better, I would suspect Lance Eddy of having his hand in that, too, but first things first. Did the techies report on the computer hard drive yet?"

"Don't think so, but I'm expecting something tomorrow from them. It's Sunday, Sheriff."

He had forgotten. In this line of work, every day blended into the next, especially when there was a major case being investigated. "Yeah, I'm glad. That means I won't have to answer Dot's nosey questions about my date last night."

"Date? You're holding out on *me*? How come I didn't know about this date?" Tommy seemed more excited to hear about that piece of news than he did earlier when inquiring about Eddy.

"Not a biggy. And it was a dud, but probably a good learning experience. So, nothin' to tell, my man."

"Shoot," Tommy replied. "Well, you know it's a numbers game. Maybe you should try one of those online sites."

"Yeah right. If I can't get a decent date as sheriff of the county, I'm in a pretty sorry position, wouldn't ya say? I'm not gonna settle, Pork. I had to fight this one off from attacking my irresistible body last night, but I'm just not gonna give it up that easily." Nathan feigned a feminine voice, sounding like he was joking, but chuckled to himself knowing he was telling the God's honest truth.

"Uh huh," Tommy answered while rolling his eyes. "It's been so long for you, I'm afraid you'll be humping anything that breathes."

"Hey, have you forgotten who you're talking to young man?" Nathan pulled the rank card on him, as he like to do when he wanted to end the bantering. He wondered why it was so difficult for guys to admit to one another that they actually wanted intimacy more than sex as they got older.

"So, let's get focused here," Nathan said while getting up from his chair and walking over to the large white board behind his desk. He picked up a black dry-erase marker. He had started a timeline of the Olwen crime, listing the day Julia apparently disappeared, followed by the day of his discovery, and the three pieces of solid evidence they had so far. He and Tommy went over the details. The truck witness, the tire tracks, and the gun. In addition, he had a few journal entries that pointed toward Julia Olwen's anger and disgust with Eddy after the acquittal. So far, she had motive and means to attempt murder, but he hadn't yet figured out the opportunity piece. How was it that she was able to access Eddy and get him to her home? He was hoping the computer analysis would lead him to that. Her cell phone was clean – no phone calls to anyone that would indicate she was harassing or stalking him in any way. Another piece of the puzzle that was missing was Eddy's agreement to go to her home and his motive to turn around and want to kill her – especially after he had just escaped conviction of her son's murder. Did this guy want to be labeled a bad guy and, stranger yet, want to do time for it? Maybe he enjoyed the publicity, despite the fact that his family worked so hard to protect their image.

"Weird, isn't it?" asked Tommy. "Ya think he hates his family so much that he wanted to show them he was a bad ass after all?"

"It's possible, but I met the guy and he seems completely content in his little luxury home that daddy bought, with his big old truck. Perverts like him enjoy getting their jollies under the radar. Ya can't molest little boys in prison."

Nathan recalled the day he met Eddy at his front door and he remembered that Eddy genuinely didn't react to Nathan's mention of Julia Olwen's name. Maybe when he went to 1126 China Grove Road, he had no idea it was her residence. He was processing this with Tommy, who clearly loved watching Nathan's mind work around a case.

"So, are you thinking she was impersonating someone else to lure him there?" Tommy asked.

"That's a good possibility, Pork." Nathan agreed. "How would she go about doing that?" He paused and sat back down at his desk to look at some papers. "I'm thinking she knew what a pervert he was and the best way to lure him there was with a little boy's charm."

"That's right!" Tommy sat up in his chair with his elbows on his knees. He loved it when Nathan was in the mood to brainstorm. "But how?"

"The internet is an amazing anonymous tool, wouldn't you say?"

"So, you're thinking she found him somehow on the internet and seduced him as a young kid?"

"Yep, that's my best guess. Just like on that *To Catch a Predator* show," Nathan laughed.

Tommy started imitating Chris Hansen's voice. "Have a seat, young man. So, what were you coming here for today?"

"Yeah, and the perv shows up with a McDonald's happy meal for the girl," Nathan snorted in disgust. "And Eddy's just the type, too. I bet he was sweating bullets when he showed up and there was no Chris Hansen…just a middle-aged ticked-off mom with a Glock pointed at him. Geez, I would have loved to be there to see the look on his face."

"You think she shot and missed? Or maybe he got the gun before she had a chance to fire?" Tommy was back in his own serious voice. "Which begs another question. Why wasn't she more careful with the evidence? She registered a gun in her name that she apparently intended to use on Eddy. She wrote stuff in her journal that showed she hated him. Do you think she knew she would be caught?"

"Probably," said Nathan. "We've seen it before. Like that father who was so angry about the guy who raped his daughter, that he shot the perp right before he walked into the court room."

"Yeah, or like Jack Ruby…Oswald's killer. He obviously knew he would go to jail, but I guess he thought he'd rather live life as a hero in prison."

Nathan considered it, but couldn't imagine a woman like Julia feeling that depressed or desperate. "Well, I don't know what Julia Olwen was thinking, other than she could live with herself in prison knowing she got rid of Eddy, rather than live on the outside knowing he was free."

"That's a little warped, but I get it."

"Yeah, me, too. None of us really know what we'd do if it were us."

"Yeah, if anyone did that to my little girl, I'd hunt 'em down myself." Tommy felt a twinge of nausea at the thought. Nathan noticed he was uncomfortable so he refocused back to the white board.

"There's a lot that's just speculation now, but I wanna do another sweep of the house to see if there are any shell casings to be found. It didn't look like he took any time to clean up the scene, so there may be some things that were missed the first time CSI gathered evidence. Also, it looked like he drug the body out of the house in a blanket or bag of some sort, but the trail ends at the back kitchen door, which means he must have put her in the truck to get rid of her. Have the forensics come back yet on the truck?"

"Yeah and there's nothing. There were no finger prints or DNA to indicate she was in there. I'm thinking he must have wrapped her up in plastic when he got her outside because there are no carpet or blanket fibers or anything that would indicate he transported a body in anything other than a non-porous material."

"There's nothing but wooded land behind her house. Let's get a team out there to look for freshly disturbed dirt. It's possible he buried her right on the property or nearby if he didn't transport her in the truck. Plus, you'd think that nosey neighbor next door would have seen him load a body in the truck. She just saw him leave."

"Yeah, he must have buried her somewhere around there." Tommy was squeezing his bottom lip together with his thumb and index finger – a habit that Nathan noticed was common when Tommy was deep in thought. Nathan thought it made him look like a fish.

"Hmmm…" Nathan shuffled through the file and pulled out the list of things they took from his house when they did the search. "When I get out there, I'll look at the line of visibility from the neighbor's back door to Julia Olwen's. Maybe he could have buried her behind the house without anyone seeing him."

"But the bag of tape and garbage bags was still in his truck. Did he go there thinking he was going to murder a kid, but then got surprised? Why didn't he use the stuff in his truck anyway?" "Don't know. I guess I need to look around in the little storage building behind the house to see if we can figure out what he might have done between the time he killed her and when he may have been searching for a way to dispose of her. If our theory is right, he didn't expect to go there and kill anyone, unless, like you said, he thought he might be killing a little kid." Nathan cringed at the thought. "And he knew he would be pegged for buying that stuff the day before, so he decided not to use it. My guess is, his original plans got foiled – big time."

"Never thought of that," said Tommy pensively, trying to track what Nathan was saying. "Maybe he got there and realized he had forgotten to bring the stuff with him."

"Unlikely. Perverted killers don't forget those kinds of details. Well, anyway, we've got our work cut out for us, Pork." Nathan got up from his desk and put on his sport coat. "I'm going out there right now to snoop around a little. You got everything under control here?"

"Yep. Let me know if you need anything." Tommy walked out with Nathan.

When Nathan got down the road a few miles, he realized he had forgotten his reading glasses, which meant he would have to stop at the drug store to buy his forty-second pair. Maybe he could have tolerated Dot's commentary about his dating life after all. Nathan smiled at the thought of being interrogated by her on Monday.

30.

Julia - April, 2012

Eddy and Joey were going out the back door on Del Mar Street, and as he turned around to shut the door behind him, he cracked a sinister smile and entered the moonlit night with her son. Then she cried out, No! But she was unable to move or scream. Or save him…

Julia shot straight up in her bed, in the dark, sweating profusely and crying uncontrollably. The nightmare was recurring more often these days and each time, Julia felt the same sense of helplessness. She wondered if she would live with this the rest of her life, or if the nightmares might go away after she carried out her plan. The worst part was waking up alone and having to sit with the terror without having any way to immediately comfort herself. It was the only time she wished she had a man in her life – someone to hear her pain in the middle of the night and soothe her with affirming words and hold her in a safe embrace. She remembered being a little girl and having her father do something similar when she would wake up afraid. Her mother was a heavy sleeper, but her father always heard her and came to comfort her with his strong whispering voice. Sometimes he would turn on the nightstand light and prove to her that there were no monsters in the room, looking under her bed and in her closet, assuring her that all was clear. Then he would rub her back until she fell asleep again. Surely, she thought, there is a man out there who was still willing to do that for a middle-aged woman. But that was an unrealistic desire given her present state of mind and plans. She wasn't really sure about why she had not had any real meaningful relationships with men. Most of it had to do with her need to protect her son from further hurt, not wanting him to get close to a man who would abandon him like his father did. Besides, when had there been time? She had to work so many crazy hours in order to make sure Joey had what he needed. When had she had time to think about romance? She regretted not having at least tried to connect with a man. Maybe that would have made a difference in Joey's life. *Maybe...maybe.* Julia's life was full of what ifs and maybes. When she started doing that to herself, she had to stop in mid-thought and talk herself through the temptation to succumb to what Dr. Pierce called the bargaining part of her grief process. If she gave into it, it tended to set her back and caused her to beat up on herself one more time for not having done something to avoid the circumstances that resulted in Joey's death. It was a no-win for her and she knew it, but when something feels senseless, it is human nature to try to make some sense of it – even if it means putting oneself into the position of being responsible, no matter how irrational that actually is. Julia understood the need, but agreed with Dr. Pierce that feeding it was only keeping her stuck, rather than helping her move through her grief.

Julia lay in the dark, having cooled down somewhat and looked at the clock. It was 4:05 a.m. She had a couple more hours of sleep left before needing to get up for her seven o'clock shift. But her mind wandered to some of her patients at the hospital who were on the edge of death in critical care. One was a woman who had contracted a flesh eating bacteria. Her right hand had been amputated and the doctors were considering lopping off the other. As strong as Julia was, she wasn't sure she would want to save her body if it meant not having any limbs left. She sometimes felt guilty because she knew she would be a coward if she was in the place of most of those in the ICU at her hospital. They had choices about the level of care they wanted and needed. She often thought that if she got close to death, she would probably choose to die, if for no other reason, than to be closer to Joey. To finally be where he was. She was reminded again of what Pastor Tucker had told her on one of his visits in the agonizing days after Joey's murder – that there is no time in heaven, so "you are already there with him, Ms. Olwen," he had said with a smile and a sweet, calm voice. Even though she was Catholic and was raised to be skeptical about anything a preacher from a small neighborhood Bible church might declare, those words still brought her immense comfort.

After dwelling for some time about what she had to face at work that day, Julia realized sleep was not going to come and she forced herself to get out of bed and make the coffee. She glanced out of the kitchen window over the sink that looked out onto the side yard and across to her closest neighbor's house. She noticed that Mrs. Timko's lights were all on throughout the house, which caused her some concern since she typically went to bed by ten o'clock and turned off all of the lights except the front porch. And the lights were rarely on when Julia got up at five thirty in the morning. It was now four forty-five and she found the lit up house eerily unusual. She decided she would go there to check on her before leaving for work.

Julia took her coffee, laced with a new chocolate creamer she had recently discovered at the grocery store. It wasn't new. It had been on the shelves for years now, she suspected, but why was she just now noticing? She sat down at her desk to log on to her computer. More and more, she was appreciating simple pleasures that she had always been too busy to notice before, or too wrapped up in her grief lately to care. As the time got closer for her plan to come to fruition, she found herself taking in the beauty of everyday life, like the periwinkle blue eggs that appeared in her backyard birdhouses. Like the blooming wisteria vine travelling up her chimney, bursting with rich lavender petals. Like the constant rippling of the brook that wrapped around her house – a sound so steady and predictable, that it calmed her most anxious thoughts. Like the yellow Labrador Retriever puppy down the street from the church that made her smile every time she saw him romping in the yard. Joey had wanted a puppy, but now she understood why. Kids had a much better idea of how to notice the good stuff. Like the dark chocolate flavored coffee creamer that she would have never bought before, thinking it was too indulgent, too fattening, or too different. Everything around Julia Olwen seemed to remind her of how precious and miraculous life was – a grave paradox to what was now taking root in her soul.

As the time got closer for her to get ready for work, she logged into her bank account to take care of some business, like transferring some money to Celeste's account in California. She knew that in a couple of months, she would not have access to her accounts anymore, and no matter how it all played out, she wanted the best possible outcome for Celeste. It was Julia's way – to always be thinking of the minutia, which could be a blessing and a curse. A blessing because it minimized the risk. A curse because she could easily get bogged down in the details and get frustrated with the larger, more important, picture. She made a note to call her insurance agent and stock brokerage firm to make Celeste the beneficiary of her life policy and her retirement funds. There were so many details she needed to take care of and she didn't want to be stressed at the last minute, trying to get it all done. Before long, it was six o'clock, time for her to shower and go to work.

She looked out of the kitchen window again to find that Mrs. Timko's lights were now off. Julia Olwen smiled, feeling relieved that her adopted mother had probably fallen asleep in front of the television and was just now going off to bed. She had a pang of sadness, knowing that would be her mundane life, too, if she wasn't on this mission that felt ordained by something other than herself. The everyday details of life now were unnerving to her, given that the plan was always looming in her brain. By the time the hot water was cascading over her body, she had stopped thinking about it and resolved to go through the painstakingly necessary motions she had to enact while waiting for the perfect plan to unfold. It had taken an unimaginable amount of strength and mental anguish to figure out what she needed do, but even more to have the patience to wait for the right time to do it.

31.

June 24, 2012

China Grove Road runs parallel to Interstate 75, but one would not know it as it is lined with Georgia pines on both sides and the homes along it are few and far between, nestled among the trees, with long driveways and large front yards. Regal is just east of both the freeway and Main Street, where Nathan lived, which runs perpendicular to China Grove Road. As Nathan drove down the road which Eddy must have driven on his way to Julia's house just a week ago, he couldn't help wondering what Eddy was expecting to find and do in a home like one of these. He didn't think Eddy would have been naïve in entering a home so isolated without a notion of what he would do if his plan was diverted. In his experience, Nathan knew that criminals like Eddy always thought three steps ahead, especially when he came so close before to blowing his freedom and a chance at all his daddy's money. But he also knew that psychopathic child molesters were inclined to feel smarter than the law, which is why so many take years to catch, and in the end, they often want to be caught to put them out of their sadistic misery or to finally be lauded for their criminal prowess. He hoped Eddy was one of those – one who would make it easy to catch this time because he was tired of his own pathetic sickness and was ready to be back in the spotlight.

Nathan was anxious to get the reports from the techies about both Julia's and Eddy's computers. He was fairly sure they had been communicating unbeknownst to Eddy. In all that Nathan had learned recently about Julia Olwen, he found himself having a strange kind of attraction to her. He knew how much courage it must have taken to plan and execute the ruse on Eddy, knowing full well that he molested, tortured and murdered her only child. Nathan shuttered at the thought. He did not have children, so he was sure it was much worse than he could imagine. All he had was a niece and two nephews, whom he loved and adored. If anyone tried to hurt them, he could only imagine what he would feel and do. The more Nathan had learned about Eddy and his family, the more he wished Julia Olwen would have succeeded in getting Lance Eddy off the streets and where he belonged – in Hell. That only made Nathan more determined to finish the job she started. This time, in accordance with the law.

Nathan turned into the driveway behind the mailbox that was labeled "1126." As he drove down the long gravel drive, he thought how much different it felt during the day than when he first visited on the night he found the crime scene. In front of the detached garage, he pulled over into a dirt area where Eddy had apparently parked and left his tire tracks. He wondered why Eddy hadn't simply parked in front of the garage. Why did he park there to the side? When he got out, he saw the reason. A large, and rather wide, magnolia tree in the side yard effectively hid the car from view if anyone next door had cared to spy. Eddy didn't know it, but in his attempt to stay hidden, his tire tracks revealed his guilt. Even more, Nathan was convinced that Eddy had not come to murder anyone or else he would not have been so careless.

Julia Olwen's front lawn was growing long and as Nathan walked to the back of the home, there were weeds that seemed to be thriving in the hot humid weather of mid-June. He peeked into the window of the storage building, hoping to see something that might indicate Eddy would have accessed materials to remove Julia from the scene. The door to the building was not locked, so he went inside to explore. There were a few shovels, a large leaf rake, and a few other yard tools hanging neatly on a rack, but nothing looked out of place. Without knowing what Julia Olwen possessed before, he would have no way of knowing if anything was missing, and since she lived alone, no one else would know either. But Nathan felt he had a sixth sense about being able to walk into a place and discern if a suspected criminal had been there, simply by looking at the condition of the surroundings and finding small clues that even the best of them would leave behind. He no sooner was thinking about that when he looked down and saw a cigarette butt lying under an old wooden table. Nathan put a latex glove on and picked it up, carefully placing it in a paper evidence bag after checking out the brand. *Marlboro.* He didn't know if Julia smoked, but doubted it. Of course, it could have come from anyone. The contents of the shed indicated to Nathan that Julia was a woman who was organized and handy. She probably would have a field day with his house on Main Street that was in desperate need of a woman's touch since his mother had passed.

There was a potting table and shelving in the middle of the shed, well-equipped with gardening tools, plant markers, and pots of all shapes and sizes. Along the walls were watering cans, soil mixes, and a variety of supplies that Nathan was not very familiar with, but that looked useful in managing a property the size of Julia's. It was obvious to Nathan that this was a much-loved hobby. Nathan thought again of his own place and how the one flowering plant that survived around his property, a hydrangea with giant soft blue blooms, consistently looked weepy and near death every day until the next afternoon pop-up shower would revive it. Nathan knew he had nothing to do with its survival and he felt sure if Julia Olwen had seen his place, she would have been elated to help him liven it up or thoroughly appalled at his neglect. Nathan laughed at himself for having such thoughts. It must be his recent return to the world of women.

A roll of thick-gauge rope was hanging haphazardly from the wall that Nathan thought could have been possibly used to tie a body in plastic tarp. He did not see a tarp anywhere, but it would make sense that Julia would have one in her shed, especially if she used the oversized rake to gather dead leaves. Nathan took the rope and put it in the evidence bag. It appeared to have been undone, but may have been replaced on the wall without having been rolled up properly. This struck him as out of sync with the organization of the rest of Julia Olwen's possessions and her neat and orderly style. If the body were ever found, the rope could possibly be matched to rope used to wrap and transport it.

After finishing his examination of the outdoor shed, Nathan decided to go inside to look for missed shell casings or holes in furniture or drywall that might indicate that the gun had been discharged. The crime scene unit said they had not found anything, but after finding the gun in Eddy's house, Nathan felt sure there was more to it than Eddy simply confiscating a gun from Julia Olwen's home. As Nathan surveyed the kitchen, he was looking at the crime scene photos to orient himself, trying to replay what might have taken place between Eddy and Julia that evening. He figured Eddy came through the front door and encountered Julia in the kitchen. If that was so, she may have had a few words to say to him, but likely was holding the gun when he saw her. Nathan looked at the walls, floors and furniture surrounding the entry into the kitchen from the front hall. Nothing. He glanced back down at the photos again and had another thought. If she had been impersonating a child, she may have asked him to come through the back kitchen door, which would be unlocked and more private. That would also explain why he parked to the side of the garage, so he could walk behind the garage and go unnoticed around to the back of the house. To the right of the door from the kitchen that led out to the back, there was a breakfast area, with a bay window and window seat that ran the length of the window and had a striped cushion covering it. The photos reminded him that the chair nearest to the door had been on its side, possibly indicating that one of them had been standing near it. Nathan moved the dinette table and chairs out of the way, got down on his knees and there it was. A bullet hole just below the edge that would have been easy to miss had Nathan not looked below the cushion. The window seat was a storage compartment, so Nathan removed the cushion and lifted up the hinged lid to see that the bullet had gone through the front façade, through the storage area and into the wall behind it. *Wow. She was either a crappy shot or Eddy was standing at the table and she had aimed for his...ouch.* Startled, he possibly knocked over the chair. She likely missed her first target area, and the bullet grazed just past Eddy's leg and into the top of the window seat. Nathan became energized. If there was a bullet shot, there had to be a casing. Nathan knew that to prove that Eddy had killed Julia Olwen, the casing would be more valuable than the bullet, since the gun had been found in his possession. He figured that Julia must have been standing near the kitchen window next to the sink when she took the first shot, which meant the casing probably flew up to Julia's right. He pulled over a chair from the table and stood on it to look on top of the cabinets above the sink and window. Nothing was visible at first glance. He placed his right shoe on the sink to brace himself so he could get a wider look, but lost his footing and grabbed onto the window curtains to rebalance, when he heard a ting-ting-ting in the stainless steel sink. He looked down and to his amazement, there was a shiny shell casing rolling around in the sink. *Sweet!* Nathan picked it up and placed it in the paper bag with the cigarette butt. He looked around a little while longer, but came up empty, still wondering what happened after Julia had taken the first shot. *Had Eddy lunged toward her after almost getting his pecker blown off?* Nathan wondered if there had been a struggle and Eddy had wrestled the gun from her to use it against her. There was also the possibility that the gun had been dropped to the floor and he killed her with something else – a knife, a meat tenderizer, a pair of scissors. There was any number of things in a kitchen that could be used as a fatal tool. Or maybe Eddy had a knife in his pocket. Regardless, Nathan knew he had nailed down the means and the opportunity, but the more difficult task in order to convince Thornton to go for first degree, was to prove the motive. This scenario would make sense to a jury, Nathan thought, especially given what he had learned from Julia's journal. He hoped to get a report from the techies on Monday to solidify his theory. Nathan finished looking around, and as he turned to walk out of the back kitchen door, an elderly woman appeared on the stoop,

"May I help you?" Nathan asked.

"Yes…well, I don't know…maybe." Her voice was shaky and frail.

"Do you live around here?"

"Uh, yes…I'm the neighbor across the way," Mrs. Timko announced, while pointing toward her home.

"Oh, yes, Mrs. Timko. Well, I was just heading out. Is there something I can do for you?" Nathan walked out onto the stoop with her.

Mrs. Timko looked over at his car. "Are you the police?"

"I'm sorry. I should have introduced myself. I am Sheriff Nathan Davis," he said while reaching in his coat pocket to get his badge. After showing it to her, she seemed to relax a little.

"Oh, it's nice to meet you, Sheriff. I voted for you." Mrs. Timko was smiling proudly.

"Why, thank you ma'am," Nathan said with appreciation.

"I have been reading the papers and hearing the television reports about what happened to Julia and I am just sick about it. Just sick about it," she shook her head in despair. "She was like my own daughter. You know, I never had children and she had lost her mama, so we just bonded, I guess." Mrs. Timko's brow furled as she thought of Julia.

"I'm truly sorry for your loss, Mrs. Timko."

"Call me Polly…please." She was looking at him with admiration.

"Okay, Polly. Since you are here, do you mind answering some questions?"

"Well, they already interviewed me…the day they discovered what had happened…but I told them I didn't have anything important to tell them other than I loved her like my own daughter…and then I remembered that I saw that red truck. Did anything ever come of that, Sheriff?" Polly Timko's southern drawl grew wider as she looked pleadingly at Nathan.

"As a matter of fact, that was very, very helpful. Thank you so much for being brave enough to mention it." He put his hand on her bony shoulder.

"Well, that's good," she said sadly and peered blankly into space. "But it won't bring her back, will it?"

Nathan could feel her loss, and for a split second he recalled a rare memory of his mother's drawn face when his sister had passed. A lump formed in his throat. "It surely won't, ma'am. It surely won't."

"Ya know, if it wasn't for her, I'd probably be dead by now," she declared dramatically as she snapped out of her daze.

"How's that?" Nathan knew to take the bait.

"I've got the sugar…diabetes," she corrected herself, "and Julia was such a help in getting me the right insulin. Those medical supply companies are so confusing sometimes. She was a nurse, ya know, so she knew all about what I needed. Bless her heart, she kept calling them until they got it right and then she had the syringes sent to me on a regular basis, just when I was running out, so I didn't have to call them and order anymore. Now, I just get the bill and pay it and they keep coming. I'm afraid if it wasn't for her, they would have found me dead in my kitchen after a shock." She looked up at Nathan to see if he was following her story.

"I'm glad to hear you are doing well now. You know, it seems that Ms. Olwen was the kind of person who had a place for everything and everything in its place."

"Oh, yes. She liked everything to be very neat and tidy."

"Have you ever been in her gardening shed?"

"I can't remember that I have," Mrs. Timko said while trying to access her memory. "Why do you ask?"

175

"Do you mind walking in there with me?" Nathan walked down the two stair steps and extended his hand to help Mrs. Timko to the grass below the steps. She was wearing a pink and white flowery house coat and light brown orthopedic shoes. Her hair was flattened in the back, but her white curls were full around her face.

"I suppose." Mrs. Timko sounded tentative.

He opened the door to the shed. "Do you ever remember being in here?"

"No, Sheriff, I don't think so."

"I am curious about what Julia may have used to do her lawn clean up in the fall. Did she use a plastic tarp or a leaf blower or anything like that to remove the leaves and debris from her yard?"

She looked confused, wondering why the sheriff cared about Julia's lawn care habits. "Well," Mrs. Timko was still struggling with her memory, a finger to her chin. "I think I do remember her using a wheelbarrow…and a big piece of plastic. Yes, now I remember. I always felt it was so much work for one person to do…you know…" Her voice trailed off. Then she had a flash of memory. "Last fall, when she was cleaning up, I took a glass of my fresh lemonade over to her, and she was raking the leaves onto a big piece of blue plastic. I remember now." Mrs. Timko looked proud of herself. "But that's about as close as I got to her shed. I'm sorry, Sheriff. I wish I could be of more help." Her drawl was wide and faltering again.

"No, you have been a great help, Mrs. Timko," Nathan said while leading her out of the shed. "I need to lock up and get on my way. Is there anything else I can do for you Mrs.…Polly?" He corrected himself.

"I guess not. I was just making sure I knew who was snooping around here, is all." Nathan could tell she probably wanted to find out what he knew about the murder, but she seemed too intimidated by his position to ask any more questions. And he knew that southern ladies were adept at demurely hiding their noses for gossip while hoping to engage a tale with compliments and sympathy.

"Okay then. If you think of anything you would like to tell me, please give me a call, alright?" Nathan handed her his business card.

"I sure will, Sheriff. And thank you for doing such a wonderful job in our county. I surely appreciate it." She turned to walk across the lawn to her small, slightly run-down cottage home.

"Well, thank you, Mrs. Timko for your support. As long as we have citizens like you, I will do my job proudly," Nathan said with a smile and turned to walk back to his car. He made a mental note, and later a written one, about the syringes. Although it probably had no significance, anything to do with a weapon or a drug always seemed noteworthy to a cop. More and more, Nathan was feeling like Julia was not the type who could take a life because she was so busy saving them. Maybe she froze and couldn't kill Eddy like she thought she could and he got the best of her. In time, he thought. The clues will tell the whole story. It just takes time.

32.

June 25, 2012

The cell was a six by eight rectangle with cinder block walls, painted glossy grey like the floors. It was clad with a steel door that had a glass peep window for the guards to keep an eye on the ones inside, and there was a screened cutout for conversing and a slit below to pass through the food trays. It had been just twenty-four hours since Eddy's arrest and he had already had two different cell mates. The first one had been in a drunken bar fight and needed to dry out. He left in the morning. The current one had beat up his wife and kept moaning about how she was not going to let him see his kids after he got out. Eddy laughed to himself about their stupidity. When they tried to ask him what his crime was, he just stayed silent and stared ahead, pretending to act subdued by drugs so they would leave him alone. It worked. What they didn't know was that inside he was seething. The more he thought about that bitch Julia Olwen and the evidence that they were using against him, the more he felt his anger grow and get the best of him.

Eddy heard a click on the door. Lunch was being delivered. "Chow!" the voice yelled. Eddy got up to retrieve the tray and he looked through the cut out window. He noticed that the trustee, or the "house man" as the guards referred to him, was a boy, not a man, looking to be seventeen or eighteen – or younger, but he knew they didn't let juveniles in this place. He liked the look of his squared jaw and youthful, tanned skin. He had a snake tattoo on his right forearm. For a minute Eddy felt aroused at the thought of him, but then the trustee walked away, leaving Eddy with the food tray. He was instantly reminded of his confinement and wondered how long it would be again before he could get into one of those young, boyish-looking men. *Damn it. I should have been more careful.* Eddy looked down at the tray and was disgusted by the two pieces of dry white bread with a piece of bologna inside, a small carton of milk, and a red waxy apple. Although it was probably healthier than his usual daily fare of a Big Mac and fries for lunch and roller food from QuikTrip for dinner, it unpleasantly reminded him of the time he spent in the Marlowe County jail during the months leading up to the kid's murder trial. He felt his face flush and the tops of his ears become hot.

He sat down on his cot and took a bite of the dry sandwich, as he thought about what mistakes he might have made that could give them something solid to pin on him. The jail smelled so strongly of disinfectant that Eddy could taste it as if it was a condiment on his bologna sandwich. He was constantly seeing the runarounds, the trustees, mopping the floors as if that was going to convince anyone they were worthy of freedom. *I don't belong in this place.* As he slowly chewed his bologna and Lysol sandwich, he went over in his head the twenty, maybe thirty, young men he had met online who had provided their IDs to him before hooking up. He had kept them all, knowing that if he were ever questioned, he could prove that he was not the one who broke the law. He went over and over in his mind the night he ended up at the house of that boy – Wonka1126 – on China Grove Road. The boy who seemed like he would be the perfect victim for Eddy to meet and befriend for his ultimate pleasure. He had not intended on hurting him that day. He thought they could meet and be friends. He would act like a kid and get his trust. He would scope out the situation and see what the possibilities were. He would not touch the child that day. He would simply play some games until it was time for his mother to come home. Eddy felt the sweat pouring out of him, his jail clothes becoming damp. His heart rate became fast and hard. He began to think about what the sheriff said to him. There were tracks that matched his truck tires. Okay. The gun? He started to feel sick to his stomach, taking a swig of milk to wash down the dry bread. He stood up, throwing the unfinished sandwich back onto the tray, and stepped over to the door and began to bang on it. A guard peeked through the window with an annoyed expression.

"I wanna speak to the sheriff!" Eddy screamed. The guard said, "Take it easy."

"I want an interview with the sheriff," Eddy said more calmly. "Tell him I have some things I need to say."

"I'll let him know." And the guard stepped away. Eddy saw him talk into his microphone, fastened to his epaulette, presumably sending his message to someone who would contact the sheriff.

Eddy sat back down on the cot, wiping the sweat off of his brow. It wasn't supposed to happen this way. *I was just going to take it slow*. He lay down on the cot, putting his forearm over his eyes, trying to think about what he would say to the sheriff. He could feel his cell mate's eyes on him and Eddy looked out from under his arm.

"What are you looking at?" Eddy barked.

The cell mate looked away and bit into his apple. Eddy was annoyed by the loud crunching sounds he was making. Had he not cared about making a good impression on the sheriff, he would have gotten up and knocked the apple clean out of the guy's mouth. *What a pansy. Who beats up on a woman?*

33.

Julia - May, 2012

It was a crisp Sunday morning and the sun was shining through the stained glass windows of St. Oliver's. Julia looked up from her regular spot, the same pew she had occupied for the last year, and examined the outline of the Holy Mother in the rainbow effect of the colored leaded glass. She had been distracted from Father Sheehan's Liturgy of the Eucharist by the reflective hues that were meant to provide hope in the miracle of life, yet in the background were the Father's words of impending doom. "Pray, brethren, that my sacrifice and yours may be acceptable to God, the almighty Father." The congregation responded, "May the Lord accept the sacrifice at your hands, for the praise and glory of his name, for our good, and the good of all his holy Church." Julia was able to mouth the last half of the response as she pulled her eyes from the colorful work of art. It seemed that as Father Sheehan looked up into the congregation, his eyes met hers and he was imploring her to do as Jesus would do – sacrifice herself. She wasn't sure if it was real or she was simply imagining father's thoughts. After pronouncing a prayer over the gifts and invoking the Holy Spirit to transform them into the blood and body of Christ, Father Sheehan declared, "The mystery of faith," and then came the part Julia liked the most, which was the sound of the congregation singing Amen in response.

The "mystery of faith" was the phrase that lingered with Julia, along with the starchy taste of bread and the pungency of the wine in her mouth, as she left St. Oliver's parking lot and traveled down the tree-lined China Grove Road toward her secluded home. She had yet to decide how her faith factored into her upcoming plans to gain emotional restitution for Joey's murder. On one hand, it felt completely right and justified given the evil corruption that allowed Eddy to go free. On the other, she thought it was not her place to mess with God's will in the universe. Yet, it wasn't that she was trying to play God as much as at every turn, she felt the hand of God leading her to this conclusion. She remembered the stories of miracles and faith of the Old Testament – how young Joseph was thrown into a hole by his jealous brothers and left to die and be enslaved and imprisoned for a crime he did not commit. It was his imprisonment that ultimately led him to impress the king, who eventually put him in charge of the very food his evil brothers needed to survive. Sometimes, God's idea of justice happens in a roundabout way, thought Julia, not via the way of the world or man's laws and rules. Julia genuinely felt her plan was the way to be sure Eddy would get his due punishment and no other little boys or families would have to endure his. It felt ordained by the Holy Spirit within her. If the priest could lay hands on and pray over the elements of the Eucharist and turn them into Christ Himself, how then could she doubt that God's hand may be guiding hers in a miraculous way, even if it was a dangerous game and could mean her sacrificing her own life in the process? It was a possibility. It was the mystery of faith and these thoughts only served to add to her resolve to trust God to lead her in knowing the right time and place to carry out her mission. These thoughts also added to her obsession, which she once again had to arrest and redirect. No matter what happened, she would find justice for Joey and relish with him, whether here or in the other world. She reminded herself, *I am already with*

you, sweetie. I am already there. That inspiration was the only thing
that seemed to snap her out of the incessant cycle of doubt and
guilt. Sometimes she had to say it over and over to find
comfort.

She walked into her house through the back door, and
thought she should eat something substantial today as she was
planning to make a considerable contribution to the "bank" as
she had come to think of it lately. Time was running out and
she needed to make sure she had an ample supply. She would
eat, and then while her food was digesting, she would attempt
to make brief contact with Eddy while playing *Slash and Burn.*
She was surprised that she had actually started to master the
game somewhat, although every time she saw his screen name
pop up, she cringed and felt nauseated. She tried to play with
other kids as much as possible first so she could gain her skill
and strength to communicate with Lance Irving Eddy.

While eating her sandwich, Julia's thoughts dominated
once again. *Lance Irving Eddy.* It was no coincidence in Julia's
mind that Eddy's initials spelled a word that personified his life
in general. He was a lie. His family was full of lies. Everything
he touched and said was a lie. She hated liars. She had
punished Joey a few times for not telling the truth. She could
tolerate a lot of bad behaviors, but lying was something she
would not abide in her child. She knew that if Joey had been
conversing with Eddy, she would have been able to detect the
lies when she asked him daily what he had done between
coming home from school and her return from work. The
rules were homework first and television once he was finished.
Absolutely no video games unless she was present. So, when
the tech investigator told her that there was no evidence that
Joey had communicated with Eddy through his gaming online,

she was relieved. *That's my boy*, she had thought. It was later determined that Eddy had been stalking the townhouse community and had simply figured out Joey's and Julia's routine. It still bugged her though. Why her son? What was it about Joey that made him a target? It was a question she wished she could ask Eddy, but there wouldn't be time for that. The biggest mistake Joey had made was in forgetting to lock the door behind him. The authorities said it may have been that Eddy had called the home phone just as Joey was walking in, so he could distract him from his regular door locking routine. A phone call from an unknown number had come in right about the time Joey usually arrived at home after school. She was haunted by that idea because she had not wanted to pay the extra three dollars a month to have her phone number unlisted. So, it wasn't Joey's fault that Eddy walked right in and took her son, probably in the middle of him eating his Bagel Bites, which was his favorite after school snack. The thought of it made Julia extremely angry at Eddy, and at herself for not being more protective of her son. But her daddy had drilled into her head to not turn Joey into a mama's boy by being too vigilant, but now she realized he was talking more about letting Joey fall off of his bike and skin his knee now and then, not letting him get abducted by a child murderer. Luckily her father had died before Joey's murder, so she didn't have to feel his guilt for having scolded her when she worried too much about Joey. She smiled, though, every time she thought of her dad and her son hanging out together in heaven. She wished she could feel both of their embraces, especially on lonely days like this one.

After eating, Julia logged onto *Slash and Burn* and within twenty minutes, Buddy666 was chomping at the bit to play with Wonka1126. She acted equally eager and was sure to throw in a few engaging comments that would give Eddy a cheap rise and prove to him that Wonka1126 was a desirable innocent. She tried to play it as if he was a kid whose sexual identity was in the balance. Thankfully, she no longer vomited after these encounters, but she usually had to take a very long walk afterwards in order to calm down. This kind of lying she excused in herself, but the words she had to use were detestable, especially when she thought of how real they must be for other kids who would actually be vulnerable to someone like Eddy. She knew she had to be careful, though, because she was sure Eddy would have his radar up for cops who might be impersonating a kid like this. She managed it by thinking about Joey and his friends and what they would and wouldn't say to someone they thought might be an older teenager or young adult. She continued to be able to convince Buddy666 that Wonka1126 was a little on the fringes and vulnerable to an older peer who could relate to his urges. Julia believed this would be Eddy's weak spot...and she was correct.

34.

June 25, 2012

"Good morning, Dr. Pierce," Nathan extended his hand to Sonya, who had agreed to meet with him first thing Monday morning to discuss Julia Olwen.

"Same to you, Sheriff Davis," Sonya said with a sympathetic smile. "I am so sorry we have to meet under these circumstances."

"Yes, I understand Ms. Olwen was a fine young woman."

"Oh, she was. And I was terribly shocked to read the news reports about her." Sonya's voice was shaky and Nathan noticed tears in her eyes.

"When was the last time you talked to Julia Olwen?" Nathan took a seat on the couch across from Sonya, imagining that it was the very spot Julia Olwen may have sat a number of times to pour out her heart. He sat back and crossed his legs, and then removed his notebook from his sport coat pocket.

"Actually, it was the day of our last session...I believe that was June eleventh." Sonya was looking down at her calendar. "We had set another appointment for the eighteenth, but of course, that didn't happen." Sonya was beginning to look nervous.

"Did you find that unusual...when she didn't show for her last appointment or had you already heard she was missing?"

"Well, yes...and no. I mean Julia was very good about keeping her appointments, but oftentimes when clients are feeling they have gotten what they need from therapy, they will simply stop coming. She had only been a patient of mine for a short time, so after I left her a couple of messages and got no return message, I simply figured she had a lot going on and would call me back when she could. I try not to appear harassing to my patients, if you know what I mean – and I try not to listen to the news because it depresses me, so I really didn't know what happened until about a week later when a friend mentioned it to me." Sonya put her head down, evidently embarrassed about not knowing about her client's death for some time.

"Dr. Pierce, just so you know, I am not here to accuse you of anything." Nathan smiled sympathetically. "I don't blame you for wanting to avoid the news. If I didn't have to know about it, I probably would choose to do just what you did. And I'm sure you did everything you could to help Ms. Olwen. It is my experience that when people decide they are going to carry out a plan like we suspect she was attempting to do, no amount of counsel or advice is going to talk them out of it. Unfortunately, it seems Ms. Olwen underestimated her opponent."

Sonya looked confused. "I'm not sure I understand...I've read some things about the case, but nothing that indicated the back story."

"Oh, I apologize Dr. Pierce. Of course you don't know. And I need to ask you to rely upon your professional ethics to not leak this information to anyone."

"Yes, I understand, Sheriff. I want to cooperate fully, although I'm not sure there is much I can reveal that will be helpful." Sonya touched a tissue to the corner of her eye to absorb a tear.

"We have reason to believe," Nathan started while sitting up on the edge of the couch, "that Julia Olwen had been planning to murder Lance Eddy, who was the man acquitted of her son's murder."

Sonya sat looking wide-eyed at Nathan, seemingly in shock.

"We think that she lured him to her home after posing as a young boy on the internet, but that when he got to her house, things went terribly wrong." Nathan did his best to break the news to her sensitively.

"And he killed her." Sonya said quietly.

"Yes, I believe so. We had enough evidence to arrest Mr. Eddy on Saturday."

"So, how can I be of any help?" Sonya had recovered slightly and tried to regain her professional demeanor.

"Can you tell me what Ms. Olwen's state of mind was in the months prior to her suspected murder? Did it seem she was mentally unstable? Did she mention any plans or thoughts of murder to you?"

Sonya sat thinking for a moment and then looked through her patient file on Julia. "Of course you understand that it is difficult for me to divulge a lot of personal information about her. Even though she is…deceased…the doctor-patient privilege extends into perpetuity. Yet, knowing Julia, she would have wanted me to help you solve this case, so I will do my best to give you information that is pertinent without compromising the details."

"I do appreciate that, Dr. Pierce," Nathan was trying to be respectful, but was a little put off by Sonya's worry about confidentiality. This was a murder case and details were important.

After a long pause, Sonya spoke in her therapist voice, slowly and quietly. "I am sorry to say that she did display great agitation when she spoke of Mr. Eddy. She shared with me that she had been having dark thoughts about him – enough so, that she felt the need to go to confession with her priest, hoping he would help her work toward some sense of closure, but I don't think she ever really got that. Having said that, I never felt at any time that Julia exhibited any characteristics of mental instability or character disorder that would lead to murder. I considered her to be a high functioning adult, able to maintain her relationships, her job and her lifestyle, despite the fact that she had experienced so much tragedy in her life. In fact, I was inspired by her undying love for her child and how she spent so much of her life taking care of others. She cared greatly for her patients at the hospital, her neighbors, her cousin in California…."

"Yes, tell me about the cousin," Nathan interrupted. "She was mentioned briefly by one of Julia's friends, but no one else seems to know anything about her."

"Well, she didn't speak of her much to me either, but I understand she was a distant cousin who was a single parent, struggling after a divorce and Julia was helping to support her so she could get back on her feet."

"Oh, okay," Nathan said while writing in his notebook. "As far as I knew, she had no living family. I was told she was an only child and her parents were gone and had little family left. The cousin threw me off a little."

"I believe this was the daughter of her father's cousin or something like that. I am not clear on the actual connection. Like I said, she didn't talk of her much and there are no details in my notes about her, so it obviously wasn't a subject she felt she needed to process with me."

"Okay," Nathan said nodding his head. "Go on."

"Like I said, I felt she was a high functioning adult, however, her grief was real and was extended I think because of the trial and the acquittal."

"Extended?"

"Well, yes, most people after a death can work through their grief in a couple of years. But when there is a murder like the one Julia was a victim of, the trial period allows for a time of stagnation and hope – hope that justice will be served. The memory of the murder victim can be kept alive for a time – in the public eye – still alive, so to speak, for the family. Then after a conviction, it takes a while for the family to grieve the sadness, but they are at least able to find solace in the justice. In Julia's case, however, the acquittal seemed to have brought on an anger that was even more intense than the anger she originally experienced after the murder. I believe that is why she came to see me last year – her neurotic projection got the best of her."

"Forgive me, Dr. Pierce. I've never been in therapy, so I will need you to explain some of these terms."

"I apologize," she said humbly. "I guess it would be the same if you started talking in police codes to me, huh?" She smiled demurely.

Nathan laughed, feeling sympathy for Sonya's evident feelings of loss around this particular patient.

"Well, in laymen's terms, projecting our anger is blaming others when we really blame ourselves. Not knowing what to do with it, so the first time someone says or does something you don't like, all of the self-directed anger gets expressed toward that person rather than at the self, which would get the person in touch with all of the guilt that goes with that. Julia felt a lot of guilt about her son's death. She thought she should have protected him from it."

"Got ya. I can understand that. Now, did she say who she was taking it out on?"

"I think it was her attorney who referred her to me. She had gotten very angry at him and he, of course, felt helpless to fix that. You know, attorneys are fixers not listeners."

"Yeah, don't I know it." Nathan wondered how Julia had gone from projecting her anger to planning a botched murder. He asked Sonya that question.

"That is where I am very perplexed," Sonya admitted. "She talked of some dark and ill thoughts about Mr. Eddy, that I thought were normal and I told her so, but she never discussed with me that she had fantasized about ending his life." Sonya paused, as if a thought had just come to mind. "Wait, she did talk about that once. She said she had encountered him – Mr. Eddy – in an online gaming site and wished she'd had the nerve to kill him online."

Nathan sat up attentively. "An online gaming site? She was playing video games with him?"

"Not exactly. She still had the gaming set up in her home from when Joey used to play, and she had turned it on one day to see if Joey's screen name was still listed. I think she was just having a moment of nostalgia. That's when she apparently saw Mr. Eddy's ID come up – I can't remember how she knew that – but she described getting physically ill after seeing it."

"Do you know if she actually communicated with him?"

"No, she said was so disturbed by just seeing his screen name that she turned the system off and became physically ill."

This was affirming news for Nathan, but he wondered why Julia would not have revealed subsequent encounters like he suspected she'd had with Eddy.

"Can you tell me when this happened?" Nathan asked.

"Uh…." Sonya checked her notes again. "It looks like she reported that to me on February sixth. But that was the last she talked about her online encounter with Mr. Eddy. After that, our sessions were more focused on how she might let go of her anger and move on. In fact, in our last session, we had discussed ways she could turn this tragedy into something good for others."

"Others?"

"Yes, she said she could probably let go of her anger if she wasn't so worried about other little boys who might end up victimized by Mr. Eddy. I told her that many families will find ways to process their sadness and anger by helping to create new legislation or starting organizations to help other families. She didn't seem ready for anything like that, yet." Sonya paused a moment to reflect. "But murder? That just doesn't seem like something she would do. Julia was the kind of person who struggled with setting boundaries so that she wouldn't give too much of herself away. Murder just doesn't fit the profile if you ask me." Sonya sat back in her chair to indicate she had said all she knew.

"Well, Dr. Pierce, you have been very helpful. May I call you again if I think of something else?"

"Of course, Sheriff. It was a pleasure meeting you and I hope you get what you need to convict this guy. It's about time he pays for the evil person he obviously is."

"That's our goal," Nathan said while walking down the hall toward the door. He shook her hand once more and took a business card from a table in the waiting area to add to his file. Sonya bid him goodbye and he walked to his car, not feeling satisfied by what he had heard. If Julia Olwen was all that Dr. Pierce and Mrs. Timko had said she was, how did she muster enough anger to even come close to attempted murder? The anger of a grieving mother must be more deranged than he thought, but obviously not as disturbed as the one she tried to murder. He felt a new respect for her. If she really had attempted to sacrifice herself because she couldn't bear the thought of another child hurt at the hands of Lance Irving Eddy, how could he blame her?

Nathan got in his car and pulled out his phone, which had been on silent during his meeting with Dr. Pierce. There was a message from Tommy. Nathan laughed out loud to hear that Lance Eddy was requesting a meeting with the sheriff. He was ready to talk. It must be divine intervention, Nathan thought, since he had been wondering if another meeting with Eddy might be productive. This could only mean two things – Eddy either knew he was toast and wanted to make a deal, or he thought he was cunning enough to convince Nathan he was innocent, as he apparently thought he had done with his attorney.

"Pork, got your message and can't wait to get in front of that guy again," Nathan was leaving Tommy a return voice mail. "I need to see if Beaudreau will allow me to have a private meeting with Eddy. Somethin' tells me that even he knows his client is scum. Also, ask the tech guys to look for evidence of Julia playing in online gaming sites, starting in January or February. Talk to ya later, Buddy."

Nathan Lee Davis smiled at the thought of cracking open the mind of a sick killer who had eluded the big city investigators. He felt the familiar adrenaline rush that flooded his brain and body when he was getting close to the answers. *You came to the wrong county, my friend.*

35.

Julia - May, 2012

She had punched in Eddy's home address and her GPS created a handy little map that led her right to his front door in Riverbridge Commons in Marlowe County. It was just after nine o'clock in the evening and the sun had descended behind the horizon, so Julia felt comfortable that she would not be noticed by anyone in the area. She had gotten his address by paying thirty-nine-ninety-five for an online service that allowed her to find out just about anything on anyone, including home addresses, work histories, phone numbers, and most everything else except social security numbers. She'd had no idea how easy it was to find out where someone lived and how to get in touch with them, which sickened her to think about how easily Eddy could have learned her home number to distract Joey. In her search, Julia had learned that Eddy had never been married, had no children, *thank God*, and had just moved into this new place six months ago, shortly after the acquittal. And he owned it free and clear, which made Julia laugh. *Yeah, right.* As far as she could ascertain, he did not, nor had he ever, had a real job, so he was living off of his trust money. It angered her to think that his boredom and lack of vocation were contributing factors to her son being gone.

The fact that he was not only free, but living like upper middle class folks, made her feel more entitled to engage in this spy operation. She had purchased an outdoor camera that looked like a rock that could be placed across from his property, which was luckily a common area with a small lake, playground, gazebo and walking trail. She got out of her car and set the rock down with the lens facing outward toward Eddy's front door. This way, she could see when he left either from the front door or in his vehicle exiting the garage. The salesman had told her that it had a wide-angle lens that would pick up activity from up to fifty feet away, at least enough to know what was going on. She only wanted to establish his daily patterns to give her an idea of his routine. The battery was supposed to last for up to three days and it would only turn on when it detected motion, which might be a problem since cars would be going back and forth all day long, but it was her best bet to ensure she understood when he came and went from his home.

After placing the camera, Julia got back into her car and drove toward the cul-de-sac to turn around and exit the neighborhood. As she was driving past Eddy's house on her way out, she noticed that his front porch light was on, which hadn't been on just a minute before, which made her nervous, wondering if he had seen her place the rock. After thinking on it, she hoped it was merely a timed light since it had just gotten completely dark a short time ago. As she was pulling out of the Riverbridge Commons neighborhood, there was a QuikTrip gas station to her right. When she looked that way to see if it was clear to pull out onto the street, she saw a chubby, dark-haired man walking toward the intersection from the QT. He stopped to cross over and she could see him clearly now under the street light. He was wearing large oversized cargo shorts, a dirty t-shirt with his large hairy gut peering beneath the hem, and untied sneakers that looked like he had just slipped them on to take a short walk. He was carrying a Big Gulp in his left hand and smoking a cigarette with his right. Julia's heart leapt as she recognized him as Lance Eddy. There was no mistaking him, even though it appeared he had gained a lot of weight since she saw him at the trial. She quickly looked away, not wanting him to notice her car or her face. As she sat there waiting for him to walk in front of her vehicle, she had half a mind to let her foot off the brake and hit the gas to "accidentally" run over him. But that would be too obvious, Julia thought, as she reminded herself of the time and effort she had invested to make things right. The temptation was great, though, and she had to take a deep breath to compose herself. A car behind her was laying on the horn because she was hesitating too long, still watching his disgusting gait. Julia looked left and then right again and pulled out onto the main street that would lead her to the freeway and back toward Regal. As she pulled away, she glanced one more time in her rear view mirror to see Eddy's shadow waddling toward his house like a penguin. She took note of his increased size since she saw him last and knew she had to be extra careful that she played everything just right to stay out of harm's way. Her energy on the way home was higher than it had ever been.

She returned to Eddy's home a few days later and discovered by looking at the recorded footage that every day at around ten in the morning and around eight thirty in the evening, he walked to the QuikTrip for his drink and smokes. It took him approximately seventeen minutes from the time he left to the time he returned. That was all Julia needed to move to the next phase of her plan.

With each step closer, she found an increasing need for a little more courage to execute, causing her to refer continually to an Eleanor Roosevelt quote she had copied and plastered everywhere – her refrigerator, her bathroom mirror, her car visor – to remind her to stay focused. It was one of her favorites that someone had emailed her when she was in the freshest part of her grief after Joey's death. It had an even deeper meaning for her now.

You gain strength, courage and confidence by every experience in which you really stop to look fear in the face. You are able to say to yourself, 'I have lived through this horror. I can take the next thing that comes along.' You must do the thing you think you cannot do.

D-Day was coming and Julia was looking fear in the face.

36.

June 25, 2012

Upon walking into the department office, Dorothy was standing at her desk with her hands on her bony hip, and said in her scratchy smoker's voice. "Well, Sheriff. What's the report? You know I've been thinkin' about it all weekend."

"Report?" Nathan asked as he walked past her toward his office, noticing that Dorothy was following him.

"Montovani's? The girl? The date?"

"Oh, that. Nothin' to report, Dot." Nathan picked up the morning mail that she had laid on his desk and was shuffling through it, hoping she would not make him talk about it.

"C'mon, hon, you had that look in your eye when you left here on Friday. What happened?"

"It was fine. We had a nice time, but it's not goin' anywhere from here, okay?" Nathan noticed his voice sounded slightly annoyed, which he didn't intend. He knew Dot meant well and was looking after him in the absence of his real mother.

"Oh, I'm sorry." She gave Nathan a pouty look. "I was hoping she might be the one."

He laughed, showing his dimples and boyish grin. "Well, don't hold your breath, Dot. I don't think I'm lookin' for the *one* quite yet."

"Whatever," Dot retorted. "That's what they all say, but we girls know that when the right one comes along, you'll be all twitterpated and ready to walk down the aisle again."

"Twitter what?"

"Twitterpated. Oh, never mind. You have to have grandkids to know what I mean."

Just then, Tommy walked around Dorothy and into Nathan's office. He took a seat, while Dorothy walked away, disappointed that she hadn't learned anything juicy to tell the others in the office.

"So, how'd it go Friday night?" Tommy teased, pretending for Dorothy's sake that he didn't already have the scoop.

"Jeez, what's up with everyone around here? Can't a man have a date without having to put an article in the paper?"

Tommy smiled, understanding, and said, "Don't mind her. She's like me – just living vicariously through your exciting life, boss. It's kinda like having our own personal reality TV show."

"Right," Nathan snorted and looked down at his phone after it buzzed. Coincidentally, it was a text from Sally Tate. It simply said, "Hey." He put it back into his belt carrier, deciding to ignore it.

"She's texting you isn't she?" Tommy could see the look in Nathan's eyes.

"Yeah, but I've got a busy day. I don't wanna get into that."

"So, be straight up, boss. What's her PPF?"

Nathan laughed. "About a six, I'd say." The PPF was an inside joke among the guys in the department who rated their dates by their Potential Psycho Factor, indicating the likelihood that a woman would be a major pest or stalker if she was ignored after being slept with.

"Well, that's not too bad, I guess."

"Yeah, she's a nice gal, but probably too young for me. I'm a little old fashioned, and she's a female progressive. I'd rather not promote something when it's clear it's not gonna go anywhere."

"Hold on, there, Nathan Davis. I've seen that girl on channel three and I wouldn't give up on her yet until, you know…it gets old."

"Okay, okay…" Nathan knew he was not going to get anywhere with Tommy. "Did you get my voice mail? What do ya think about Eddy asking for an interview?"

"Odd, I'd say, but he must be desperate. He actually thinks he can convince us that he's got an explanation for the evidence we have on him. Amazing how delusional these guys can be, isn't it?"

Nathan was looking through his card file and located Wayne Beaudreau's number. "I'm gonna talk to Beadreau first and then head on over to the jail. Wanna sit in?"

"I wouldn't miss it for the world." Tommy got up from his chair and walked out.

Beaudreau had not heard that his client was requesting an interview with the sheriff and said he needed to talk to his client first before he'd allow Nathan to sit down with him again. He agreed to meet Nathan at the jail within an hour. Tommy and Nathan walked past Dorothy's desk, where Nathan grabbed his reading glasses and they headed out of the double-glass doors. Nathan's Crown Vic was sitting in the sun, while Tommy's cruiser was in the shaded sheriff's spot. Nathan looked over at Tommy, who was silently gloating. Nathan smiled and shook his head jokingly, knowing what Tommy was thinking. "See ya over there," he said as he watched Tommy get into his cool vehicle.

Dorothy noticed that the sheriff and Tommy looked confident and serious as their respective car doors opened and closed in unison, and both pulled out of the lot on a mission. She sat staring with pride at them through the glass doors for a few seconds. Even she had been surprisingly shaken lately by the recent events. Dorothy was a mother and a grandmother who shuttered to think of what Julia Olwen must have gone through. "Good luck, boys," she said under her breath while turning toward her computer screen to start the day's work.

***

The Calhoun County jail is situated just north of downtown Regal, the county seat, on a road lined with bail and bond businesses, affectionately referred to as One Call Row. As Nathan drove north on State Road 520, he remembered his days as a young deputy on night watch at the jail, anxious to get promoted to a street beat so he could catch the criminals, not herd them around like sheep. The night watch was the worst, as there was rarely any real excitement, which was the only thing interesting about working the jail – the possibility of an altercation of some sort, or an out of control inmate who might require a heavy hand. Nathan marveled at how much his life had changed since being a twenty-something, to now a man in his mid-forties. Those were the days, he thought, when it took nothing to get a woman to go to bed with him and he could drink like a fish and still make it to work the next day. These days, he found he was no longer interested in a one night stand, and after two glasses of wine, he couldn't be trusted to act his age. He was envious of the younger guys, but knew if he had it to do over again, he would not likely change much. His memories were fond, even if he did marry the wrong girl and took a detour on the road to happiness. Maybe Dot was right. Maybe that right person will be just around the corner. Nathan nearly laughed out loud as he realized that his thoughts had gone quickly from thinking about his jail days to settling down with a woman. *Unreal.* It reminded him of Sally Tate and how he had left it with her. He didn't know how long he could continue avoiding her, since they had never gotten around to discussing what she knows about the Eddy family and their connections to Judge Seeger and District Attorney Luckinbill. He thought he should text her back sometime during the day, but now that he was turning into the jail parking lot, he put that out of his mind temporarily.

Nathan went through the security gate, nodding at the guard who let him through. He pulled into the personalized pole position reserved for him, and on this day, he was glad to take it since the outdoor temperature, as well as the humidity level, were both in the nineties. He and Tommy walked through the doors on the sally port side of the building, acknowledging the chief jailer, Chuck "Picker" Goolsby. He got his nickname from being a full-time jailer and a part-time banjo player in a bluegrass band. "Hey Pick," Nathan said, waiting to get the update on Eddy.

"Good mornin', Sheriff. We got a talker, wants to spill his guts and convince you of his *in-no-cence*," Goolsby drew out the last word, while exchanging a look of mutual skepticism with the sheriff.

"Good," Nathan replied. "Let's see what he's got."

Goolsby led the way into the small interview room that contained a utility table and two metal chairs. When Nathan opened the door, he saw Eddy sitting with his hands folded on top of the table, and his leg bouncing up and down like a jackhammer. Tommy leaned up against the wall behind Nathan.

"Mornin' Mr. Eddy," said Nathan in a business-like tone. "I understand you requested to talk with me. Where's your attorney?" Nathan sat down and slammed a thick file of papers onto the table for effect.

"I told him I wanted to do this myself. I have nothing to hide, Sheriff." Eddy was visibly agitated, but trying not to show it.

Nathan was shocked at Eddy's arrogance. "So, let's not waste any time. What was so important that I needed to rush down here this morning and hear what you had to say?" Nathan was looking Eddy straight in the eye, determined to maintain control.

"Ya see, Sheriff, I think there has been a big mix up. This so-called evidence that you have against me must have been planted 'cause I didn't kill anybody." Eddy's voice rose to a high-pitch whining.

"Okay, well, let's look at this evidence." Nathan opened the file and while looking down at it, he put his elbows on the table and rubbed his palms together. "For starters, it says here that a neighbor saw a red Ford F150 enter Ms. Olwen's driveway around eight in the evening on the sixteenth of June and that the tire track imprint that was taken from the scene matches perfectly with the tires on your red Ford F150." Nathan saw Eddy wince a little and look down at his shaking leg.

"Yes, but I can explain that..." Eddy started, but was interrupted by Nathan.

"Mr. Eddy, if I recall, you denied ever being at Ms. Olwen's home, but *now* you say you can explain? Were you lying to me Mr. Eddy?" Nathan did not take his eyes from Eddy's. His voice became more forceful with each word.

"No, well, I did go to that address that night, but I had no idea it was the home of Ms. Olwen. I swear."

"Where did you *think* you were going then?"

"There was this guy I met in a gaming site online and we were gonna get together for a beer or somethin'. He gave me that address. But when I got there, no one answered, so I just left. I figured I got it wrong. And he hasn't been online since."

"A beer or somethin'? What was the somethin' Eddy? Somethin' like you had with that Olwen boy?" Nathan pressed harder, feeling his own blood pressure rise. Up until now, Eddy's eyes had been hollow, but with the mention of the Olwen boy, he saw fire come into them.

"No! Not like the Olwen boy…and I didn't kill that bitch of his mom either!" Eddy screamed, pushing himself away from the table.

"So, can you give me this guy's name? A phone number? Something to prove that you are tellin' the truth?"

Eddy hesitated nervously. "I don't know! All I have is a screen name. It was Wonka-somethin'."

"Wonka? Really?"

"Yeah, you guys took my computer and my game system. So, check it out. You'll find it. Then maybe you can find the guy…or the kid."

"Oh, the *kid*. You piece of lying shit." Nathan shook his head in disgust, with pursed lips and clenched fists. He fantasized for a moment about throwing a punch square in the middle of Eddy's face.

"Listen, do you have something important to tell me or are you just here to waste my time with your whining?"

The fire in Eddy's eyes was growing more intense and Nathan felt sure he was about to crack him. Eddy broke his gaze with Nathan and leaned forward, placing his forearms on his thighs, shaking his head back and forth, eyes looking at his cuffed hands.

"Let me continue, Mr. Eddy." Nathan was looking again at the file in front of him. "There was a gun found in your home that is registered to Ms. Olwen, and yesterday, I found a shell casing in her kitchen that will probably match the weapon. Now, when you combine that with the fact that there was over five pints of blood in that kitchen – her blood – I think there's a pretty good chance there is a dead body somewhere. So, why don't you just stop wasting everybody's time and tell me where you put the body?"

"I have no idea where that gun came from and I don't know anything about a body. In fact, it seems to me that someone, maybe one of your boys, killed her and decided to set me up to take the fall for this thing. I know the cops watch me online, so I bet one of them is Wonka." Eddy responded as if this news might be enlightening to Nathan.

"What site would that be? You mean on that stupid game, *Slash and Burn*?" Nathan was glad that Tommy had filled him in right before the interview that the techies had found a connection between Julia's online gaming system and Eddy's. He flashed Eddy a sinister grin. He knew he had the goods on Eddy and was hoping he would just give up and confess.

"Whatever. Ask one of your cronies to explain why they killed that woman to get to me. If you ask me, that's pretty sick." Eddy felt dejected. If the sheriff knew about *Slash and*

Burn, then he already knew about Wonka, which meant they were all in on the dirty game to convict him.

"Oh, I get it. So, what you're saying is a police officer broke into your house and hid the gun, and then killed Julia Olwen to make sure you went to jail? I'm sorry, Mr. Eddy, but do you take me for a fool?" Nathan's eyes were inches away from Eddy's. "Your story is ridiculous. And unless you have something to say that doesn't make you sound like a cold-blooded killer, then this meeting is over."

Nathan got up to indicate he was leaving. "Sergeant Goolsby, we're done here," Nathan barked while picking up his file from the table.

Goolsby came into the room and escorted a fight-ready Eddy out of the room. Goolsby had to strong arm him to get him through the door. Nathan and Tommy exchanged disgusted glances. They heard Eddy's voice scream as he walked down the hall toward his cell. "Fuck all of you!"

"Whatdya think, Sheriff?" Tommy inquired as they were leaving the room.

"There's no doubt in my mind that he killed that kid. I could see it in how his eyes shifted and burned when I mentioned it. The other stuff, I don't know. I think his daddy is dead now and can't get him out of this one, so he's in a panic, knowing he's really made a mistake this time around."

"Yep, I agree," Tommy said. "Like a caged animal with no way out. Maybe if he thinks about it for a while, he'll accept his fate and lead us to Ms. Olwen's body. Without that, we've still got a lot of work to do."

"I know, Pork. What else did you get from the techies that might be helpful?"

"Oh, yeah. Conversation between Wonka1126 and Buddy666 is clear. Like I said before, she was definitely luring him to her home by posing as a boy. What went wrong when he got there is anybody's guess. Do you think she just wanted to talk to him?"

"Maybe, but with a gun to his head. I think Eddy had the gun because she had the gun on him when he was there. How else would he have gotten possession of it? So, I don't think she was intending to have a friendly conversation, it that's what you mean."

"I guess you're right. It's just hard to believe she would have the guts to do it." Tommy sped up his pace to keep up with Nathan, who was clearly amped up and on a mission.

"Maybe she didn't…have the guts to do it after all." Nathan looked pensive. "Anything else from the computer that might be helpful?"

"Not much on her hard drive that was suspicious other than a few interesting internet searches."

"Like?" Nathan was walking out of the jail toward his car.

"Like *life in a women's prison* and *how much blood can you lose without dying*," Tommy replied matter-of-factly.

"Hmm….that's weird." Nathan snorted while thinking about what Tommy just said.

"What do you make of that?" Tommy had stopped at Nathan's car to finish their conversation.

"Nothin' right now. Anything else?"

"No, but they are still working on looking at her online banking and recent transfers – that kind of thing."

"Perfect," said Nathan. "I've got something to do right now and then I'm gonna pick up some lunch. I'll be back there around 2:00, I guess."

"Okay, boss. See ya later." Tommy walked over to his car and Nathan got into his. He looked at his phone and saw another text from Sally Tate.

"Damn it," Nathan muttered to himself. It said *Are you upset with me?*

Nathan thought for a moment and then punched in *Course not...Tater Tot.* He figured humor was the way to get things back to normal. He waited for a few seconds and another one popped up. *Okay :-)* He replied. *Busy day. Gotta go. Talk later.* He pulled out of the parking lot and felt like he had done enough to keep her at bay until he needed to talk to her about the case again. After he returned to the office, he noticed she had responded once more while he was driving. It said *Any more details on the case?* But by that time, he was on his way back to the office, too distracted to try to play the game with her.

37.

Julia - May, 2012

She raised the firearm and aimed it at the target of a human silhouette, male she presumed. With her right arm straight in front of her body, slightly to the left, and her left hand bracing her right wrist, she steadied her gaze. She was fixated on the goal, peering through the two sights on top of the gun. In her gun safety class, she had learned this was called the Weaver stance, and in this moment, she found herself wondering who Weaver was and what was so special about this technique. How does someone get his name assigned to something that is seemingly so common and taken for granted? It's like Lamaze classes or the Heimlich maneuver. Why aren't they just called breathing lessons or the squeeze and release? Was it really such a big revelation that taking a few deep breaths might ease pain or that if you practically broke someone's ribs, they might spit out their food? Julia thought that maybe after this was all over with, her plan would be called the Olwen revenge. She refocused and took a deep breath, aware of the acrid smell of gun powder – the odor that had nearly taken her breath away the first time she had come to the shooting range. With eye and ear protection on, the only sound she heard was her heart pounding, first in her chest and then the rhythmic swishing of her pulse between her ears. She could barely hear the other shots from the men at the range who appeared to be police officers, their bodies pumped up and ready for a physical challenge. In contrast, Julia felt small and incapable, nervous that the others were watching and wondering why she was there. Practice makes perfect, she told herself, and everything had to be perfect. One miss could throw everything off kilter.

She had seen Eddy in person several times. She had learned he was five foot ten and weighed two hundred and sixty pounds. She knew his pants size and inseam. She knew the distance from the floor to his heart, the ceiling to his head, and to other parts of his body. She had placed targets in her house to simulate his frame. She had done her homework. This practice was to make sure she got it right. She took a deep breath and without exhaling, she pulled her index finger against the trigger and braced herself for the jolt. In a split second, she could see a hole, several inches to the left of where she was aiming. *Not bad.*

She felt a tap on her shoulder and turned around to see a chunky young man, with a wide chest and massive biceps, grinning at her. She pulled off her ear protection.

"That's pretty good," he said through a glimmering smile that didn't look like he meant it. He looked to be Hispanic, with a short crew cut and a tattoo of an anchor on his left arm. She thought of Popeye and smiled.

"Oh, thanks," Julia responded, not knowing if he meant it or was flirting with the only female in the place. "I've only been here a few times."

"Do you mind if I give you a pointer?"

She didn't really want one, but felt like it would be rude to say so. Julia shrugged. "Sure."

"Next time, try looking through the front sight only instead of through both. And line it up with where you want to shoot." He had a smile like Mario Lopez from the old television show *Saved by the Bell* that she had watched as a teenager.

Julia took his advice and was surprised that it made sense. She gave him a nod of approval. "Okay," she responded positively.

She put her ear protection back on and lifted her right arm once again, cupping her right wrist with the palm of her left. She steadied her body, closed her left eye and looked through the front sight and aimed it at the target. After a deep breath, she pulled the trigger. In a split second a black hole appeared just between the silhouette's legs.

"Yay!" Julia exclaimed while jumping slightly off the floor, her hands still clutching the gun. She turned to look at the man whose advice she took, and he was wincing, but still smiling. She saw him point to his crotch and mouth the words, "Is that your target?" Julia's face felt hot with embarrassment and she nodded affirmatively. He walked away, shaking his head in disbelief and she saw him saying something to the other guys. She imagined he must have thought she was practicing to get revenge on a cheating husband. *You have no idea.*

After a few good shots, Julia wrapped up and left the range feeling confident that she was ready for the next step. As she was walking to her car, she could feel her cell phone buzzing in her purse. It was Claire.

"Hey sweetie," she answered.

"Hey girl, what are you doing? I stopped by your house on my way home from the grocery store and saw that you were gone. I hope I'm not bothering you on a date or anything. It is Saturday night, ya know."

"Oh, yeah, I can't talk long or I'll keep Romeo waiting." Julia rolled her eyes, knowing that Claire wished so badly to be free and single.

"Really?" Claire's voice was soft and eager.

"Right. I'm just out running some errands. Sorry to disappoint you."

"Errands? On a Saturday night? Like what?"

Julia hesitated, not having a good answer. "You know…uh…picking up my dry cleaning and buying stamps at the post office kiosk."

"Oh my God, Julia. You need to get a life."

"Like going to the grocery store on a Saturday night?" Julia laughed.

"Okay, well, I have a family and responsibilities," Claire blurted out without realizing how painful that must be for Julia to hear. "And Steve doesn't mind hanging out with the kids on a Saturday, so it's the best time to go." She attempted to recover, but Julia understood.

"Jeez. Why are you defending yourself? And why do I have to give you a play by play of my evening?" Julia asked.

"You're right. Let's start over. How are you?" Claire's voice was less animated.

"I am doing well," Julia replied. "I'm headed home now, did you need something when you came over?"

"Nah, just thought I would say hey and I bought you a little something at the store that I was going to give you, but it can wait until I see you again."

A thought went through Julia's mind that these times were going to be over in only a few short weeks. "Well that's sweet of you. Why don't I stop over now…or is it too late?"

"Well, I've gotta put the groceries away and I think Steve wanted us to do a family movie tonight. Raincheck?"

"Sure, but let's get together soon, okay?"

"You got it," Claire said. "Love you."

"Love you, too." Julia hung up and she could feel the sting of tears in her eyes. If there was one reason to not do what she was preparing to do, it would be Claire. She turned left onto China Grove Road and before she pulled into her driveway, her cheeks were wet. *Damn it. I'm so sorry.* She hated the thought of the guilt and sadness Claire would probably feel when it was over. But there was no way to avoid that. She resigned herself to the thought that ultimately Claire would understand it had to be done. *For Joey.*

38.

June 26, 2012

It had been ten days since Nathan had found Julia Olwen's kitchen in a bloody mess. There was some satisfaction in getting Eddy behind bars, but some things had been nagging at him that were like puzzle pieces forced into place, but not exactly fitting. Where was the body? He had sent out a crew to look for a fresh grave, but nothing was found. How did the body get from the house to where Eddy hid it or destroyed it without leaving behind a drop of trace evidence? Why was Eddy so insistent this time that he had not done it, going against his attorney's wishes to stay silent? Nathan had watched the interrogation videos of Eddy after the Joey Olwen murder. A guilty Eddy was smug and silent. He had also studied the television news reports to see what he could discover in Eddy's eyes in certain moments. When the juror said "not guilty" at the end of Eddy's trial, Nathan detected a guilty relief in not only Eddy, but in his attorney's eyes as well. This was different. If he didn't know Eddy's history or the evidence in this case, he may be inclined to believe that Eddy was telling the truth. But how could that be? The gun was in his house. The tire tracks were his. A witness saw his truck there. He admits he was there, but not to see her. He says he was framed, but Nathan was not aware of any one person or group who would go to such lengths to set him up. Not in this way. Not in a way that would put Julia's life in danger. And then there was Julia. She was obviously smart, sensitive, caring...beautiful. Was she really willing to go to jail for Eddy's murder if she was caught? Was she so despondent that she was willing to risk her own life, especially if it meant Eddy might live to escape justice once again? Did she want him to murder her and get caught, sending him to jail as she thought he deserved?

Nathan took a long drag on his cigarette, while sitting on his back patio, the same place he and Sally had been just a few nights before. His feet were propped up on a chair and he felt a wave of embarrassment when he recalled the moment Sally's hand ended up on his crotch and he had refused her. *I'm turning into an old man.* He smiled and took a final drag before stamping it out on the stone patio. It was a balmy evening, but the mosquitoes were more active tonight than Nathan liked, so he got up and went inside. He poured out the last stream of warm beer that was in the can he had been drinking. *Maybe I should call her.*

He picked up his phone from the kitchen counter and saw that she had beat him to it. Sally Tate had left a voice mail, telling him she was free on Friday if he wanted to try again and she promised she would not be so forward this time. Nathan thought it was kind of her, glad that she apparently had not been too scarred by his rejection. He found her in his speed dial and her phone rang four times, her voice mail picking up after that. Nathan hung up, as he wasn't big on making recordings of himself saying perfunctory phrases. *I'll call her in the morning.*

Nathan fell asleep on his bed, with his shoes still on and his reading glasses propped up on his nose from when he had looked up Sally's number in the kitchen. When he woke up, an old rerun of *CSI, Las Vegas* was blaring on the television – a show he routinely made fun of because of its corny lines and unrealistic drama. He heard Grissom say to Catherine that things were not always as they seem. *Duh. Who writes these lines?*

Sometimes the victims are as sly as their perpetrators, was the message Grissom was clearly trying to relate. Nathan turned off the television, pulled off his shoes and pants and crawled under the covers, leaving his t-shirt and socks on. As he was drifting off to sleep again, memories came to mind of times when life had thrown him unexpected curve balls. *Things aren't always as they seem.*

He had grown up without knowing that his parents had any money. His father had been a city councilman in Regal, Georgia, and had owned a hardware store to feed the family. Nathan's mother had stayed at home and took care of him, his older brother Wade, and his sister, Caroline. They ate meat and potatoes most of the time and rarely went out to dinner. He thought it was because there was no money to do such things. He worried about his parents when he went off to college because the hardware store was being overshadowed by the big emerging home improvement chains, and he thought they were surely going to struggle financially. Even after his father had died, his mother was always watching her pennies and scolding Nathan for not saving his. It wasn't until after she passed away that Nathan discovered she was worth a million dollars, half of which she gave to her church and the other half was bequeathed to Wayne and Nathan. That never bothered him because he knew how devoted she was to her faith and it felt like she was placing the same amount of importance on her children as she did on God, which was okay in his book. *Things aren't always as they seem, indeed.*

Nathan's sister Caroline had died of cancer when she was only twenty-two, which was tragic and could still bring feelings of guilt in him. He had been too young to try to be a real brother to her and then she was gone before he had a chance to stop caring about only himself. Nathan had thought at the time it was such a dirty trick that God would take her so early because she had faulty ovaries, even though she had never been married, never had children, and as far as he knew, she had never had sex. She hadn't deserved such a cruel ending. Before Nathan was twenty-seven, he had slept with every young female who had a pulse in Regal. He remembered thinking after his sister's death that *he* was the one who deserved to die, not her. That he had squandered all that God had given him, and more, and there was his sister who barely got to live life and had probably never felt the joy and pleasure of making love to a man. He had tortured himself with this thought until a couple of years ago, after his divorce, when he had attempted to clean out the attic and accidentally stumbled upon a box, labeled "Halloween costumes." Thinking it would be cool to see what was in it, he had opened it up to find it was full of his sister's things. He had wondered why it was in the attic, but could only conclude that his mother found it too painful at some point to keep the box where it was easily accessible, so she had hid it away in a place she would have had to intentionally visit. On that day, when he had pulled out the items one by one, he had found himself getting more emotional than ever before and had chalked that up to his increasing, as well as annoying, middle-aged sensitivity. There were trinkets and stuffed animals that presumably came from her friends or old boyfriends. He had found an old cheerleading outfit and a swim meet trophy. There was a jewelry box and a slew of birthday cards and flattened Mylar balloons. At the bottom were several booklets that turned out to be her personal journals that, according to the dates, had been written when she was sixteen to nineteen years old. He had put everything else back in the box and had taken the journals with him for later reading. It wasn't that he wanted to pry into his sister's thoughts or violate her privacy in any way. Truth be told, he had wanted to see if she had written anything about him. When she had died, Nathan was only in his late twenties, and like all twenty-somethings, he had been more focused at that time on his life and his own conquests than his sister's. Her cancer had come quickly and she had died within a year. Even though they had said their goodbyes and all the expected sentiments family members are supposed to say to each other, Nathan wondered what she had really thought of him before she got sick. Had he been the kind of brother she looked up to? Had he given her the kind of protection big brothers are supposed to give? Later on, after finding the journals, Nathan had settled down with a Jack and Coke and decided to pore over them to see if he could get some insight into a part of his sister's life he had been too busy to notice or care about prior to her death. He had begun laughing immediately as he read the first page because she was a typical sixteen-year-old, clinging to the never-ending drama with her friends. He had smiled as he read about her trying to fix her friends' problems. She had always been the therapist in the group, yet none of her friends ever seemed to give back much to her, other than a reason to laugh. He had enjoyed reading about her feelings and her aspirations and her pain. It allowed him to reengage with the memory of her that had been too quickly forgotten in an attempt to assuage the pain. But enough time had passed that he had felt close to her while reading, without feeling particularly sad. To his dismay, she had not mentioned him at all in her writing, except in a matter-of-fact way like, "Nathan is coming home this weekend from college, which means I won't get to have the car." That had made him laugh, as it was a real depiction of their relationship. She was just being a teenage kid, and he had realized how silly it was to think that she would have had any deep, emotional words to say about him. It had only made him wish he could have known her as a forty-year-old, maybe with a slew of kids and a great career. As he had read through her last journal that was presumably written when she was nineteen, his eyes were opened to her becoming a young woman. Back then, she had a boyfriend named Tuck, who Nathan never cared for, but no one was ever good enough to date his sister. Even though Tuck ended up being a fancy attorney in Marlowe County, Nathan had dismissed him as a loser back then. As Nathan had read Caroline's accounts of her and Tuck, he became enthralled, like a sex-hungry woman reading a romance novel. He had been surprised by Caroline's mastery of the language as she described her sexual encounters with Tuck in detail. She had said he was the most romantic man on earth. She compared him to Michael Douglas, and said he kissed her all over and made her wildest dreams seem small in that moment of climax. Nathan had blushed upon reading his sister's words that were so full of passion and romance. He was horrified to think that his mother had read these same words about her daughter. What must she have thought? But then he had remembered that his Aunt Carol had pulled out a vibrator in his mother's bedside table as they were going through her things after her death. Carol had gasped and then laughed uproariously at the paradox. "Nathan, look," he had remembered her saying, as she lifted it up in full view for him to see. He had groaned and said, "You gotta be kidding me. The church lady had a vibrator?" Then they both had a long-overdue belly laugh. Remembering that, Nathan had reconsidered his mother's reaction to Caroline's words. Just as Nathan was relieved and full of joy to read that his sister had, after all, experienced that kind of pleasure before her untimely death, he imagined his mother had been grateful as well. *Yes, indeed, things are rarely as they seem.* With that thought, he drifted off into a restful sleep.

Grissom's last words did not make a connection with Nathan until about five minutes before his alarm went off in the morning. In a state of clarity, between sleep and awake, Nathan grabbed onto a thought that would haunt him the rest of the day.

Why would Julia Olwen be willing to go to jail for this? Maybe she wasn't.

He popped out of bed with a new spring in his step and headed to the office. He had to stop thinking about the obvious, and start seeing this case through the eyes of a grieving, yet intelligent and sophisticated mother, who could not rest until justice was served on a silver platter to the cold-blooded killer of her only son. *Thank you, Caroline. Julia's trying to tell me the answers. I just have to start listening to what she's saying.*

39.

June 27, 2012

"Lance, dear, don't use such words," said Penelope Eddy, peering through the prison plexiglass at her son.

"Well, who do they think they are? I didn't do it, Mama, you gotta believe me." Lance's face was twisted, as he faked his good-boy routine.

"Of course I do, and I am doing everything to convince Uncle Charles to let me get you a better attorney, but he is insistent that Wayne is the best." She looked at him pleadingly.

"If he's so good, then why am I still in here? And why do you have to listen to him? Dad's money is yours now, and you can do what you want."

Penelope's lip began to quiver. "It takes time for these things to get worked out." She hesitated. "Your father has only been gone for a few days and we're still waiting…." Her voice trailed off. There had been a lot of red tape in getting Clyde Eddy's remains shipped back to the states for a proper burial and memorial service. Eddy noticed that his mother had a look of guilt behind her eyes. He dismissed it as her usual penchant for martyrdom.

Lance Eddy tried to draw pity from his mother, even though he knew that he should be showering her with it. He hated that she had been so easily controlled by his father, and now his uncle. He knew Uncle Charles would be a more formidable competitor for his mother's control than his father had been because at least his father had cared for Lance in some roundabout way. Uncle Charles, on the other hand, hated Lance and would be happy to see him rot in prison.

Lance reached up and placed his palm on the glass. He knew he needed to appeal to her emotion if anything was going to move forward for him. In a sickeningly sweet voice, he said, "Mama, you know I love you." He widened his eyes like a small child.

Penelope dabbed her small nose with a tissue. "Yes, I know. It's just that there is so much going on at the same time and I can hardly think straight. They've got me on some anti-anxiety medication that makes me a little cloudy, Lance. So, I need your Uncle Charles right now. Please understand that."

"I do, I do, Mama. I just want you to be okay." He could barely get the words out, as his anger seethed in his gut. "I think it's time to go now...it's about time for lunch," Lance said abruptly. Penelope looked relieved that the meeting was ending.

"Okay, dear. I hope they are feeding you enough in here," she said, not knowing how to end the conversation.

"Actually," Lance replied, "You could bake me a cake and put a little somethin' in it so I could break outta here." He smiled.

"Now, Lance…" A smile broke through her devastated face. She got up from the hard metal chair and placed her crumpled tissue in her Coach purse. She watched Lance walk away without another word before she turned to leave the visitation area.

Lance did not look back at her. As soon as he turned the corner, he pummeled his fist into the lacquered concrete wall that was representative of his temporary home. The guard led him back to his cell and visions swirled in his head of Julia Olwen, his father, Sheriff Davis, Uncle Charles, his mother, and every smug Sunday School teacher who had ever tried to mold him, as he pictured his hands around each of their necks. And all of them were pleading for Lance Eddy to let them live. As Eddy lied down on his cot, he crossed his feet and folded his arms beneath his head. Thoughts of Joey Olwen unexpectedly surfaced and he felt his brain and body finally calm a bit. *I had to kill him or he would have talked.* It was the boy's innocence. Even if for only a few hours, Joey Olwen had been someone who did not, could not, control Lance Eddy and it felt strangely loving as he remembered the boy's eyes, full of childish fear. The way he remembered looking at his father when he was enraged. He needed to feel that kind of power and innocence again. He needed to get out of this place.

Eddy nodded off to sleep, but after about an hour, he was awakened by a guard who announced that Wayne Beaudreau had arrived for a visit. A sleepy-eyed Eddy was led out of his cell back into the interview room. He saw the overweight, swarthy looking attorney sitting at the table poring over a thick manila file, presumably Eddy's.

The top button on Wayne Beaudreau's oxford shirt was undone to accommodate his oversized neck. Eddy noticed that his tie was loosened a bit under the unbuttoned collar, which gave Eddy the impression that he was not having a particularly pleasant day. *It's about to get worse*, Eddy thought.

"Good afternoon, Lance," Beaudreau said.

"Hey," an unenthusiastic Lance replied, while lazily plopping down in the same chair he sat in two days ago when the sheriff was there. He felt shaky, needing a cigarette.

"They treatin' you okay in here?" Beaudreau folded his hands on the table in front of him, while looking through the cloudy pane of glass.

"What kind of question is that?"

"Nevermind…we need to discuss your case…"

"There is no case!" Lance leaned forward and glared at Beaudreau. "I didn't do it, so what is there to talk about?"

"How did your little talk with the sheriff go? Ya know, I'm still miffed that you refused to let me be there. You're gonna bury yourself if you don't keep your mouth shut. And then there won't be a damn thing I can do to save you."

"Well, that's the problem – you think I need to be saved." Lance shook his head in frustration and then got close to Beaudreau's face. "It didn't go well, *Wayne*. That guy thinks I'm guilty, so no matter what I say, he's gonna try to convince everyone I did it. I swear, they are all mad that I got off on that kid's murder because of their fucking mistakes, so now they've made something up to get me back."

"Because of *their* mistakes?" Beaudreau lowered his voice and peered intensely at Eddy. "You got off because your daddy paid some damn good attorneys to make sure you got a second chance. Don't you forget that. Your daddy is gone now and, quite frankly, I'm pissed off that you don't even seem to care about that."

"You don't know what I care about." Eddy sat back in his chair and looked past Beaudreau at a woman and a couple of kids who were apparently visiting their father. He noticed the little boy, who appeared to be about eight or nine years old. *Too young.*

"Listen, I could take myself off this case and you could get a public defender if you want. Your Uncle Charles would be fine with that, ya know."

Lance rolled his eyes. "Uncle Charles," Lance scoffed. "What a waste of skin. I don't give a rat's ass about Uncle Charles. My mother is the one I care about and I need to get out of here so Uncle Charles doesn't milk her for everything she is now worth."

"C'mon, Lance. Charles is not that way. He doesn't need your mother's fortune. But I do think he cares about her."

"Yeah, and hates me."

"Well, you have caused this family a great deal of anguish."

"A great deal of anguish," mocked Lance. "What about what Clyde did to this family? If mom only knew about the hundreds of women he's screwed. Actually, she probably did know, but she's so fucking weak that she just turned a blind eye to it – kinda like she did when her husband was beating the shit out of her son!" Lance got up abruptly, knocking the chair out from underneath him. "We're done here." He turned and left to go back to the cell.

Wayne Beaudreau shook his head, while gathering up his file papers. He yelled, "I'll be in touch, Lance."

"Whatever," Lance yelled back, while waving his arm in the air.

40.

Julia - June, 2012

The calendar said June, as Julia turned its page. Claire's husband Steve owned an insurance agency in town and she could always count on him to keep her in calendars. Today, she wished she didn't know what day it was because it was getting to be that time. She felt a rush of sadness and for the first time in a long time, she was confronted with doubt. This happened occasionally, especially as she was closing in on an important part of the plan. The camera at Lance Eddy's house had been successful. She had managed to accomplish what she needed, although it felt sneaky and unlawful. It was the only really unlawful thing she had done in the scheme of things. She was glad she had managed to be unnoticed and was thankful Eddy's father had set him up in a good quiet, neighborhood where it seemed no one noticed what was going on around them. She felt good about her firearms training and practice, and she was making headway with Eddy on the online gaming front. Just yesterday, she got him to start asking her some fairly personal questions.

"What do your parents do for a living?" He had asked just after he annihilated her in the sixteenth level of *Slash and Burn.*

"Parent," she responded, hoping he would get the reference to only one parent in the house.

"Oh, which one?" he had asked after some hesitation.

"Mom. She's a bartender." Julia wanted Eddy to be thinking *night shift.*

"Cool," he had responded. "Do you get to see your dad ever?"

"Dead. Motorcycle accident. Don't like to talk about it."

It was weird that she was beginning to see him as a person because of their conversations, so she had to continually remind herself that this was not just some kid on the game system. But that it was the monster who had tortured, mutilated and murdered her son. Eddy stopped talking after that, but Julia felt she was gaining his trust. They had been playing online regularly for a few months. She had been careful to only play with him during after school hours and weekends when it was conceivable that Wonka's mom was either at work or in bed sleeping, like early morning or late at night.

Summer was here and she only had a couple of more weeks before she had to make her move to invite him to visit China Grove Road. The timing had to be perfect. It was the one part of the plan that had to work just right or the rest of it was out the window. As she sat down to pick up the gaming controls, Julia thought to herself that she would be a good children's book author. After having spent so much time listening to Joey and his friends, she had become very good at believable dialogue. She had also studied a little about pedophiles and their propensity toward the vulnerable ones. The ones who were neglected. This would be the key to Julia reeling Eddy into her web. Before she could put in a request to play with Buddy666, there he was already poised for a challenge.

Wonka1126: *Hey*
Buddy666: *Ready to get taken down, dude?*
Wonka1126: *Yeah, but can't play long. Mom didn't work last night..be up soon.*

Buddy666:	*OK. Haven't seen ya in awhile*
Wonka1126:	*Got caught after hours. Restrictions.*
Buddy666:	*Sucks*
Wonka1126:	*Yep*
Buddy666:	*U don't want to get in trouble again*
Wonka1126:	*No. She said an hour a day. So ur my hour to day…if I get caught :-)*
Buddy666:	*Thx. I like playing with you*
Wonka1126:	*Me, too. Maybe you can come over sometime. Meet my mom.*
Buddy666:	*She wouldn't like me. Too old.*
Wonka1126:	*How old?*
Buddy666:	*Too. Old as ur mom probably.*
Wonka1126:	*Oh. My uncle plays and he's 24! Well, he used to play. In jail now.*
Buddy666:	*that's a bummer. He lives around here?*
Wonka1126:	*No. California.*
Buddy666:	*Oh, too bad. Well maybe sometime I can meet ur mom.*
Wonka1126:	*OK. She's only 32. She's pretty.*
Buddy666:	*That's nice. Oh, she's young. And you?*
Wonka1126:	*I'm not supposed to say.*
Buddy666:	*Oh. Sorry. Hey, let's play.*
Wonka1126:	*Yes! You will be sorry!*
Buddy666:	*You wish*

Again, Eddy managed to put Julia to shame by dominating the game, but she was surprised that the more she played, the more adept she got at the eye-finger coordination it took to keep up. If nothing else, she figured it was good Alzheimer's prevention for later. Julia hoped she hadn't been too forward with Eddy, but he seemed to be taking the bait. She would wait for him to bring it up in the next few days. That's when she would know he was getting hungry for his next encounter. The more he was craving his little boy fix, the weaker and more he would be prone to making mistakes. If her plan succeeded, it would be the worst mistake of his life and the best decision of hers.

41.

June 27, 2012

Tommy greeted Nathan when he walked into the building, handing him the blood analysis report he had requested the day before. "Nothing out of the ordinary here. Why did you want this extra test done? I mean the lab already determined it was all Julia's blood." Tommy shrugged. "What else is there to find out?"

"Just doin' my *due* diligence." Nathan emphasized his drawl, indicating that he was in charge and didn't feel the need to explain himself. Tommy hated when he got cryptic like this. It usually meant he had something up his sleeve that he was not going to reveal until he could be sure about it. "Let me know if there's anything else I can do," Tommy said with a frustrated tone. He started to walk away, and then turned back around. "Oh, by the way, that Sally chick called this morning. Told Dot she had some information you might be interested in."

"Thanks," Nathan said, appearing not to be interested. Tommy walked off and Nathan thought it was weird that Sally hadn't called his cellphone to tell him that. She had been avoiding him as much as he had been avoiding her in the last couple of days. That was good, he thought. That put her down to about a four on the PPF scale. She wasn't psycho. But she probably was hurt. He would call her back after he looked at the blood analysis report.

Potassium EDTA. Nathan didn't remember seeing that chemical on an analysis report before. He turned to his computer and Googled it. It quickly came up under a web site about vacutainers, the tubes used to collect blood for testing or donation. Apparently, EDTA was a blood coagulant used in vacutainers for blood donation to be stored at blood banks. He was aware that when there was a body at the site of a crime scene, his guys used yellow-topped vacutainers to draw blood from the victim. They contained a preservative of some sort, so he wondered if that's all it was. But EDTA was not in the yellow-tops according to this web site.

"Hey, Dot," Nathan spoke into the intercom on his phone. "Could you get Terry at the lab on the phone?"

"Sure, boss," Dot said. A few minutes later, she broke in. "Terry's on line two."

"Thanks, darlin'." He picked up the line that was flashing. "Terry, how's it goin'?"

"Fine, Sheriff. What can I do for ya?"

"I'm workin' on a case and I just needed a chemistry lesson, if you don't mind."

"Oh, yeah, sure," Terry replied. Nathan detected her Great Lakes accent. She was a transplant from Northern Michigan, and so light-skinned it could blind you when she walked into the room. Her pasty pallor and bleached blonde hair were unattractive to Nathan, but he liked her personality and attention to detail. If anyone knew her chemistry, it was Terry.

"When we take blood from a murder victim, and use those yellow-top tubes, isn't there something in them that preserves the blood for testing?"

"Yeah, it's ACD...acid citrate and dextrose. It aids us in the DNA testing, so we can eliminate individuals or, of course, nail the perpetrators."

"Oh, I see. Do we ever use any other colors...vacutainers,

I mean?" There is a universal color-coding system, with each color indicating what chemicals are added to the tubes used to collect the blood. In his search, he read that pink, blue and purple tops contain EDTA.

"Not since I've been here. The yellow-tops are the most reliable as far as I'm concerned."

"Now, when we take blood samples from a scene, is there anything added to them…any chemicals that might show up on a blood analysis report from you all?"

"Not usually. If anything, distilled water is added to get a wet sample from a dry piece of evidence. Occasionally, ethanol or acetone may be used to pull dried stains off of hard surfaces to get the best DNA yield, or if we're doing some other analysis on the blood, but that's about it. Most of the time, large enough dried samples gives us all we need, as long as we have a good collection sample from the victim using the yellow-tops."

Luckily, in Julia's case, she had just had her yearly physical exam, a few days before the murder, at the hospital where she worked, and a fresh sample of her blood was still available at the lab for testing. It was a stroke of luck that Nathan almost felt was divine. Nathan had interviewed her co-workers the day after the crime scene was discovered, and they had reported that she took a couple of hours off work three days before she went missing to have her yearly exam. *Was that a coincidence?*

"You've been real helpful, Miss Terry. You have a great day now."

"My pleasure, Sheriff. Have a good one," Terry replied and hung up.

Nathan was puzzled, but didn't want to jump to any conclusions before getting more facts. Why did the blood sample used to prove her DNA also have EDTA in it? The sample the doctor took at his office the day before did not show EDTA. It had another chemical in it to preserve the glucose factor so that her blood sugar levels could be assessed. There was enough blood at the scene that he was sure the detectives were able to get an ample amount of wet samples – in places there had been puddles of blood where it appeared Julia had laid for a time before getting up and fighting back. The wet samples had been tested right away, as far as he knew because he got the testing back very quickly. The smaller dryer samples always took a little longer. Why was the EDTA to prevent coagulation present in Julia's blood? It's possible she had been taking some form of blood thinner that might contain the chemical, but the doctor Nathan had interviewed said she was as healthy as could be. Had she been self-medicating for some reason? It didn't make sense, but he decided it probably didn't mean anything. There may have been an herb or something she was taking that had the same makeup. He knew she was into Yoga, so those types tended to follow all kinds of Eastern remedies that could have included something that thinned the blood. He filed the report away in his notebook and turned in his chair to look at the whiteboard, where he and Tommy had drawn a timeline with the known evidence. He decided not to add the EDTA fact to the board yet. As far as Nathan was concerned, they had all they needed by way of actual concrete facts. Even so, he was struggling to put together the story behind the motive. He sat staring at the board when Tommy interrupted him.

"Here's one more thing to make Eddy guilty as sin," Tommy said, throwing a piece of paper onto Nathan's desk.

"What's that?"

"The cigarette butt you retrieved from the shed at the Olwen house?"

"Yeah?" Nathan had completely forgotten about that. *I'm losing my touch.* "Eddy's DNA. He's a Marlboro man and you hate those." Tommy smiled, glad to know something Nathan didn't for a change. "Well, well, well..." Nathan put aside his doubtful thoughts. This is when he would go into attack mode. He stood up and grabbed his sports coat from the back of his chair. "Let's go pay Mr. Eddy another visit. It's confession time." Tommy eagerly smiled. "You got it."

"Oh, by the way," Tommy said. "Centipede got picked up and brought into the jail this morning."

"What? Damn it. What did he do now?" Nathan stopped and turned around to look at Tommy, who was following close behind as they walked toward the door. He hated when his snitches got taken off the streets. "Got into a fight with a dealer. Beat him up pretty bad. Convenience store clerk called one of our guys, who said he tried to call you, but your phone was off or something – it was about three a.m."

I was dreaming about my sister, Nathan remembered. *Dead to the world.* "Looks like we've got two people to visit this mornin' then."

At the jail, Nathan walked into the room where he typically met with prisoners and Eddy was sitting slumped over, elbows on his knees, acting like he was bored. When Nathan opened the door, Eddy looked up and feigned excitement. "Sheriff, I am honored you wanted to see me. This must be visitation day, today. You're my third visitor. Ain't I popular?" He sat back in the chair and crossed his feet in front of him. "I hope one of them was your attorney," Nathan said. "Cause you're gonna need him." Eddy sat up, looking more serious. "I already told you, and everyone else, that I should not be in here."

"Is that right?" Nathan scooted his chair up close to Eddy's and got within inches of his face. His voice was low and intense. "Listen, you dirt bag...the evidence just keeps mounting and mounting. Every damn time I walk into my office, somebody is telling me there is one more thing that shows up pointing to you as the killer. The neighbor, the truck, the gun, you admitting to being at the house on the very night of the murder, and now, low and behold, there's a cigarette butt found in the back shed with your DNA on it. What a coincidence, Mr. Eddy. You a Marlboro man?"

Eddy silently stared into Nathan's eyes. For a few seconds, neither man spoke. Then Eddy broke the silence. "You guys think you're pretty smart, don't ya? Can't you see that somebody on the inside is framing me?" Eddy's voice matched the pitch and intensity of Nathan's. "I just want to know who the hell broke into my house and planted that gun and took a cigarette butt from my place to plant at hers? 'Cause when I find out, my attorney and my wealthy family will be all over your ass, suing you and your so-called genius deputies to high heaven."

Nathan sat back and let out a roar of laughter. "That's rich, Eddy. How old are you? That's sounds like somethin' I used to say to my teacher when the dog ate my homework." He flashed his white smile. "Let me tell you what I think happened. Julia Olwen couldn't stand that you got away with killing her son. In fact, she burned with hate for you. So, that night you went there to meet with some young man? It was her who pretended to be a little boy, Eddy." Nathan was in Eddy's face again. "Yeah, that's right. She pretended to be a little boy online and you took the bait, didn't you?" He could see Eddy squirming at the thought of being deceived by a woman. "You drove over to 1126 China Grove Road, hoping to find some little pre-pubescent kid to fondle and instead, you found Julia Olwen there, didn't you?" Nathan noticed beads of sweat forming on Eddy's forehead. "What then? Did she have a gun pointed at you? I bet she had a few choice words for you, too, didn't she? What'd she say, Eddy? What'd she say?" Nathan had his hands on the arms of the chair Eddy was sitting in. Eddy had moved his head back to create a more comfortable space between them.

"She didn't say nothin'. I'm telling you I didn't go in the house. No one was there!"

"That's bullshit and you know it!" Nathan's voice was getting louder. "She taunted you, didn't she? She made you feel like the little *pecker* you are and you didn't take that well, did you? In fact, I think she took a shot at that little thing and missed, do you remember that? Then, I guess you decided you wanted to keep it, so you wrestled the gun from her and shot her didn't you? You killed her in cold blood, just like you did her son, didn't you?" Nathan was shouting now. "Then what? She fought back didn't she? There's nothin' tougher than an angry mama bear, is there? She fought back and you overpowered her. I'm surprised you didn't rape her, but then again, you can't get it up with women, *can* you?" Eddy appeared to be hyperventilating. "She fought until she didn't have any fight left in her. Then you went out and had a cigarette so you could decide what to do. You found a tarp and some rope in the shed, where you dropped your butt, wrapped her body in it and trucked it off." Nathan moved his chair back and sat still, looking at Eddy's pitiful face, contorted in anger. "Then," Nathan continued, "you drove her somewhere and dumped the body. So, that's what I'd like to know now. Where is she? Eddy, you might as well tell us and admit to all this and then maybe, just maybe, the judge will have some kind of mercy on you. If not, you're gonna fry. Now, I know you just lost your daddy, and I'm truly sorry for that," Nathan said, faking sympathy, "but I wonder what he would be saying if I told him what you had done? I wonder what your *mama* is gonna think?"

"You leave her out of this!" Eddy was more than agitated.

"Well, I would if you would just come clean. She doesn't have to know anything other than you did it. But if this goes to trial, she'll know every sordid detail about who you really are. How you like to rape and kill little boys. Don't ya, Eddy? How'd you kill that little Olwen boy? Did you overpower him, too? Remind me how you do it," Nathan taunted.

"Go to hell!" Eddy shouted and then sat silent for a few seconds, trying to regain his composure. Nathan shot him a disgusting glance. "And just for the record," Eddy continued, arrogantly, surprising Nathan. "I don't shoot my victims. I like to put my hands around their necks and watch the blood drain from their faces. I don't even own a gun…oh, except for the one they planted in my house." Nathan remembered that Joey Olwen had died by strangulation. He felt the blood rush to his face and he jumped out of his chair and went for Eddy, but Tommy anticipated it and grabbed Nathan before he could make contact.

"Whoa, whoa," Tommy said calmly, restraining Nathan. "C'mon Sheriff. I don't think he's gonna talk."

"You got that right," Eddy said. "I have nothin' to say to you jokers."

"Mark my words," Nathan said as he turned to walk out of the room, straightening his jacket. "I will be sitting in the front row on the day of your execution. Then we'll see who the joker is." Nathan shoved the chair against the table and left the room.

It occurred to Nathan that Eddy, in fact, did not own a gun and as far as Nathan knew, he had never shot one. In all the media coverage, it had come out that Clyde Eddy, who owned a quite elaborate hunting lodge in the North Georgia mountains, never could get his son to take an interest in hunting or anything that would look like he was one of the male members of the family. That didn't mean he couldn't have shot Julia, or cut her up into pieces. Eddy was definitely deranged enough to have done it. Still, Nathan couldn't shake the feeling that Eddy was right about a few of the details.

"You wanna go pay Centipede a visit while we're here?" Tommy asked in the hallway.

"Not today. I'm likely to try to kick his ass, too, with the mood I'm in." Nathan leaned against the wall. "I'll come back later. I need to cool off."

"I know. Man. I thought you were gonna strangle Eddy right there," Tommy marveled. "I would have let ya, but then I would have had to explain to the judge at your hearing why you had clocked the guy," he teased.

"Yeah, thanks, Pork. I wasn't really gonna do it. I just wanted to scare the bejesus out of him. There's somethin' about wanting to see a piece of slime like that have the fear of God in his eyes, ya know?"

"Yep. I feel that." Tommy nodded in agreement.

"Let's get outta here." Nathan said, while pointing to the door. As they walked to the car, Nathan couldn't stop thinking about his interview with Eddy. "I'll be damned," Nathan said. "That bastard just admitted to killing the Olwen kid and there's not a damn thing we can do about it...shit!" Nathan kicked the front tire on his car in frustration. Then he pulled out a pack of cigarettes to light up. *There is no immunity for the disease I'm gonna plague you with, Eddy.*

42.

Julia - June 11, 2012

"You seem distracted today," Sonya said. Julia looked as if she would rather be having a root canal than sitting on the couch in front of Dr. Pierce. "Oh, I'm sorry," said Julia. "I guess it's just been a busy week. I have a lot on my mind." She fidgeted with a paper clip she had picked up from the coffee table. Her mind was racing with thoughts of impending events, wishing she could spill her guts to Dr. Pierce, but knowing she had to play this coolly until the very end. "I talked with my cousin the other day."

"The one in California?" Sonya asked.

"Yes, Celeste. She has been working and is doing much better, so I'm thinking about going out to visit her." Julia had no idea why she was telling Dr. Pierce this, but it was helping her fill the space in the room.

"That sounds like a plan." Sonya shifted her body in the tapestry chair she always sat in during Julia's appointments. Julia noticed that she appeared to have gained some weight as she looked slightly more uncomfortable in the chair than usual. "So, I'm going to go out on a limb here. Something tells me you are not okay. Has something happened that you would like to talk about?"

Julia regretted not having cancelled today's appointment because she knew it would be hard to fool Dr. Pierce. She was worse than a mother who had eyes in the back of her head. Somehow she had this incredible guilt radar that detected the slightest signal in Julia. "I can't really say something has happened, except for in my own twisted brain." Julia scoffed, and then hesitated before going on. She put the paper clip down and sat back on the couch, tucking her foot under her thigh to get comfortable. "This is going to sound strange, I know, but have you ever felt like you didn't really exist? Like you were just going through the motions and at some point, your life would just end, and everything you thought and felt had no real meaning?"

"Yes, I suppose I've had times like that."

Really? Julia couldn't picture that. "I mean, it's like you spend most of your life worrying about getting a job, paying the water bill, what to make for dinner, burying your only son, and after a while, it all seems to be a big blur. Does any of it really matter?" She knew she was being facetious.

"You're trying to minimize Joey's death?"

"What?"

"You included his death in a list of mundane events, even though you were being sarcastic...I think. Maybe you are tired of trying to find meaning in that – and you would like it to be as meaningless as paying the water bill. But that's not possible. You're tired of it." Sonya raised her eyebrows, waiting for Julia to respond.

Julia felt undone, revealed, naked before this woman who barely knew her, but seemed to be able to turn her inside out, even when Julia was simply trying to pretend to have something to say. She guessed Dr. Pierce was probably right, even though it was all said in frustration.

"That makes sense, I guess. I am tired. Tired of thinking about it all."

"It's okay to not think about it."

"Is it? Really? How? How does a mother just start over? As if nothing happened?" Julia was surprised that she was actually asking something that would have real significance to her in the near future.

"Is that what you want to do? Start over?"

"Maybe. A whole new life. One that doesn't include pretending that everything is okay. It will never be okay, so I have to keep thinking about it or else it feels like I'm pretending."

"I think I understand, Julia. It's common for victim's families to be afraid to let go – to let go of the memories and the tragedy – or else someone like Joey will slip into the past and be forgotten. Are you afraid you will forget him?"

Julia had thought about this deeply in the last few weeks. *Forgetting? No. Avenging? Absolutely.* "I will never forget him. That's impossible. I will think about him every day, I am sure of it. I just don't know what to do with myself after the grief. First there was the initial shock of it all, then a year of preparing for a trial, then the trial and the total disappointment of that. Now, there's the grief about the lack of closure. But then what? I can't seem to make sense of anything. I guess that's what I was trying to say in the beginning. It makes me question my very existence. It's like you feel when you are standing at the ocean or the Grand Canyon and you feel incredibly small and insignificant. What part could I possibly play in this world that would matter compared to the universe that is full of complicated processes that have nothing to do with me?"

Sonya was listening intently, nodding with interest at every word Julia uttered. "Every great philosopher who ever lived has asked these same questions, Julia. You are asking them because you have experienced a great loss, followed by a huge disappointment. Sometimes it takes loss to help us gain our bearings of appreciating what we have and what we can and cannot control. You just don't have your bearings yet. Give it time."

As Sonya said those words, Julia's eyes were drawn to the plaque on Sonya's desk behind her therapist's chair that displayed the Serenity Prayer. *The courage to change the things you can and the wisdom to know the difference.* She was right. This tragedy had made Julia understand clearly what she could and could not change or control. She relished in the few things she had determined she could change, even though she had to contemplate them in private.

"I guess…" Julia went silent. "Do you believe in Karma?" She decided to switch topics.

"Do you?" There was that blasted answering a question with a question thing that Sonya did so masterfully. *Was she always on guard?*

"Not in the theological sense of the word. But I guess I believe that good increases the chances of good, and bad, bad. Lance Eddy. Do you think he'll eventually put out so much bad that only bad can come to him?"

"Would that help you achieve closure? To know that he is suffering?" Sonya questioned again.

"I guess my question is about him eventually bringing on his own suffering, through his own negative actions."

"I suppose it's a tenant of most religions," Sonya replied. "In the Christian religion, it's the golden rule. In Judaism, it's about the sacrifice. I wonder if you can walk away from this and start over, even if you cannot witness his suffering. Maybe it will be internal and you will never know about it. Would that be enough for you?"

Julia hadn't expected Dr. Pierce to be so insightful with her today. She was planning on announcing she was going to take a break because she was doing much better, knowing she would not be coming back anytime soon. This was supposed to be a pleasant goodbye, but it was turning into a discomfort that Julia hadn't anticipated. The last thing she needed right now was to be feeling doubt or, God forbid, indifference toward Lance Eddy.

"No, in fact, it would not." Julia felt her heart quicken as she spoke emphatically. "He hurt my little boy. My sweet, innocent little boy." The lump in her throat was growing. "He tortured and raped him. He put his hands around his neck and watched the life disappear from my son, for God's sake. And I should just hope he suffers some internal pain? He's a freaking monster. He doesn't have the capacity to suffer!" Julia put her face in her hands and wept quietly. Sonya Pierce sat motionless, nodding her head in agreement, but not saying a word, letting Julia feel the gravity of it. Julia was painfully reminded that no matter what she did, a man like Eddy would never be capable of feeling even a sliver of remorse, even if he was within an inch of his own demise. That created a wave of hopelessness in her that she had felt before, but sitting here, only a few short days before she would transform her own life, she needed to be absolutely sure she was doing it for the right reasons.

"It's the other boys," Julia said, wiping her wet nose and taking a deep breath to gain her composure. "I could walk away and start over if I didn't worry about who else he was going to victimize. That haunts me every day. Every night, I go to bed and worry that he's preying on someone just like Joey and it makes me sick to my stomach. That's why it's so hard to walk way."

"I understand," Sonya said. "So, you will find a way eventually. Maybe to create awareness, to help other parents, to work on prevention – create a new law." Sonya was smiling. That's what people do who have experienced what you have been through. You find ways to stop the pain by making sure it doesn't happen to someone else. You'll find your way, Julia, but you may not be ready for that yet. Like I said, give it some time."

The session ended without Julia saying a proper goodbye to Dr. Pierce. She couldn't very well tell her she was "all better" after she had just had a meltdown on her couch. It was obvious she was not okay and needed another appointment, which she scheduled for the following week when she was pretty sure she would not be available to attend. For the first time, she reached out and hugged Dr. Pierce as she was leaving. Dr. Pierce hugged her back, to Julia's surprise, as if she knew – or maybe Julia was simply sensitive to the moment. She left the office feeling like she did have a plan to find her way. It didn't include creating awareness or forging a piece of legislation in Joey's name. It included making Eddy pay and she knew exactly what had to be done.

43.

June 27, 2012

Lana's Diner hadn't changed in forty years. Nathan remembered his parents taking him there when he was a little kid. His favorite dinner he had ordered every time was meatloaf and mashed potatoes, with a side of fried okra and collard greens. Lana's had the best southern cooking in the Southeast, although Nathan had to admit that he didn't exactly travel the countryside testing the kitchens. He just knew that it was a treat when he was younger because his parents didn't eat out much, but when they did, it was usually at Lana's. As far as he knew, Lana herself never really worked there. Legend has it that there was no one ever called Lana to begin with. The Mercers, J.D. and Marge, opened this place in the 1960s. Apparently, Marge's first grandchild had an oversized tongue and couldn't pronounce "Nana." Instead it came out as "Lana," that Marge took on as a new identity, and consequently, Lana's Diner was founded. Nathan wondered if anything would have been different had it been called after its real namesake, Marge's Diner. As he contemplated that thought, he heard the bells on the door clang and in walked a crisp and beautiful Sally Tate.

"Sorry I'm late," she announced as she scooted into the booth across from Nathan.

"No worries," Nathan said while taking a drink of his sweet tea. He felt unusually awkward.

"Now, wait a minute, Sheriff Davis. I know we now have this little history, or whatever you want to call it, but since when do you not greet me in a proper manner?" Sally set her purse aside and folded her hands on the table.

"Excuse me?"

"Tater Tot? I don't get a Tater Tot anymore?"

Nathan laughed. "I thought you hated that."

Sally scolded him with a stare. "Women 101, Nathan. You should have learned this in kindergarten. A girl only knows if a guy likes her by how much he teases her. We say we hate it, but it's actually a pretty good gauge."

Tish, with her Dolly Parton hairdo and chest to match, walked up to the table just then to get Sally's drink order.

"Just water please…with lemon," Sally said. Tish gave her a look that seemed to say *Damn Northerners*.

"Okay, Tater," Nathan said, "I hear you've got something to tell me. We never did get to talk about your experiences with the Eddys, but at this point, I think we've got him nailed to the floor, so I'm not sure I need to know much more."

"That's great," Sally said genuinely. "He's quite the monster, isn't he?"

"Yep."

"Well, you know Clyde Eddy died in that crash last week, so I've been covering the developments around that for the station. It's rumored now that there may have been foul play."

"Yeah, I heard about that. Not surprising, though, given his business dealings. I suppose there's a long list of suspects – people who would have benefitted from his death."

"Like his brother Charles." Sally waited for that to sink in.

"Charles?" Nathan looked surprised. "Why on earth would he want his brother dead?"

"It's not clear yet, but there are rumors – a leak to the press, actually, but don't quote me on this – that Charles and

Penelope – Clyde's widow?" She gave Nathan a suggestive nod. "They had it goin' on." Sally moved her head back and forth, and smiled proudly.

"You're kidding me." Nathan sat back and pondered the implications. He knew that Charles hated Lance for the grief he was causing his mother, but Nathan never once suspected that it was because of a love interest between the two. Maybe Charles hated Lance because he loved Penelope and had planned on being with her, sans her deranged son. Is it possible that Charles may have framed Lance so that he would be out of the way, too? He might not have wanted to waste any more time or money on that sick and wayward son of hers. This could be a problem, thought Nathan. He knew he had to be absolutely sure the right guy was going away for Julia's murder.

"Wow, I've got to make sure this is a solid case against Lance Eddy, don't I?"

"That's why I thought you might want to know what I've found out, but not yet confirmed. It could be really big. Let's just say Charles and Penelope are found to be conspirators, and if Lance Eddy gets acquitted again, then he ends up with a big chunk of the Eddy fortune. That would be a nightmare."

Nathan realized that Sally and he were not thinking about this the same way. She was thinking it had to do with where the Eddy fortune would end up. Nathan was going in a completely different direction, but he didn't want to let on to Sally. He just wanted to nail the right guy. Neither Sally, nor anyone else for that matter, knew the doubts that Nathan had been having about Eddy – his insistence that he was innocent, the lack of a body, or evidence of the transportation of it, and the murder being a shooting or stabbing, not a strangling, which was Eddy's preferred method. Also the weird chemical in Julia's blood that is used for storage in blood banks. Had Charles Eddy stolen Julia's blood from a blood bank and used it to look like Lance had murdered her? If so, where was Julia's body? Why would he hide the body? Nathan's brain was a tangle of wires all firing at the same time. *She had a physical three days before the murder.*

"Hey…you still with me?" Sally asked.

"Oh, sorry. This puts a different spin on things for me, so I'm going to have to take another look at what I've got and process." Sally noticed that Nathan had stopped looking at the menu.

"Can we actually order and finish a meal this time?" Sally asked. "I'm starting to get a complex." She smiled.

"Absolutely. I'm having the meatloaf, what about you?" Nathan replied politely, but wanted in the worst way to bolt out of there and get some answers.

44.

Julia - June 15, 2012

_____

The air was crisp, but perfectly warm. Julia felt the cool sand under her feet, perfectly packed and form-fitting to her arch. The sound of the ocean waves crashing against the reef melodically comforted her. She knew she was in an awesome place, but had no sense of space or time. She felt light and free, with a strange content sense of anticipation. As she turned from the azure horizon to look toward the coastal land, a crowd of people all dressed in white cotton was walking toward her. Each one was smiling with an unusual sense of joy. There were young boys and girls, as well as older men and women. A few she recognized. Oh my, there is Grandma Mackenzie. Normally, Julia would have felt tears coming or an anxiety about not understanding what was before her. But instead, she simply felt happy at the expectation of what was about to happen. Then she saw her mother, walking hand in hand with her father. There were other she did not know by name, but somehow she instinctively knew who they were. One was a younger cousin, whom she had never met, but yet she knew her somehow in this place. Everyone in the crowd began to clap and shout and sing songs of praise so glorious that Julia was rapt with pleasure. It occurred to her that they were clapping for her arrival into this paradise. She looked toward the end of the crowd and saw Trent, Joey's father, bringing up the rear. She had never seen such a beautiful smile in all of her life. *He made it*, she said quietly to herself. And she felt genuine love for him and all the others. And then she saw Sheila, who was beautiful with all of her hair and her breasts intact. Made whole again. *Good for her.* She noticed how beautiful her mother looked, with her hair pulled up into a wispy bun. There wasn't a wrinkle on her face. And her father! He was strong and tan. She wanted to run directly into his arms so he could twirl her around like he did when she was a little girl. Just as she was about to run toward him, the crowd parted and a young boy came walking through the middle. At first, it didn't register with Julia who he was – just that he was a young boy, almost a teenager, with dark blond hair and a charming grin. It was Joey. "Mom," he shouted, to Julia's delight.

"Yes!" Julia was overcome with nothing but pure elation and happiness. They embraced and she smelled the familiar fragrance of his hair, the way it used to smell after he had bathed, before she kissed him goodnight. In that moment, Julia forgot why she was there. It was if she had always been there, with him. They sat down on the beach, while everyone gathered around, watching them build a sandcastle together. They laughed and talked and smiled lovingly at each other. Julia loved having her parents there to witness the moment. Occasionally, her mother reached down and added to the artwork. Memories faded...and Julia had no idea why she was in this place other than she was supposed to be. This was where everyone was supposed to be.

A loud ring began to pierce the air. It got louder and louder until Julia was startled out of her dream to hear her cell phone ringing. It took her a few seconds to get her bearings. She picked up her phone from the bedside table and noticed it was Claire calling. She silenced the phone, knowing she could not possibly talk in this moment. She wanted to go back to sleep and reenter the dream. She closed her eyes, but knew it would not happen. Julia Olwen turned over and buried her face into the cotton sheets and began to softly whimper. *Already there. I am already there, Joey. I can't wait to see you. I can't wait.* She cried until the phone rang a second time twenty minutes later. It was Claire again. And Julia silenced it again.

She got up and drug herself into the kitchen to make the coffee, without being able to shake the dream from her thoughts. It was so perfect, so beautiful, so right. She couldn't help wondering if what she was about to do would jeopardize her chances of getting to that place. She poured coffee into her favorite cup that Joey had bought her for their last Christmas together. It was purple with a big "J" on the front. *Huh.* She stopped at a thought. *Trent made it.* Julia smiled at the idea that Joey's father was with him and she felt a slight wave of jealous urgency. *Please, God, don't punish me for what I am about to do.*

45.

June 27, 2012

"So, what's going on?" Tommy asked, sitting across from Nathan's desk with pen and notebook in hand. Nathan had called Tommy and Dorothy and asked them to meet him as soon as he returned from lunch.

"Yeah, it sounded like you were all worked up over something when you called earlier," Dorothy added. Her hair was in an up-do, which reminded Nathan of his mother.

Nathan got up and closed the door to his office. "Okay…" He took a deep breath. "We've got a lot to do in a little bit of time." Tommy began to write in his notebook. Nathan continued. "I'm looking for emails that she may have exchanged with anyone in the Eddy."

Tommy interrupted. "Whoa, slow down, what are you thinking we're gonna find?"

"Damn it, Pork, I don't have time to go into all the details. I'm asking you to get some specific information for me. Can we just leave it at that for now?" Nathan felt annoyed that Tommy was pushing him for more than he was ready to give.

Tommy shrugged. "Sure." He looked disappointed.

"Sorry, but I've just been handed some information that could take this case in a different direction, but you know how I am. I know where I'm going with this, but I just need you to trust me. Got it?"

"Got it," Tommy said, more relaxed.

"So, emails between Julia and anyone in the Eddy family. I also want to know if she had any online journals, where she may have recorded her thoughts and feelings. I have this abbreviated one she wrote by hand, but it's pretty generic. Also, emails to close friends, like Claire Brownlee, that might have indicated what she was thinking and doing right before her disappearance. Oh yeah, and there was something mentioned before about her doing an internet search of women's prisons. Find out more about that." Nathan turned his attention to Dorothy.

"Dot, I need to meet with Penelope Eddy, ask her a few questions about her son. If she can do it tomorrow, that would be awesome. I need to be gentle on this one, so don't push too hard, but you'll have to jump through some hoops to get to her, I'm sure. If she wants her attorney present, that's fine. I don't want it to seem like I'm going after her, but that I just need to clear up some things about Lance and could use her help."

"*Are* you going after her?" Tommy asked.

Nathan shook his head and stayed focused on Dorothy.

"I think I can take care of that for ya, Sheriff," Dorothy responded.

"Okay, next, I want both of you to dig up everything and anything you can on Charles Eddy."

"Which one is that?" Tommy asked.

"Clyde Eddy's brother, Lance's uncle. Pork, you do the legwork and Dot you put it together in a timeline for me if you can."

"What are we looking for?" Tommy asked.

Nathan ignored Tommy after giving him a *don't start* look.

"Okay, okay...I'll see what I can find."

"I wanna know all about his history, his character, his mistresses, times in rehab, his favorite toothpaste, and what time he eats dinner every night."

256

"Seriously?" Tommy asked, joking.

"Yes. Seriously."

"Should I set up an interview with him as well?" Dorothy asked.

"No. He's gonna be sly. He has a lot to protect, so I'd rather know all I can about the guy before actually talking to him. Just get me into see Mrs. Eddy. Any questions?" Nathan knew he had to get answers before the big news broke about Charles' suspected involvement in Clyde Eddy's accident. He was thankful to Sally for the tip and had a passing thought of sending her flowers, but quickly turned his thoughts back to the present.

"Yeah," Tommy replied in two syllables, indicating his frustration. "But I'm gonna leave the details up to you, just like you asked, Sheriff."

"I appreciate that, my man. I've got a hunch about a few things, so the sooner I can get information from you two, and talk to Mrs. Eddy, the sooner I can confirm or not. Got it?"

"Yep," Tommy and Dorothy replied in stereo.

"Great. You guys are the best. Who loves ya now?" Nathan held up his hand to do a fist bump.

"You're a dork," Tommy said, shaking his head and smiling, as he turned to walk out. Before leaving, he turned back around.

"Oh, by the way, I did learn more about Ms. Olwen's financial dealings from the tech department. Apparently, she had been transferring large sums of money to a personal bank account in California — in the name of that cousin of hers. Made me wonder if she knew she might not be around to spend it and wanted to make sure it didn't get tied up in probate or something."

Nathan sat up to focus on Tommy's revelation. "Interesting. Like how much money?"

"Well, she must have gotten a big settlement in that civil suit against Lance Eddy...we're talking hundreds of thousands."

"Uh-oh." Nathan looked worried and sighed. "I hope that doesn't mean she was playing dirty with Charles Eddy."

"Huh?" Tommy looked perplexed.

"Never mind...thanks for the info. Did they find anything else suspicious on the hard drive about her spending habits?"

"Nah, she's pretty squeaky clean...shopping for shoes, med supplies stuff like that."

Nathan remembered his conversation with Mrs. Timko and the diabetic syringes. "Okay, thanks, buddy. I think we're closing in on something. Not sure, what but something. Can you get me a copy of the receipts from the med supply company? I just wanna check something out."

Tommy was tempted to inquire again about why that might be important, but knew it was futile, so he got up and walked out of Nathan's office. Nathan sat back in his chair, putting his feet up on the desk while thinking through what he was going to ask Penelope Eddy. After a few minutes, his thoughts turned to what he knew so far and what he still needed to learn. He turned around and looked at the white board. *This changes things.* Nathan pondered the fact that up until now, Eddy was the obvious suspect. He looked down at his case notebook, where he had written the chain of evidence:

- *Red Ford F150 seen by Mrs. Timko at victim's residence the night of her disappearance*
- *Cast of tire tracks taken at residence match Lance Eddy's red Ford F150*

- *Gun registered in Julia Olwen's name found at Lance Eddy's home*
- *Cigarette butt with Eddy's DNA on it found in shed behind Olwen's home*
- *Large quantity of Julia Olwen's blood (5 pints+) found scattered in her residence*
- *Chemical Potassium EDTA (use to preserve blood at blood banks) found in the blood*
- *No forensic evidence found in Eddy's truck to show that he transported a body*
- *Tarp that Mrs. Timko said Julia used to do yard work was missing from shed*
- *Eddy insists on his innocence; defying his attorney; unlike when he was guilty of Joey Olwen's murder, he stayed silent, following his attorney's advice to the letter*

Nathan added to the list:

- *Eddy says he kills his victims using strangulation, not weapons; believable*
- *Eddy does not own a gun; and presumably has never shot one*
- *Charles Eddy and Penelope Eddy suspected of having an affair; maybe orchestrating Clyde's death; maybe wanting Lance out of the way, too*
- *Large sums of money transferred to California account*

He put his pen down, and thought about the possibilities. Could Charles be the one who was framing his own nephew? If so, how did all that blood get in Julia Olwen's home and where did it come from? Where was Julia? Suddenly, Nathan stood up and started pacing. *EDTA used to preserve blood in blood banks. Julia can't be found. Charles and Julia? Had she made a deal with him to frame Eddy and then disappear into a new life? Was she transferring money from Charles Eddy to a California account or was she setting herself up to disappear?* It would make sense, thought Nathan. She was a nurse. She could have drawn her own blood, over time. He knew that no one else would have the means, access or motivation. This would be genius. Nathan felt a sense of uneasiness about it, though. They were an unlikely pair. Everything he had heard about Julia Olwen would point to her being a moral, upstanding citizen. It was hard to see her as anything else but a grieving mother. Nathan had come to like her and understood her anger toward Eddy. It didn't make sense that she would make a deal with the devil to avenge her son, if it meant she would indirectly participate in Clyde Eddy's fatal accident. Would she really be motivated by money? Nathan didn't think so, but knew anything was possible. *If my first hypothesis is true, I'm gonna take them both down.*

If she had done this on her own, Julia Olwen was a freaking hero.

46.

Julia - June 15, 2012

Julia, still relishing in her dream, loved this time of morning that was so full of hope and positive energy. In a few short hours, she would say goodbye to life as she knew it. There were a lot of unknowns, but maybe for the first time in two years, she could end her obsessive thinking, her anger at the universe, her constant sense of helplessness, and just simply be. It was a welcome thought, but then she remembered Claire, and Mrs. Timko, her church friends, her co-workers. Mr. Peabody at the dry cleaners. Tiffany at the bank. The guy with the weird name at the post office who always flirted with her. What was his name? Walford Pukenberry, she remembered. No wonder he didn't have a wife or a girlfriend. She managed a sleepy smile. *My name is Julia Pukenberry and this is my husband Wally. Oh my. It takes all kinds to make the world go 'round.* Julia laughed to herself. One kind she was glad the world would be rid of was the likes of Lance Irving Eddy. For that, she felt an anticipated sense of accomplishment. Her efforts would pay off, she was sure of it. She just had to keep her cool for one more day, she hoped.

Today would be the day that Julia would make the invitation to Eddy and hoped he would take the bait. If that happened, she had to make some final bank transfers and talk to Claire one last time. It had been plaguing her thoughts all night long. She wondered how she was going to say "goodbye" without sounding like she was saying goodbye. Chances were slim that she would ever see Claire again, and if she did, it would be under unpleasant circumstances. She also needed to make sure Mrs. Timko had everything she needed. The last thing on her list was a final visit to Precious Gardens to see Joey. She dreaded that the most. If he were in her shoes, would she tell him to do what she was doing? Probably not. On one hand, she felt like a guilty child, needing to apologize to her son for what she was about to do. On the other hand, she wanted him to give her a high-five for accomplishing what justice could not do for him after his death.

She took her coffee onto the front porch to enjoy the coolness before the heat of a June summer day expanded everything. She liked the early morning in summer, when everything living was waking up and making "good morning" noises. She loved her country setting, where life was isolated, safe and innocent, apart from civilization. As the sign said above her front door, it truly epitomized "Rest for the Weary." She was undeniably weary, but this normally innocent and safe place was about to turn into the black widow's web for Eddy. And the fact that she would soon be inviting him to place his disgusting footprints on her soil, turned her stomach upside down and into knots. She thought of how he had violated her previous home, and her child, without a second thought. She took one last gulp of her coffee and an equal breath of fresh air. It was time.

Julia sat down on the couch in front of the television. This would be a prime time for a twelve-year-old to be doing his morning game playing. Julia remembered that Joey was still an early riser at that age, but in a couple of years, he would probably be one of those teenagers who would sleep until noon on a summer day. She had relished in the fact that she had been able to have mornings with him in the summer before he died. She felt saddened at the thought that there would never be the opportunity for her to yell at him to get out of bed in the afternoon, hear his voice crack and deepen, or see the hair growing softly on his chin and upper lip. She would miss all of that because of some sick person's urges to hurt and kill a child. Julia picked up the game control and typed in her ID and password to log on. Buddy666 was furiously playing like a child himself.

Wonka1126:	*Mornin'*
Buddy666:	*Hey, wonkie*
Wonka1126:	*Hate that*
Buddy666:	*I know ;-)*
Wonka1126:	*Guess what?*
Wonka1126:	*I got some new games yesterday. Pure Pestilence and the Stalking Dead*
Buddy666:	*Cool. Those aren't online yet.*
Wonka1126:	*I know. I might have my cousin come over sometime to play*
Buddy666:	*That's good*
Wonka1126:	*You still wanna meet my mom?*
Buddy666:	*??*
Wonka1126:	*You'd like her*
Buddy666:	*Maybe. She might not like me.*
Wonka1126:	*I could tell her ur comin over to play Stalkers. She always wants to meet my friends first.*
Buddy666:	*Dunno. Maybe I could meet you first. Moms don't like guys online too much*
Wonka1126:	*Oh yeah. Ur probably right.*

Wonka1126:	*She is working tomorrow night. Five til midnight I think. Wanna come over? You can see her picture.*
Buddy666:	*Maybe just to meet for a minute. I can bring you a game I like but never play anymore. Soldiers of Doom. Whats ur moms name?*
Wonka1126:	*Janie*
Buddy666:	*That's pretty*
Wonka1126:	*So is she*
Buddy666:	*Ur really tryin to fix her up, aren't u?*
Wonka1126:	*Yeah with someone I can game with, man!*
Buddy666:	*How do I know where to go?*
Wonka1126:	*We're in Regal*
Buddy666:	*Oh. That's a little drive from her in Marlowe*
Wonka1126:	*Maybe. You have a car?*
Buddy666:	*Sure do*
Wonka1126:	*What kind?*
Buddy666:	*Ford truck. F150*
Wonka1126:	*Cool. What color?*
Buddy666:	*Red*
Wonka1126:	*Cooler*
Buddy666:	*Are u sure she would be okay with it? If she's not there?*
Wonka1126:	*Don't know. If she finds out, I'll tell her ur a friend from the online games. She'll be okay. She likes to play sometimes, too, so u guys could play together.*
Buddy666:	*Awesome. Ok. Well, I'll let you know tomorrow if I'm comin or not.*
Wonka1126:	*Okay. I hope you do. I like u. U r cool.*
Buddy666:	*Thx. Lets stop yappin' and start playin'!*

Julia knew she had taken a risk at the end of her messaging, and hoped it had not sounded too suspicious. But they had played on enough occasions that she felt they had built some trust between them. She was hoping that Eddy was hungry for admiration from a young boy, which would cause him to take risks to get more of it. Julia played a few rounds of *The Annihilator* with Eddy, and then before signing off, she messaged her address to him without another word. She hoped that if he lost contact with her, he would be more likely to come by. She would check back later in the afternoon to see if he had responded.

She leaned back and sat quietly, eyes closed, meditating on all that she had done so far and what she may have missed or still had to do to be prepared for the next day. She was glad her contact with Eddy would soon come to an end. She was tired of the bitter aftertaste, the psychological stain, she was always left with after encounters with him. Not much longer now. One more deposit and she would be ready. Her thoughts turned to Claire and she picked up the phone to call her back.

"Hey, sweetie. Sorry I missed your call. Wanna get together today?"

47.

June 28, 2012

Lance Irving Eddy lay on his six-foot-long cot, trying to pass the time that went by so slowly that he thought he could feel the hair growing out from underneath his scalp. He hated the anxious feeling of wanting time to go by quicker than the clock would allow. He was tapping his toes together to the beat in his head from a Metallica song he used to listen to when the high school jocks would piss him off.

Just then, Eddy was interrupted by the guard, announcing he had another visitor. *For God's sake*, thought Eddy. *Why don't they leave me the hell alone? If it's not my attorney busting me out of here, I couldn't care less who wants to see me.*

"Who is it?" Eddy snapped at the guard.

"Don't know. Not my job to tell ya who it is. My job is to get your ass up there, now let's go." The guard walked into the cell, prepared to manhandle Eddy, but he got up from the cot, seeing what was about to happen.

"Okay, okay." Eddy shot the guard an angry glance, stepping out of the cell and allowing the guard to cuff him for the walk down the long, blank hallway.

Eddy opened the door to the visitation area and was able to see the outline of a tall, lanky man with gray hair sitting at the table on the other side of the glass. He plopped down into the metal chair and let out a deep sigh.

"Well look what the cat drug in," he said to his Uncle Charles after picking up the phone receiver.

"Good afternoon, Lance."

Eddy thought his uncle looked beat up and disheveled. It was a change from his usual wool sport coat and crisply ironed oxford shirt.

"Whatever." Eddy was unenthused. "Is my mother okay? Why are you here?"

"Yes, Penelope is fine. She's still shaken up, of course, but doing as well as can be expected. Still no word about when we can expect your father's remains to return from Australia so that we can have a proper memorial service."

"Well, I'm in no hurry for that. I don't think they're gonna let me out of here anytime soon." Eddy leaned forward toward the glass, as if he was about to whisper something to Charles. "Listen, I don't know what you've been told about why I'm in here, but I didn't do this thing. I swear it. Somebody is framing me for some reason – I bet it's one of those cops who investigated the other case and is pissed off that he didn't get me thrown in prison before. Somebody offed that stupid bitch and then decided to pin it on me. So, I need you to hire somebody – a PI or someone who can dig deep into this and figure out who put the evidence there."

"Lance, I'll see what I can do, but…" Charles hesitated.

"But what? Shit, Charles, you've got more money than God, I bet. Can't you just do this one thing for me? Tell my mother. She'll make it happen." Eddy's eyes were piercing through Charles' blank gaze.

"You aren't the only one in this family the cops are after," Charles said. Eddy detected a hint of fear. "You are probably going to be hearing some rumors in the next few days, which is why I am here. I wouldn't give you the time of day if it wasn't for your mother…but now that some things have been discovered, there is no way to hide it. She asked me to come, but I doubt I can get you to understand."

"What the hell are you talking about? Hide what? Understand what?" Eddy was showing his agitation.

"Some of what is being said is true, but the worst of it is not. You have to believe me, Lance. I know I haven't been your favorite person, just like you haven't been mine, but in times like these, family must stick together."

"Damn it, Charles!" Eddy's voice was rising, and the guard stepped forward to warn him to keep it down or he would end the visit.

"Okay, calm down, Lance. It's your mother and me...we have gotten close over the last couple of years."

"Close? What the hell does that mean?"

"You know your dad has never been much of a father or a husband..."

Eddy noticed that Charles forehead was becoming moist with sweat. Suddenly he realized what Charles was trying to tell him.

"Are you tellin' me that you've been boinking my mother?" Eddy leaned back, clearly racked with disbelief. "Well, well, well...you have some balls after all."

"Lance, please."

"Please, shit! You fucking piece of garbage. If there wasn't glass between us, I would be kickin' your ass right about now." The guard stepped up again and gave a hand gesture to show he was serious.

"Listen! There's no time for this macho crap right now." Charles' hands were shaking, even though they were folded on the table.

"What time is it, then Uncle Charles? What time *is* it? Time to take the wife, let the kid rot in jail, and live in the lap of the luxury that my father created. You're pretty good. Yeah, you're good. So, why did you need to come here and tell me? You wanna apologize for stickin' it to my dad and boinkin' my old lady?"

"No." Charles lowered his head for a second, then looked at Lance intently. "Your mother asked me to come because she's just so distraught over everything that has happened lately."

Figures, thought Eddy. She had never been able to show any backbone, especially where her son was concerned.

"Lance, they are trying to say that I had something to do with your dad's accident. That I somehow conspired to have him killed...so...so your mother and I could benefit from his estate. I am now being investigated because someone leaked information to the press about my affair with your mother."

"Geez." Eddy shook his head. "I bet Aunt Marie is just rollin' around in her grave right now, angrier than a hornet. She just died last year, for God's sake. How long have you and my mother been carryin' on like this?"

Charles looked at Eddy as if he had just been caught with a girly magazine.

"Are you kidding me?" Eddy began to do the math in his head. "You and my mom were doin' it while Aunt Marie was on her death bed, weren't you? You piece of scum..."

"Wait a minute, let's talk about who the scum is in this room, boy." Charles regained his confidence for a moment, as a vein popped out on his right temple. "There's no doubt in my mind what happened to that little kid and I think your daddy was dead wrong in making sure you got off. He should have let you take your punishment." Charles got up to leave. "That's what I'm gonna do. Have a nice life, Lance. It's clear, you are not gonna be of any comfort to your mother, so don't expect anything...anything...from me." Charles started to walk away.

"Wait!" Eddy yelled after him.

Charles looked back in disgust. "Go to hell, Lance." And he walked out of the visitor area door.

Eddy was escorted back to his cell, where he kicked his cot with as much force as he could put behind it. "Damn it!" He knew he had blown it with his uncle. As he began to put together the pieces, he realized that Charles may have been prepared to help him out if Eddy had listened. It was clear to Eddy that his mother had sent Charles to him to break the news, hoping Eddy would not judge her. Instead, he had once again alienated his uncle, and now, his mother. Eddy knocked fiercely on the door to get the guard's attention.

"What is it?" the guard yelled.

"I need to speak to my attorney! I need to speak to Wayne Beaudreau." Eddy sat down on his cot and leaned over, elbows on his knees, staring at the floor. *She's a slut. A no good slut.* Thoughts of his mother who played the good Christian dominated his mind. The one who never protected him, but acted like she did. The one who enjoyed his father's money while screwing his uncle. *No good slut.* He grimaced, anxious to talk to Beaudreau and get out of this place. He would make sure Charles Eddy ended up in jail instead.

48.

June 28, 2012

It had been almost a week since Nathan had been in front of the Eddy's opulent home, arresting Lance for Julia's murder. He noticed it looked much different in the daytime. In the middle of the circular driveway where Nathan had put Eddy into his car, there was a large white marble angelic statue, with a fountain of running water cascading over it into a small pond, which was surrounded by mature shrubbery and every kind of rose bush imaginable. The fragrant roses nearly overwhelmed Nathan, as he got out of his car, nodding at the Asian gentleman who was carefully pruning them. The stairs were marble as well, wider at the bottom and narrowing toward the door. He approached the front door and before he could ring the doorbell, the door opened and a short, elderly woman in an apron greeted him.

"Good morning, Sheriff," she said pleasantly. "Mrs. Eddy is expecting you."

Nathan was led through the wide and open foyer, into a sitting room furnished with antiques and a vast array of what looked like expensive China in huge glass front cabinets. Maybe Meissen, or something of that sort. Nathan's mother had a few pieces of the good stuff, but nothing like this. He was glad to see that Charles was not with Penelope when she entered the room. He hoped that Charles would be lying low, not wanting to be seen with her these days, but maybe he didn't care what anyone thought about their so-called affair. Seeing her alone, though, meant Nathan would have a better chance of getting the kind of information he was looking for.

"Good morning, Mrs. Eddy." Nathan extended his hand to hers, which was small and cold, and she only offered him a few fingers. Hating limp handshakes, he grasped her tiny fingers and used his left hand to cover her whole hand to show his confidence.

"I apologize for the way I had to visit your home last week, and I didn't get to tell you how sorry I am for your loss of Mr. Eddy."

"Thank you, Sheriff. That means a lot." She motioned for him to sit on the embroidered settee behind him.

"I hear you are experiencing a delay in getting his remains back to the states."

"Yes, well, Charles is handling that, but...." Her voice trailed off and then she motioned for her maid to leave the room. Her voice became like a whisper and Nathan turned his best ear toward her to grasp what she was saying.

"What they are saying about him...about us...it's terrible. I hope that is not why you are here. I don't think I can take any more nonsense. I just want to know what you can tell me about my son."

Nathan felt genuinely sorry for Penelope Eddy, as she seemed to be the type who had been protected all of her life from the real world, and lately, she'd had her share of needing to face reality.

"Well, I don't listen to what the news people are saying, I can assure you of that. I'll leave the rumors up to the Marlowe County guys. I'm here to ask you a few questions about Lance, if you don't mind."

Mrs. Eddy's face softened, and Nathan hoped his demeanor had won her trust. "Of course. I know you think he did this horrible thing to that boy's mother, but I just can't think of why he would. It makes no sense to me and I can tell you that he was very distraught when he heard about it." Penelope Eddy looked worrisome, past Nathan, toward the window where the gardener was pruning the rose bushes.

Distraught? Right. Nathan knew that Eddy hadn't even remembered the name of his young victim's mother, let alone have any sympathy for her. But he was not going to correct Mrs. Eddy.

"Did Lance say where he was the night of her murder? He told us where he was, but there is no one to corroborate his story. I thought maybe you may have remembered something about that." He saw in her eyes that she was searching her memory for anything that might be a match to what Lance had claimed. Eventually, she lowered her head and stared at her thumbs that were revolving around each other in her clasped hands. "I'm sorry, Sheriff. My memory is not what it used to be. In the last few months, Lance and I haven't talked that much. You know his father...well..."

"Go on, Mrs. Eddy." Nathan could hear the soft buzz of the gardener's electric shears trimming close to the window. A good thirty seconds went by before Mrs. Eddy spoke, but he was determined to wait her out.

"I really can't talk about Clyde right now. I'm sure you understand."

"Of course," Nathan said. He could already tell the rumors about she and Charles were correct. He detected more guilt than sadness in her. "I'm wondering, though, if you can recall anything your husband may have said, or Charles even, about what Lance had been doing on the night of the murder. Anything could help, Mrs. Eddy."

"No, no...there's nothing." He believed her.

"Okay, I know this is difficult." Nathan moved closer to her and put his right hand on her forearm, covering a diamond tennis bracelet that he figured was worth more than his car. "Let's go in a different direction. You said Lance was distraught to hear about the death of little Joey's mother. Why was that?" Nathan could tell she was nervous, probably recognizing that she had only attributed the quote to Lance to make him sound innocent.

"Oh, I can't really say. I don't know if distraught is the right word. He was upset to find that out. You know he did not hurt that boy, and he would never hurt anyone else. He has his problems, but kill a little child and then kill the mother? My son is *not* a monster, Sheriff." Penelope's gaze was stern.

"Well, for your sake, Mrs. Eddy, I hope you are right. Your family has endured enough pain in the last week, and years for that matter." Nathan hesitated before going on. "If I were you, and I am surely not…but if I were, I could imagine how hard it would be to have the men in your life coming under so much slander. First your son is accused of a murder he did not commit, then your husband being blamed for paying off a judge to get an acquittal. Then your son being accused for another murder, your husband getting killed, and now this thing with Charles…" He watched intently has she absorbed his words. "It's more than most women could take I imagine. Have you seen Lance lately? I stopped by the jail a couple of times and he seems to be getting his rest and enough food. But he is surely angry that we are focusing on him."

"Yes, well, I have not been able to make it there with all that's going on." She looked at Nathan with pleading eyes. "But I know that Charles visited him this morning and reported that it did not go so well."

Nathan's interest was piqued, as he had not anticipated she would be so open. "Oh, that's good, Mrs. Eddy. I'm glad to hear that family members are taking some of the burden from you. Do you think Charles might know something about Eddy's whereabouts on the night of Julia's murder? I mean, if they are close…"

Penelope Eddy interrupted. "Oh, no, I am not saying that. Charles and Lance were very different people. I simply asked Charles to go and talk to Lance. I was afraid he would hear things, but I didn't think I had the strength to address it with him." Her head went back down to staring at her thumbs again.

Nathan's curiosity was growing. *Why would Charles visit his nephew in jail to break the news about the affair to him?* Then it occurred to Nathan that Charles might be afraid that Lance would make up stories about his and Mrs. Eddy's involvement in her husband's accident, just to get Charles out of the way. This was clearly a battle between uncle and son for the mother and her money.

"So, what did Charles have to say about it? It sounds as if you have talked to him since yesterday." Penelope looked up, realizing she had made a mistake in divulging this level of communication between her and Charles.

"Not much, I am afraid. He called me briefly to mention that he had talked to Lance, but that it didn't seem to help Lance feel any sense of security. You know, Charles is helping me with finances, paying for Lance's attorney and such, until everything is cleared up…" Penelope's voice cracked and she began to cry.

"I understand. There is a lot to think about and I'm sure Mr. Eddy didn't bother you with the details of his business dealings."

"Never," she whimpered. "I never wanted to know. That's why Charles…"

"Why Charles?" Nathan waited, holding his breath.

"Charles assured me that everything would be okay. That whatever happened, it would all be okay. I don't know, Sheriff, I really can't tell you anything more."

Nathan realized that if she was guilty of anything, it was allowing men to be in control of her life to the point that she could easily ignore what was going on around her. He got up to leave, confident she had nothing more of value to tell him.

"I appreciate you talking to me, Mrs. Eddy," he said.

"I'm afraid I haven't given you anything to help Lance, have I?" She patted her tear-stained cheek with her fingertips.

"Well, you've been honest with me, and that's all I can expect." He handed her his business card. "If you think of anything that might be helpful to us, please call me any time – day or night."

"Thank you, I will." Mrs. Eddy's summoned the maid, who escorted Nathan through the foyer again, and out of the home. As he was exiting, he noticed a man's wool sport coat hanging over a green overstuffed upholstered chair in the foyer. *Charles is either here now or hasn't gone far.* The maid closed the door behind him. The gardener was gathering cuttings from the ground, but didn't look up this time. Nathan got in his car and drove out of the golf course neighborhood.

The eyes always have it, he thought, as he nodded to the gate guard and pulled out onto the main road. The maid was nervous, the jacket was conspicuous, and Mrs. Eddy was conveniently clueless, but likely came by that honestly. If anyone can clear this up now, it will be Charles Eddy.

"Dot," Nathan said into his Blackberry. "I need Charles Eddy to come down for an interview. Tell him it has to do with his visit to Lance Eddy yesterday. Now that I know he was there, I have a good reason to interview him again."

"Okay, Sheriff. By the way, not much on the guy, except he is a successful business man. He's actually quite the philanthropist. No skeletons that we can dig up so far."

"Not surprising. Keep looking. I want to make this guy squirm when he comes in, so any dirt will be helpful."

Initially, Nathan had done a general interview with Charles Eddy after Lance's arrest to find out if he had any information about Lance Eddy's life and recent whereabouts. The only thing he remembered from their conversation was that Charles clearly had no respect for his nephew, but wasn't willing to throw his family under the bus to satisfy his own disdain for the man. He claimed that he had not seen Lance much since the murder trial and had no idea what he had been up to since. That seemed plausible at the time, but now Nathan wondered if they were more connected than he had let on. He thought he could eliminate Charles and Lance conspiring to murder Clyde Eddy, as it seemed clear that they had no affection toward one another, but Nathan also knew to never rule out the seemingly impossible. Just when you think something doesn't make any rational sense, a critical puzzle piece could connect in a way that would make the whole picture seem rational. Nathan wrote a few notes in his casebook, one of which was *Penelope Eddy is not capable of conspiracy, but she wouldn't refuse the benefits of someone else's plan. She needed to continue living the life she had.*

49.

June 29, 2012

Wayne Beaudreau put his keys, wallet and cell phone in the plastic bin to be scanned by the metal detector near the Calhoun County jailhouse door. His thoughts turned toward how he was going to convince Lance Eddy to accept a plea deal. The evidence seemed clear, and once District Attorney Thornton got it in his head to win a case, he was rarely wrong. The deal seemed fair, given what Beaudrea knew about Lance Eddy's dark side. Now that Clyde Eddy was gone, and with all the rumors about Charles and Penelope, he was ready to be done with this family for good. Yet, in the last twenty years of his law practice, the Eddys had provided him with the bulk of his income. At fifty-nine years old, though, he figured it was a good time to begin slowing down and letting the younger partners in Coates, Collins and Beaudreau to deal with the difficult cases.

"Hands up," the deputy instructed Beaudreau as he walked through the X-ray booth. Beaudreau raised his hands above his head, revealing his ready-to-pop shirt buttons holding in his oversized gut. Getting older, coupled with a poor diet and stressful job, had allowed him to gain forty pounds that his doctor wanted him to lose. *Why bother?* That's what the cholesterol and hypertension meds were for. After being cleared, he retrieved his belongings and walked down the long corridor to the visitation room, where he had a seat in the familiarly dank interview room, noticing the coldness of the metal chair beneath him. He pulled out Lance's file from his weathered leather brief case and waited for Eddy to appear.

"Hey Wayne," Eddy said, more subdued than Beaudreau was used to from Eddy.

"Good afternoon, Lance," Beaudreau spoke up while looking through the file. He looked up to see a fatigued Eddy. "They treating you okay in here?"

Eddy just nodded, staring at the file that Beaudreau had opened. He had one hand on his thigh, and the other was nervously tapping on the table.

"What's this about, Lance? They said you demanded to see me. Is there something new you want to talk about?" Beaudreau tried not to show his agitation, especially after Lance's last disobedient move when he had demanded to talk to the sheriff without his attorney. He had no idea why Lance would care to talk to him again when he clearly had no intention of taking his legal advice.

"I gotta get outta here, Wayne. Charles came to see me yesterday. Told me a bunch of crap about him and my mother. Do you know anything about that? What the hell?"

Beaudreau had never seen Lance this genuinely upset, almost human, not even during his last murder trial. He wanted to believe it was because Lance had somehow acquired a heart, but he knew it likely had to do with money or control – wanting to make sure Charles did not get any of the family fortune or the opportunity to be the dominant male in his mother's life.

"There's a lot of rumors going around right now, but you need to stop listening to those and focus on how we can create a solid defense for you. If you want to help your mother, the best thing you can do is get out of here so she can stop worrying about you."

"*Create* a defense?" Lance's eyes became wide and piercing. "I don't need to fucking *create* a defense. I didn't murder that bitch. The proof has to be somewhere that shows I'm innocent. What I wanna know, *Mr.* Beaudreau, is why you haven't hired a PI or someone to investigate this the right way. That derelict of a sheriff is only interested in fingering me and he'll get his way if someone doesn't dig a little deeper."

"Okay, Lance. I understand you are angry, but you have to understand that every piece of evidence points to you. So, tell me, what is your alibi? How did your tire tracks get into that woman's driveway on the very night of her murder? For God's sake, how did her gun end up hidden in your home?" Beaudreau began to sweat with disgust at Eddy's arrogance.

"I don't know, dammit! Somebody is framing me and ya know what? I think it might be Charles. That guy has always hated me and now that he's got my dad out of the way and is into my mother's pants, wouldn't it be convenient to get rid of me as well?" Beaudreau thought he detected tears in Eddy's eyes – the kind that might well up in a spoiled ten-year-old who couldn't get what he wanted. Beaudreau sat back and let out a heavy sigh. He looked down and noticed that one of his buttons had, in fact, popped off, exposing his grayish white t-shirt underneath. Eddy kept going.

"Son of a bitch," Eddy leaned forward, shaking his head. "You're worthless, ya know that? I was lucky you got me out of that last one, but I don't think that had a damn thing to do with your lawyering because my dad…" Eddy stopped, realizing where he was headed. He remained silent for a few seconds before Beaudreau chimed in.

"Your dad. Yeah, your dad bailed you out all right. He's been bailing you out since you were a kid, Lance, and this time…" Beaudreau moved forward, realizing he was getting loud, and reduced his words to a whisper. "This time, your daddy's not here anymore and your mama is now relying on Charles to take care of business. Something tells me Charles will not be so interested in setting you free. If I were you, and thank the good Lord I am not, I would take the DA's deal and be done with it."

"Are you fucking crazy? They want me to spend twenty years in prison. Twenty years! I'll be as old and decrepit as you before I get out."

Beaudreau's level of disgust hit a high point and he got up, shoving the metal chair against the table. "Yeah, I'm crazy all right. Crazy for gettin' involved with this fucked-up family." He gathered his file and placed it back in his briefcase. He threw Eddy a look of disdain and said, "Take the plea deal, Lance. I don't care if you did this one or not. You killed that kid, so do your time, son." Beaudreau opened the door and walked out. Lance Eddy sat stunned. *If I get outta here, Charles Eddy is a dead man.* Lance Eddy went back to his cell and fantasized about how he would torture Charles first and then maybe Beaudreau. Later, he dropped off to sleep on his small little cot, with visions of putting the fear of God in the eyes of both men. For the first time in his life, he wanted to talk to his father.

50.

Julia - June 16, 2012

Her shift ended at seven in the morning, giving Julia plenty of time to make ready her plans for the day. She had prayed. She had spent a little extra time with the gang at work, letting them each know in small ways that she appreciated their camaraderie. An extra "thank you" here and "can I do something for you?" there. She had simply been more mindful of her tone and gratitude than on a regular day. Julia had baked Mrs. Timko's favorite sugar-free chocolate cake with peanut butter icing and delivered it to her in person, making sure she had all she needed to continue getting her medical supplies. She'd had a painful conversation with Claire the night before, trying not to lead on that it might be their last. Claire was more quiet than usual, causing Julia to wonder if something may be wrong at home. At the same time, she didn't want to inquire, for fear that would make her want to stick around rather than carry out the task at hand. She had been very careful not to let emotion of any kind get in the way of what she was about to accomplish and discovered it was one of the most difficult parts of the entire operation, especially with Dr. Pierce. She had trusted Julia was being totally open and honest, and Julia felt a wave of guilt, knowing she would not be showing up for their next appointment. She wondered if Dr. Pierce would think of her as irresponsible or flighty. Then she laughed at herself, as she compared that worry to what she was about to do. *If only I could be irresponsible.*

The pieces were in place, except for one unknown. If Eddy decided not to take the bait and come to the house this evening, she would have to delay her plans. Exhausted, she walked to the hospital parking deck, got in her Nissan Murano, and left the hospital for the last time. With a lump in her throat, she fought back tears and turned on the radio to distract her from thinking about what she was doing. The oldies station was playing an old break-up tune that still could make her surprisingly angry. The driving beat filled Julia's car and she thought how strangely music could mirror real life.

After showering and grabbing a quick breakfast of oatmeal and orange juice, there was still time to check online to see if Eddy had responded to her bait when she had messaged her address to him before signing off the night before. She was both excited and scared when she logged on and saw that he had sent her several messages in response that she had not answered. It seemed he was anxious at her silence. There were several in a row, all from him.

Are you serious about me comin over to ur place?

I dunno if I can…

Will ur mom be there?

How old are u again?

Talk to ya tomorrow.

Then they dropped off with nothing further until this morning. He apparently had decided not to pass up an opportunity after all.

Be there round 7:00 tonite. That a good time?

Julia suddenly gasped and thought for a few long minutes about how best to answer to ensure he would indeed come. Then she wrote:

Cool. Too bad mom works 3-11 tonite, but best that we meet first, huh? You can meet her next time.

Julia's heart skipped a beat when after a brief pause, Buddy666 popped up on her screen again with a simple, *C ya @ 7.*

She only had a few more hours to get ready. It would be the worst and best day of her life, she thought. She would normally go to bed after the night shift, but she knew that sleep would be impossible on this day. The adrenaline in her veins was providing emotional fuel that was foreign to her. *The creep is coming. He's really coming.* The intense mix of fear and elation was something she had not felt until today. She could only hope the natural high within her would allow her to carry out every detail with great precision. This had to be a mistake-free day, and she reminded herself how many people put their lives in her hands every day, as she was able to avoid messing up when the stakes were high – like life and death. She stayed focused on Joey and his pride in her for making sure Eddy would pay for his evil deeds. Before finalizing her plans, Julia Olwen had one more errand to run – a trip to the cemetery to pay her respects to her little boy, her inspiration, her heart. One last trip to visit Joey and place a bouquet of roses from her cutting garden near his headstone. One last opportunity to visit Precious Gardens. It was June 16th. It was time.

51.

June 29, 2012

"Do you recognize this woman?" Nathan slid a recent picture of Julia Olwen across the table toward Charles Eddy, watching closely for anything that would prove to him that Charles was more familiar with her than simply having seen her face on a television new report.

"Sheriff, what…" Charles hesitated, seeming confused. He gave Nathan an imploring look. "I have no idea who this is. And I have no idea what this has to do with me or Lance."

"Really?" Nathan tapped the photo with his index finger. "You have no idea who this is? It's Julia Olwen, the woman your nephew is accused of murdering." Nathan had shown him a photo that had not been released to the press.

"Oh…oh, yes, I guess I do recognize her now…from the trial." Charles shook his head, while staring at the picture. Then he gestured in a way to Nathan that seemed to say *help me out here*. Nathan was somewhat relieved that Charles appeared genuinely confused.

"Have you ever met her personally? Other than maybe at Lance's previous murder trial?"

Nathan watched his eyes intently.

"No, I couldn't have picked her out of a line-up if you needed me to. It's been a long time since then, and quite frankly, I've been a little too busy to watch the news reports."

"Yeah, so I've heard." Nathan grinned, watching Charles Eddy squirm with embarrassment.

"C'mon, Sheriff, I've got enough going on in my family. Could you tell me why you asked me to come down here?"

There was a hint of exhaustion in his demeanor. Nathan decided to take another route. "Just a couple of more questions, Mr. Eddy, and then you can go." Nathan pulled the photo of Julia toward himself and sat back in his chair.

"What do you know about potassium EDTA?"

"Potassium what?"

"EDTA," Nathan responded. "It's a chemical compound used to preserve human blood – such as in blood banks for example. You know, if someone wanted to gather a lot of blood for a specific purpose." Nathan waited to see if Charles' eyes would reveal any discomfort or guilt at his suggestion. He needed to know if she was partnering with Charles or working alone.

"For *what*?" Charles Eddy looked disgusted now, getting even more agitated at the curious line of questioning.

"That's what I was hoping *you* would tell me." Nathan leaned in, this time glaring at Charles Eddy while waiting for his answer.

"Listen, if you think I somehow had something to do with that woman's murder, you are dead wrong!"

"Did I say that?" Nathan asked.

"No, but it seems you are being awfully mysterious here. Just come out and ask me what you are trying to find out, won't you?"

"I apologize, Mr. Eddy. It seems you are getting upset and that was not my intention." Nathan thought he should back down as Charles Eddy was showing his seventy-some years. His hands revealed a slight tremor, his voice quivered, and his eyes looked fearful, as if he were being threatened.

"Let me get to the point," continued Nathan.

"Please do," Charles said.

"What kind of relationship do you have with your nephew?"

"Not a very good one, I'm afraid." Charles backed away from the table and wiped his moist forehead with a handkerchief he had retrieved from his suit coat pocket. "My brother, God rest his soul, tried very hard to do the right thing by that boy, but there was always a problem. When he was a kid, they diagnosed him with something called conduct disorder, whatever the hell that is – excuse my French. Then as he got older, they said he was a sociopath, which I translated to be a simple criminal. Clyde did his best to keep Lance out of trouble – usually by buying his way out – but his mama never could accept that Lance was different. She just thought Clyde was too harsh and that's why Lance was so troubled. At least that's what Lance wanted her to believe. But I knew my brother, dammit, and he was not a child abuser – I mean, he gave him a good whack when the kid needed it, but nobody could have beaten that boy into submission. That's just the story he tells to justify his sick and twisted behavior." Nathan noticed Charles' breathing was becoming labored.

"Mr. Eddy, are you okay?" He touched Charles sleeve.

"Yes, I'm fine. It's just too much…too much to deal with. If you wanna know the truth, Penelope and I were more than just friends because my brother was never around and she needed someone to help her deal with Lance. I gave that to her and now the press has me on trial, thinking I had something to do with Clyde's accident. That's craziness, I tell you – pure and utter craziness." Charles shook his head and gave it another swipe with his handkerchief.

"Well, ya know, Mr. Eddy, the press has to have something to report every day, don't they? What do you think should happen to Lance? Do you think he is guilty of this crime?" Nathan knew the answer to this was the one that would tell him what he needed to know.

Charles Eddy hesitated for about thirty seconds, while he was considering his response. He sat up to the table again and folded his hands on it. "I really don't know, Sheriff. For his mother's sake, I hope he didn't do it and he decides to get some mental help. That would be her greatest desire – and because I care for her – mine, too." Nathan noticed that Charles looked beaten up by his own thoughts. "But if he did kill that boy's mother, just like we all think he killed the boy, then that kid ought to be put away for the rest of his life. The world would be a better place, I hate to admit."

Charles Eddy's eyes met Nathan's boldly. There was no reservation in his gaze, no desire to lead Nathan in one direction or the other. Nathan relaxed, knowing he had what he needed. "Well, you have been very helpful, Mr. Eddy. I am sorry if I upset you, but I'm just trying to do my job. I hope you understand." Charles Eddy was apologetic. "No, no…I apologize for getting so frustrated with you." He shook his head in dismay again. "I haven't slept much in the last few days."

"I hear that," said Nathan. They shook hands, and Nathan patted Charles Eddy on the back as they walked out of the interrogation room together. He watched Eddy leave the building. Then he looked back at Dorothy who was looking on.

"How'd that go?" She asked.

"I'm gettin' closer, Dot."

"Here are copies of those medical receipts you asked Tommy to dig up from Julia Olwen's credit card statements." She handed him a few sheets of paper.

Nathan studied them closely. Most of the orders were for insulin products, which reminded him of his conversation with Mrs. Timko and the arrangement she made with Julia to help her get the proper supplies. Then his eyes were drawn to the first order receipt. Not insulin. Vacutainers. Pink tops. The kind that contain EDTA.

Dorothy noticed Nathan's mouth widening into a full-blown grin. "You look like you just won the lottery," Dorothy mused.

"Hot diggety dog, Dot!" Nathan shouted while slapping his hands together.

"What?" Dorothy looked at him quizzically.

Nathan quickly calmed his enthusiasm and then asked excitedly, "Get me a plane reservation to Santa Barbara, California, ASAP. I'm gonna pay a visit to one Miss Celeste Edmund."

"Who?" Dot stared with a worried gaze.

"Never mind. Just get me that reservation. I need to leave as soon as possible."

Nathan walked briskly back to his office, with his heart pounding in anticipation. He stopped abruptly and walked back to Dorothy's desk to cover his tracks.

"Do me a favor, darlin'. Don't mention my excitement to Tommy just yet. It's a hunch, but it might be nothing."

Dorothy swiped her fingers across her lips as if zipping them shut. "Secret's safe with me, boss."

He didn't want to be too confident, but he was pretty sure he was about to expose the secret of the century.

52.

June 29, 2012

Nathan put two pair of Dockers, a couple of golf shirts, socks and boxers in an overnight bag, with his Dopp kit, and rushed out of the house to get to the airport by five o'clock. Dot had indeed gotten the earliest flight out of Atlanta, which he hadn't expected to be that evening. He was glad, though, to be on his way to getting this case settled once and for all. Tommy had done some background work and discovered Julia Olwen's cousin's address in Santa Barbara. Celeste Edmund was the woman Julia had apparently been helping financially and who would likely be the key to helping Nathan place the last puzzle pieces together. If his suspicions were right, he would return to Atlanta with one less burden on his shoulders.

The plane to Santa Barbara was luckily not full, so Nathan was able to spread out among the two empty seats next to him – laying out his files and laptop to work on some other cases that he had put aside in the past two weeks. Two hours into the four and a half hour flight, he was getting sleepy, so he leaned back in his seat to rest his eyes, placing the ear buds to the inflight radio in his ears. He drifted into a light sleep, listening to an unfamiliar, but haunting Maroon 5 tune.

He saw Julia Olwen's face, her chestnut brown eyes communicating a kindness and warmth to him that he had not experienced from a woman before. He reached out to touch her face with the back of his hand, and she smiled, then blinked slowly, looking as sleepy as he felt. Her skin was as soft as silk, her breath warm on his hand. He couldn't hear her, but she mouthed the words "Thank you," then closed her eyes, pressing his hand more firmly against her cheek. He wasn't sure what he had done to illicit her words, but he liked her light grip that was meant to keep his hand against her longer. He reached out with his other hand to pull her closer. He wanted to kiss her lips – they were glistening – pink and inviting. Her dark hair fell around her face naturally, landing on her shoulders, turning up slightly at the ends. He longed to feel her near him. Just as he put his hand gently on the back of her head, she relaxed her grip on his other hand, pulling it down in front of her. She began to laugh, pulling back and teasing him. He noticed the cross on her neck, like the one in her photos, lying against her smooth neckline. She lifted his hand and placed it this time on the golden cross. He felt the coldness of it in his fingers, against the warmth of her chest and the roundness of her breasts on his palm. He smiled at her playfulness, but felt uncertain. He couldn't figure out what she was trying to communicate to him and he felt completely within her spell of beauty and kindness. Then she came closer and allowed him to move in to kiss her. Their lips touched lightly, just enough to send electricity through his veins…

"Sir…sir…please return your seat to its upright position," Nathan heard a voice, but it was distant and muffled.

"Sir?" It became clearer.

Nathan opened his eyes and a brightly bleached, blonde fifty-something flight attendant was looking at him, slightly annoyed. "We're about to land in Santa Barbara, sir. Please put your tray table up and return your seat to its upright position." Her voice was robotic and monotone.

"Oh, sorry," he said while pushing the button to adjust the seat and lifting the small plastic table into its locked position. Nathan stretched his arms over his head, and then rubbed his eyes, looking out of the window to the lights below. Somewhere down there is the light of Celeste Edmund and he couldn't wait to darken her doorstep in the morning.

53.

June 30, 2012

The vibrant coral hibiscus was in full bloom on Julia's back patio, flanked by soft pink bougainvillea trailing up the trellis that divided the patio area and her neighbor's back yard. The inviting fragrance of fresh flowers on a June morning was something she had missed in the last few years. She had been too busy grieving to notice that the aroma could symbolize anything other than funeral decorations. She was now ready to live for her future, rather than dwell anymore on the past. She picked up her coffee cup and sipped from it – this time tasting the Bailey's Irish Creamer she had picked up at the grocery just the other day. She took in a deep breath of cool summer air and felt like she could float away if she willed herself to do so. It was in moments like these that she felt she could feel Joey's laughter and happiness surrounding her. Maybe she was crazy, but in the last couple of weeks, it seemed she had an assurance that he was finally okay – that he could be released from having to take care of her any longer. She was content to live her best life now, knowing she would see him in due time, whenever it was her time to have the privilege to do so. Yet, at the same time, she knew she was already there. She could live in both worlds at once. She now had a renewed sense of wanting to help the children who she was working with at her new job on the children's cancer ward at the hospital. Their smiles and fight to live amazed her every day. She often saw a smile like Joey's in one of them and truly believed he was helping her make their lives easier, healthier, worth living. She didn't have to do this work. After all, the settlement from the

Eddy family civil suit was quite substantial. She would be set for life. But no amount of money could change her or change what had happened to her. The kids that she helped would get to live. The ones who didn't would tell Joey that she tried.

Through the back screen door that led out to her patio, Julia thought she heard the doorbell ring at the front door. She got up and put her ear to the screen, and determined that someone must be at the door – maybe one of the neighborhood children who wanted to play with her new cat Chelsea. She opened the screen door and went through her kitchen to the front of her small, Victorian bungalow. She opened the door, and to her surprise, found a handsome, somewhat familiar-looking gentleman.

Nathan was instantly blown away by her beauty. It was just as he had seen her in the photos, only more real, warmer, more feminine. She had no makeup on, nor did she need it. Her hair was pulled up, but youthful wisps of it framed her face. She looked happy. Nathan flashed his most charming smile and she returned it, just like in his dream.

"May I help you?" she asked politely.

"Celeste Edmund?" he asked.

"Yes, what can I do for you?"

54.

June 30, 2012

Standing at Celeste Edmund's front door, Nathan was guarded about how to proceed, as it was entirely possible that Julia Olwen's cousin was the spitting image of her, but he rather doubted it would be to this degree. "Sheriff Nathan Davis. Calhoun County, Georgia." He showed her his badge. "May I come in?"

Her smile turned to what looked like a concerned surprise. "Uh…of course." She stepped aside, motioning for him to enter. "What is this about?"

Nathan grinned to himself as he took a seat on her Pottery Barn couch, which looked bright and new – not something he would expect to see in a struggling single mother's home.

"Do you have children, Ms. Edmund?" He looked around.

"Why do you ask?" she fidgeted nervously.

"Oh, no reason, other than we may be discussing things you wouldn't want them to hear."

"I see," she said. "No…no children."

"I'm here on official business…regarding the disappearance of your cousin Julia Olwen. I understand she had been in contact with you recently."

"Uh…yes." She stood up. "Would you like a cup of coffee, Sheriff?"

"As a matter of fact, that would be wonderful. I'm a little groggy from the long flight here."

"Cream or sugar?"

"Yes, both…thank you."

She left the room and went into the kitchen. Nathan got up and began to look around the room. It was obviously a newly furnished place in a big ticket area of town. *Civil suit…Eddy's money…awesome.* There were pictures of Joey Olwen scattered everywhere – on the fireplace mantel, on the sofa table, and on a table next to an overstuffed chair. The one on the mantel was the familiar photo often shown in the media – with his baseball cap on, posing in an at-bat stance. She came back into the room with two cups of coffee. Her eyes tried to hide the worry, but Nathan could not be fooled. She handed him his cup and noticed he had been looking at Joey's photo on the mantel.

"When is the last time you talked to your cousin, Ms. Edmund?"

"Celeste, please call me Celeste." She lowered herself to the couch with coffee in hand.

"Okay, Celeste." Nathan nodded and smiled, knowing this would not last long.

"It's been a while, really, I can't remember exactly."

Nathan took a seat next to her, deciding to be as kind and gentle as he possibly could.

"What do you know about the chemical compound potassium EDTA?" He said, matter-of-factly.

"What?" She was caught off guard.

"It's a compound that is in those pink-top vacutainers – you know the ones used to collect blood to be stored at a blood bank. I understand you are a nurse, so I figured you would know something about that."

Julia's face paled.

"Are you okay…Celeste?"

"Yes." She had spilled a bit of coffee on her Nike hoodie and was patting it dry. Nathan thought she looked extremely sexy in her relaxed attire. He also knew by her eyes that he was piercing her soul. He decided to end the charade to calm her discomfort.

"Listen," Nathan said with generosity. "I am not here to create any problems for you. You have not committed any crimes that I know of. I'll have to look, but I don't think it's a crime to totally trash your own house with your own blood and then disappear. That's your prerogative." He noticed her take in a deep and sudden breath. "Now, I do have questions about how you got that gun into Lance Eddy's home without his knowledge, but I might be willing to overlook that tiny possible break-in if you'll kindly tell me how you pulled the rest of it off." Nathan was using his most gentle, soft and southern drawl to indicate to her that he was not a threat. Her shoulders dropped and she placed her coffee gently on the table in front of her. Then she lowered her head into her hands.

Nathan put his hand on her back and began to pat it gently.

"Julia. It is Julia, isn't it?" He whispered to her. She nodded affirmatively.

"You've been through a lot in these last few years. No one could possibly understand. I know I can't imagine the pain and heartache. When I see pictures of that precious little guy of yours, it's unbelievable how anyone could hurt him, let alone torture him, like Eddy did. Every cop I know within a hundred miles of Atlanta has wanted to see him pay for that." Nathan started laughing heartily. "And who da thunk a smart, sexy little thing like you would finally be the one to pull it off?" He reached down and put his hand under her chin, pulling it up until her eyes met his. They were watery. "If I were you, though, I'd not make a shrine of your kid in this house or your new friends will be asking a whole lot of intrusive questions." He smiled kindly.

"I...I don't know what to say." Her bewilderment touched Nathan.

"It's okay." He felt genuine admiration for her. "We'll figure this out." He pulled her close and she leaned into him and began to sob. He held her there for several minutes, his arm around her shoulder and her head buried in his chest. He had never felt so much respect for anyone's pain as he had in that moment.

"Now what?" she asked softly, through her tears.

"Now, Julia Olwen, I get the pleasure of hearing the whole story – how you made it happen. I wanna know every detail. And to think all this time, I thought *I* was the smartest detective in Calhoun County. Now I got me some competition, I do believe." He poured on the Southern charm.

"I have one question first," Julia said sheepishly.

"Shoot."

"Where is he now...Lance Eddy?"

"He's in the Calhoun County jail waiting to be tried for your murder. Rumor has it, no one, not even his own attorney, is standing by him. He'd be smart to take the plea deal Thornton is offering, but I actually think he's arrogant enough to go through a trial. God knows that family has enough money to drag it out. We'll see."

Julia smiled for the first time since he arrived. "Good. That's very good." She sat silently for a moment, taking in the news. "Another cup of coffee?" She asked, while getting up to head for the kitchen. She wobbled a little, not realizing the toll this visit from Nathan was taking on her.

"Whoa…you okay?" Nathan asked, concerned, as he reached out to steady her.

"Yeah." She balanced herself for a second before standing up. "Maybe too much caffeine…and a little too much excitement. I was planning on this being a fairly normal day off."

"Right," Nathan said apologetically. "You sit here and I'll get another cup. How about some orange juice or something for you instead?"

"That would be great." Julia sat back down, emotionally exhausted. "There's some on the top shelf of the fridge."

Nathan made his way to her kitchen, his mind reeling with questions, and also with anxiety about what this meant for the future. Eddy was exactly where he belonged. But Sheriff Davis was a man of honor. For the moment, though, he was going to enjoy the present company and listen to the most intriguing tale of his life.

55.

June 30, 2012

"So," Julia started after taking the glass of juice from Nathan, who was settling back down on the couch with a fresh cup of coffee. "How did you figure it out? How did you know I was framing him?"

Nathan smiled slightly and took in a deep breath, knowing this was not going to be a short conversation. He had hoped he could be the one asking the questions, but he knew he needed to put her mind at ease if he was going to get her full story.

"First of all, there were a lot of things that didn't add up." He went on to explain to her that all reports pointed to a healer, not a killer, so even though she had intended for everyone to think it was an attempted murder gone wrong, he had trouble buying into it. He also reported that although Eddy was a terrible human being, it was believable when Eddy said he didn't do it.

"I have a thing about how to read a person's eyes," Nathan said confidently, but a bit embarrassed at his obvious pride. He noticed Julia's face going from serious to adoring. He continued. "My gut was telling me he didn't do it, even though the evidence was overwhelming. And there was no evidence that a body had been removed and transported anywhere...God, I have so many questions for you...but I'll finish my side and then you can fill in the blanks." Nathan told her about Clyde Eddy's accident and his brother's indiscretions with Clyde's wife. He also mentioned his suspicions that she and Charles Eddy may have conspired to frame Lance Eddy, to which she choked and nearly spewed her wine.

"You're kidding, right?" she asked. "That would never happen. I was definitely acting alone, but that is so interesting that the plane crash happened and the affair came to light as you were investigating. I couldn't have planned for a better smoke screen, huh?" Julia was now smiling proudly.

"Well, that's true, but you had no idea whose county you were in, *Ms. Olwen*. I'm the kinda guy who leaves no rock unturned." Nathan was enjoying the banter, forgetting for a moment that he still had to make a decision about what to do with the beautiful woman sitting next to him. "So, all I needed to do was talk to Charles and Penelope Eddy and it was clear to me that there was no conspiracy going on, but there were unexplained facts – such as the preservative chemical that seemed to be in all the blood that was at your home." He waited for Julia to respond.

"Yeah, if I made any mistake, it was in not considering anyone would notice or care about that stuff in the pink-tops. I didn't even remember the name of the chemical until you told me today. Dumb, dumb, dumb." Julia thumped her head with the heal of her palm.

"Okay, now my turn," Nathan said anxiously. He sat up on the couch leaning his forearms on his thighs, intent on getting the final pieces of the puzzle explained. "How did you gather so much of your blood? How long did that take?"

"Oh...well, that took a few months. It all started when the medical supply company screwed up an order for insulin syringes for my neighbor." Julia looked sad at the memory. "They sent me pink-top collection tubes instead. I was so angry and understood why she was so frustrated with them, but then the light bulb went on that I could actually draw enough blood over time, preserve it, and use it to cover the crime scene. So, I ordered more of them and kept my own blood bank. I figured I drew about a pint every three weeks – you really can't do more than that and stay healthy."

"That's why you searched the internet for how much blood can you lose before you die. You needed to know how much you would have to leave behind."

"Ooops, you saw that. You guys are good," Julia responded.

"And you used your credit card to order the pink-tops."

"Ahhh…I didn't think that you would try to get the actual order receipts. Okay, I'm an amateur, what can I say?"

"Did you see the search on my computer for life in a women's prison?" She asked eagerly, while pulling a pillow from the couch to her chest. "That was a plant I wanted you to find."

"We did, but I had a hard time buying that one. You? In a women's prison?" Nathan chuckled. "Not so much."

Julia laughed in agreement.

"What about the gun and the cigarette butt?" Nathan asked more seriously.

"*That*…" Julia hesitated. "Maybe I shouldn't…" She was concerned that Nathan would think poorly of her.

"C'mon," Nathan cajoled. "The ante is up, so you might as well tell all at this point."

"Okay, well, I placed a hidden camera across the street from his house to figure out his daily patterns and noticed that he never locked his door when he left to make his morning and evening visits to the local QuikTrip."

"Hidden camera?" Nathan laughed, still amazed at her chutzpah. She continued without reacting to Nathan's enjoyment. "So, I went there one morning and waited for him to leave. I knew it took him seventeen minutes to do what he did each time, so I figured I had half that time to get in and out without being noticed." Julia became silent and put her head down as if she was being chastised.

"Hey, keep going...this is good stuff," Nathan said eagerly.

Julia looked up and smiled slightly, feeling the deep emotion of what she had done for the first time in weeks. "It was difficult," she continued. "I entered the devil's den that day – the home of the man who murdered my son."

Nathan realized he had gotten caught up in the story and had forgotten her pain for a moment. He reached over and patted her shoulder. "I'm sorry," he said. "I bet that was awful."

"Yeah, to say the least. But I was determined to stay focused. So, I ran in there shortly after he left, put the gun in the box in the top of his bedroom closet and on my way out, I noticed an ashtray full of butts next to his easy chair, and just grabbed one. I neded DNA. The smoking gun." Tears had formed in Julia's eyes.

"So why did you put it in the shed? The cigarette butt. I might not have found it. I only went out there because I was trying to find out how he might have gotten your body out of there."

"Exactly. I didn't want it to be too obvious." Julia smiled.

"You thought of it all, didn't you?" Nathan shook his head in amazement.

"I'm a nurse. I always have to be thinking about the process necessary to help someone recuperate. You can't afford to miss a step. So, I tried to view it the way someone like you might approach it – only backwards."

"Hmmmm...that makes sense, I guess. Now tell me when. *When* did you decide to do all of this? Frame Eddy and completely leave your friends and life in Regal?" He saw that he had stung something in her.

"I'm sorry, Sheriff. This is a lot to process. Can we take a break for now?" Nathan wanted to hold her in the worst way because he could see she was still tortured by what she had done. "It's a huge relief to be able to talk to someone like this about something I've been keeping to myself for almost a year. But my head feels like it's going to split in two."

"I understand." Nathan was not satisfied and had more questions to ask, but he also understood her fatigue. "We'll process this a little at a time." Just then, Nathan's phone rang – the Bonanza theme song. Julia looked at him and chuckled. "Really?" she said teasingly. He grinned back at her and looked down at the phone screen. It was Tommy.

"Hey, Sheriff," Tommy said when Nathan answered.

"Pork. What's up?"

"Just thought you might want to know that Eddy took the deal."

56.

June 30, 2012

Nathan's heart skipped a beat at the news that Eddy was prepared to go to prison for a crime Nathan now knew he had not committed. "What?" Nathan wanted to be sure he heard Tommy correctly.

"Yeah, apparently Charles Eddy and that attorney, Beaudreau, got together and pressured him. Told him that he was gonna face a trial alone with a court-appointed attorney if he didn't take the deal. Guess that's what happens when you're a despicable human being – when the chips are down, nobody believes you, not even your own family."

"Wow...that's amazing." Nathan was still stunned, looking at Julia who was trying to figure out what was making the handsome sheriff look so bewildered.

"So, how's it going in California?" Tommy asked.

"Well, doesn't much matter now, does it?"

"Guess not, but you never know when these guys are gonna rescind. Until he gets in front of a judge, he could turn back the other way."

"Yeah, I hear ya," said Nathan. He reached over and took Julia's hand and squeezed it. He sat speechless for a few seconds. Then he looked at Julia's face, and thought she couldn't look more innocent and lovely. "No leads here," he continued. "It was a dead end, so I'll see ya tomorrow, I guess?"

"Okay, boss. Have a safe trip back."

Nathan hung up the phone and sighed. "He took the deal...Eddy copped a plea." He was staring into Julia's eyes, not sure whether he should dance her around the room or finish his coffee and leave. Now that he had put the puzzle pieces together, the adrenaline rush for him was over and in a split second a strange dilemma began to form within him. He loved putting away the bad guys, and Eddy was definitely a bad guy – but Julia Olwen was alive and well. She was sitting in front of him with tears of joy covering her angelic face. She looked up and said, "Thank you, God." Then she turned to Nathan and took both of his hands in hers. "Thank you, Sheriff. You could have told whoever that was that I was not dead. But you didn't." Julia's demeanor changed when she saw confusion in Nathan's eyes. "Oh...oh no. I've misread you, haven't I?"

"I don't know what to say," Nathan said. "It's not like an innocent man is going to jail. He may be innocent of murdering you, but we all know what he did to your boy."

"Yes, Sheriff, I know that better than anyone." Her voice began to shake with anger. For the first time in months, Julia was afraid her plan was about to dissolve right before her eyes – her new life would abruptly end and then what about the children? What would Eddy do if he was set free? Her tenacity was unmistakable. "My son," she declared emphatically, "my son was sexually assaulted, tortured and strangled to death at the hands of that...that thing. All for his own pleasure. I cannot...I *will not* let him do that to another child...to another mother. I won't!" Julia had gotten up from the couch without even realizing it, and was looking down at Nathan with fury in her eyes and a finger in his face. "So, Sheriff, do what you have to do, I suppose, but no matter what happens to me, as soon as I am able, I will *kill* that man. In fact, this was his easy way out. I always knew that if this didn't work, I would have nothing to lose by finding a way to torture and strangle him myself. Without Joey, I have very little to live for and I know where I am going when I leave this God-forsaken world. In fact, I am already there." She sat back down and crossed her arms like a stubborn child. "I'm already there. So, just do what you have to do." Her voice trailed off while Nathan sat silently, trying to absorb all that had just transpired.

"Julia," he said calmly. "May I call you Julia?"

She nodded without looking at him. He got up to take off his sport coat and returned to the couch to face her.

"And please call me Nathan," he continued.

Julia was exhausted with emotion, but was relieved by Nathan's kindness. There was something about him that comforted her. Maybe it was his stature or the fact that he was so impressed by what she had accomplished. Whatever it was, she desperately wanted him on her side, not on anyone else's.

"From everything everyone has told me about you, there could not be a more loving, caring mother and friend. I never met you, but with all I have learned about you, it's felt like I've really known you. You are not going to murder Lance Eddy. You can't."

Julia interrupted. "You did meet me." She smiled slightly. Nathan looked puzzled.

"A few months ago. I almost got into an accident on Route 42 and had pulled over to compose myself. The next thing I knew, blue lights were flashing and a tall, handsome man approached my car to make sure I was okay." She could see the wheels turning in Nathan's head.

"Ahhhhh...I think I do remember that. That was *you*?"

"Yeah, I guess I made a great impression, huh?" she teased.

"Well, it was dark...."

"Uh huh, and I had been crying, and had my hair in a ponytail, and wasn't exactly looking like a fashion model."

"You were crying? I hadn't noticed, but then again my ex-wife always accused me of not knowing when she had been crying either." Nathan laughed. Julia wondered if he was still single.

"Well," she responded, while thinking of the present irony. "I had just purchased the gun from the sporting goods store and it was lying on the front seat. I was so freaking worried that you were going to know it was there. I can't tell you how relieved I was when you didn't ask me what was in the shopping bag."

Nathan laughed. "Oh, no...that's another thing I learned from my ex-wife."

Good looking and witty, thought Julia. She wondered if she still had it in her to charm him into her way of thinking about the crime-that-wasn't-really-a-crime she had just pulled off. Not being a very good manipulator, she decided to keep trying the honest approach.

"So, what are *you* going to do?" Julia became serious again. "Either way, I know what I am going to do, so the ball is in your court." She was hoping her confidence would weaken his doubt.

"You do, do you? What are you going to do? If I leave here today and keep your secret with me, what will you do?"

"I will live my new life, knowing that maybe a hundred little boys are safe from Lance Eddy. And I'll take some pleasure in the fact that he will not be free to live his life after he took my son's."

"And if I take you back with me to announce to the world that you are alive and well?" Nathan was most interested in this response. Julia looked away, as if feeling shamed. "I will face the consequences." She sat staring ahead, lost in the thought of that kind of defeat. "By the way, what would they be? Could you prove I was purposely misleading you? If so, what is the charge? And what is the punishment, Sheriff?" She demanded smugly.

"*Nathan,*" he corrected her, with a smile. "Well, it's hard to say what the district attorney would want to do with you. I don't think I've ever encountered a situation like this, and I doubt he has either, so there would definitely be some scrambling going on to appease the wealthy Eddy family, especially when the general public is not sympathetic at all toward Lance Eddy." Nathan was amused at the thought of Thornton trying to handle this one with the media in light of the fact that he is up for re-election in another year.

"I know I am not a perfect person," Julia said. "I have not lived my life like I wanted to. I should have never gotten involved with Joey's father, but I did, and I got Joey out of that. Sometimes I wonder if that's why Joey was taken from me...because I had made poor choices and he deserved to have a good father...so the good Lord took him to give him what he deserved." Julia had softened and Nathan could sense the depth of her pain. "But I think I have worked through most of that now. Honestly, for Joey's sake and for everyone else's, I just needed to find a way to get him off the streets. I didn't want another little boy hurt or killed before that happened. I had to try this. I had to. Please believe me. That's all I can ask." She leaned her head back on the couch and closed her eyes. Nathan wondered if she really had resolved herself to either possibility and maybe the decision truly was up to him now.

"Like I said, I don't think you are capable of torturing and killing Eddy," Nathan responded. "I know you wish you could do that because he has caused you and Joey so much pain, but I've been doing this a long time. People like you simply can't do what people like him are capable of doing. Believe me, I encounter bad guys all the time and wish I could take the law into my own hands and squeeze the living daylights out of all of them, but I'm not capable of that either. So, I do what I can, which is enforce the law. I know you were only doing what you felt you could do, given that the law had failed you. You were only doing what you knew you could do, and frankly, I am blown away that you had the guts to go through with it." Nathan became animated. "I mean, when the light bulb first went off in my head, I thought, wow...this chick is like Dirty Harry in a skirt! And now that I know how it all came together, I have to say, it was a little deranged," he teased. "But I get it." Nathan patted Julia's thigh, which got her attention. "I get it."

"So, what should we do?" Julia knew she was at his mercy. Nathan noticed she had said *we*. He paused, appearing uncertain, and making Julia aware that time was very much a factor in the mortal world they were still living in. Seconds felt like hours. She unexpectedly surrendered her heart when he finally spoke. "I don't know,' he replied coyly with an astute smile and a calm voice reminiscent of her father's quiet assurance. "But we have twenty years to think about it."

Epilogue

Nathan looked down at the bloodhound he had affectionately named Watson and rubbed his loyal head. Watson looked at him the way Julia did, with affection and anticipation. Their California home was modest, the way the newly married couple both liked it – simple and honest. Two short years after meeting, Nathan and Julia were like two peas in a pod, thankful for each other and the series of events that had allowed them both to live in peace, and within their own values of honor and justice.

"Here ya go, sweetie," Julia said affectionately, while handing Nathan his coffee. He took a sip. "Did you put that weird creamer in this?" He scrunched his nose. She smiled, knowing that if she was ever going to get him to try anything new, she would have to sneak it in. "Ooops, sorry." She wasn't really. "I'll dump it out if you want."

"Nah...it's actually not that bad." He smiled lovingly back at her, aware that it was his job to be the one to question everything, even though living with her in the last few months had opened up a world he had always wanted to see, but never allowed himself to explore. She, on the other hand, had learned to appreciate Nathan's steady and stable predictability. Together they were more similar than either wanted to admit, but their differences had added exactly what was missing to each other's lives. She gave him joy. He was her rock.

They knew from the first time they had met that there was a spark between them that was fueled by more than the drama surrounding Eddy's incarceration. In those first few months, Nathan had taken time to process all that had happened, keeping Julia's story safe and secure. Eventually, he had flown out to see her one more time to talk about revealing their secret and finding another way to protect children from Eddy. But just about the time they were prepared to reveal the truth to the world, they learned that Eddy had hung himself in his cell after realizing his prison mates were not going to allow him a day without torture. That had thrown Nathan and Julia into a complicated mess of emotions about how to go on. At that point, there seemed to be no reason to tell the real story since no one stood to gain from it. Nathan was thankful that Eddy was gone from the world, but Julia struggled with the idea that she had set events in motion that had led to anyone's death – even Eddy's.

Nathan figured it all had happened the way it was supposed to because he was now with the most amazing woman he had ever met. Surprisingly, she had managed to motivate him to quit smoking, which generated a fair amount of teasing from his old buddies in Regal. In fact, once the Eddy case was closed, he chose not to run again as sheriff, sold his family home place, and left the few friends he'd had in Regal to make a life with *Julia* – as he called her in private. She had successfully assumed the identity of her fictitious cousin Celeste Edmund, and later Celeste Davis, and he was okay with her continuing what she had worked so hard to protect. He knew she still had a lot of mixed emotions about what had happened, which caused him to be even more in love with her. He had been exactly right about Julia Olwen. Even though she had lost her son in a horrific way, she wasn't capable of accepting Eddy's death as a substitute for her son's. She had only wanted him contained, not dead. Penelope Eddy's name came up quite a bit in their conversation as she wrestled with knowing the pain of a mother's grief. In that way, Nathan saw her as a true angel on earth. He had never known anyone with such a heart and he felt blessed to now have her as his wife.

"What do you want to do today?" Nathan asked while reading the Wal-Mart ad from the newspaper. "Doesn't matter," she responded, with her knees pulled up to her chest and her hands cupped around her warm coffee mug. She loved her life. Her cozy home, with the sun porch where they sat every morning and talked to each other about life, and politics, and religion, and the ridiculousness of television. It didn't matter what they did with one another on any day of the week. She was just glad to have the love of her life in the here and now, knowing her son was smiling with her here...and there.

8

Diane Chambers Dierks is a Marriage & Family Therapist who has authored the non-fiction work, *Solo Parenting: Raising Strong & Happy Families*, as well as numerous articles and publications regarding parenting and divorce. This is her first work of fiction. She has two grown children and a granddaughter. She and her husband Eric live in Atlanta, Georgia, with their dog Max.